RAMZA

Contemporary Issues in the Middle East

RAMZA

OUT EL KOULOUB

Translated and with an Introduction by
NAYRA ATIYA

SYRACUSE UNIVERSITY PRESS

First Edition 1994
94 95 96 97 98 99   6 5 4 3 2 1

Ramza was originally published in French in 1958 by Éditions Gallimard,
Paris.

The paper used in this publication meets the minimum requirements of
American National Standard for Information Sciences—Permanence of
Paper for Printed Library Materials, ANSI Z39.48-1984. ∞™

Library of Congress Cataloging-in-Publication Data
Out el Kouloub.
  [Ramza. English]
  Ramza / Out el Kouloub : translated and with an introduction by
Nayra Atiya.
    p. cm.
  Translated from the French.
  ISBN 0-8156-2618-5. — ISBN 0-8156-0280-4
  1. Women—Egypt—Fiction. I. Title.
PQ3989.2.O86R3613   1994
843—dc20   93-42382

Manufactured in the United States of America

I dedicate this translation to my mother, Lola,
with love and admiration;
and to Asma el Bakri, who inspired it.

OUT EL KOULOUB (1892–1968) was an Egyptian author who wrote in French. She belonged to the Muslim aristocracy and fled Cairo in the early 1960s after Nasser came to power. *Ramza* is one of five of her novels that tell stories of Egyptian women from various social classes.

NAYRA ATIYA was born in Egypt and educated in the United States. Her oral histories of five Egyptian women, *Khul-Khaal* (Syracuse University Press), won the 1990 UNICEF Prize for the best book on women, children, and development and was translated into several languages. Ms. Atiya lives in New York City.

CONTENTS

TRANSLATOR'S
ACKNOWLEDGMENTS

I would like to thank the following friends for their help, some in reviewing the manuscript at various stages, others for hosting me as I worked on the translation: Mercedes Volait, Melissa Solomon, Henriette Sakakini, Donette Atiyah, Ülkü Bates, Lilianne Dammond, Mary Frank, Sam Sieber, Gary and Karlan Sick, Lucy and Steve O'Connor, Andrea Rugh, Kevin and Sybil O'Connor, and particularly Robert Alford for reading all final drafts with passion.

Very special thanks to my friends Mary Dungan Megalli, Amina Megalli, and Janet Lippman Abu Lughod, as well as to my children Adam and Katrina Walker, for their help and encouragement.

Last but not least I am grateful to my editor Cynthia Maude-Gembler for her diligence and support.

TRANSLATOR'S INTRODUCTION

The story of Ramza is the story of many Oriental women, a story of life in the harem at the turn of the century, of life behind the veil, and of one woman's rebellion. Out el Kouloub wrote it as a novel, yet it reads like a personal account. *Ramza* is rich in what appears to be autobiographical, and certainly biographical, detail. The heroine's name means "symbol" and alludes to the central theme of the book, the liberation of women.

In translating the novel, I have chosen to highlight the oral historical flavor of the story as told by an aging Ramza to a companion while sitting on the terrace of a hotel in Aswan—the Old Cataract, perhaps. To that end I have added a final sentence to Out el Kouloub's prologue: "The following is Ramza's story, told in her own voice." I have understood the companion to be Out el Kouloub herself.

Out el Kouloub el Demerdashiyyah (1892–1968), known as Out el Kouloub, was an Egyptian who wrote in French, the preferred language of the upper-class woman of her time. She belonged to the Muslim aristocracy, to a family that both founded and constituted a Sufi order. Some members fled Egypt after the extensive properties owned by the family and the order in midtown Cairo were confiscated in the early 1960s. Scholars writing on contemporary Egyptian Sufism assert that the family resolved not to return home as long as Gamal Abd el Nasser was in power. The author herself died in exile.

Out el Kouloub was very much drawn to French literature; and when she became a widow at an early age, in addition to raising her children, she devoted herself to writing and entertaining writers. She held a literary salon in Cairo that both Egyptians and Europeans attended. It is said that she was eccentric but, as her personal history is shrouded in mystery, scholars of Francophone literature have relied on hearsay and on her own pen to piece together the scant picture we have of the woman and the writer. J. J. Luthi's biographical sketch of Out el Kouloub in *Le Français en Egypte* (Beyrouth, 1981), for example, is only four short paragraphs.

Ramza is one of five novels by the author that recount stories of Egyptian women of different social classes and of family life in a traditional society. They appeared between 1937 and 1961 and include *Harem* (1937), *Zanouba* (1950), *La Nuit de la Destinée*, (1954), *Ramza* (1958), and *Héfnaoui, le Magnifique* (1961).

Out el Kouloub was a keen participant-observer of her world. Her stories are often set in historic quarters and old dwellings where dramatic as well as ordinary activities of daily life occur. She interlaces her descriptions of architectural detail with an intimate knowledge of folklore, allowing the world of the harem—its superstitions, magic, and rituals—to emerge vividly.

In translating *Ramza*, I have chosen to ornament Out el Kouloub's sometimes stark prose as performers have ornamented a composer's melodic lines with turns, mordents, and appoggiaturas. I have taken the liberty of adding some detail to certain scenes in order to enrich the texture of the setting and to help the reader better visualize a world she may be unfamiliar with. One such example is the description of pollinating the palm trees, a yearly ritual that the little girl, Ramza, watches with enchantment. Another is the way that new earthenware water bottles were cured, filled, and set on the harem balconies to cool amidst blossoming jasmine climbers. The first I have observed closely myself; the second was described to me, when I was a little girl, by one of my great aunts. I have also added adjectives about feelings where they were hinted at, or expressed summarily, and filled out the dialogue where I believed it would enhance the story. For this reason also my rendition of *Ramza* might be called an ornamented translation.

When Ramza recounts her life as a girl born in the harem of a rich family in nineteenth-century Egypt, we quickly get a sense of her ambivalence about that world. She flourishes, secure in the embracing safety of the harem, but she also clearly hates its constraints. She describes her growing awareness of the life of women in her elite milieu and the complicated feelings and conflicts that this awareness raises in her mind and heart. In so doing, she paints an intimate picture of her own life, that of Out el Kouloub herself, no doubt, and the lives of similarly born contemporaries.

Ramza struggles with a complex identity. She is the daughter of a Circassian slave mother, Indje—a talented musician who has more education than the other members of the harem that becomes her home—and an Egyptian aristocrat, Farid Pasha, who has been educated both in the Orient and in France.

Ramza has tender feelings for her mother and the women who nurture her, but as she grows up, she also experiences feelings of rage against them. She loves them but also despises them for their subservience and unquestioning acceptance of slavery and the cloistered life of the harem. She describes them as "a community of females looking inward." Their lives are limited. Few of them read or write, and their days trickle away in domestic activity, the celebration of folk and religious rituals, superstitious practices, visits, eating, and gossip.

The young Ramza wants something more. She is drawn

to her father's world of books, poetry readings, philosophical and political discussions, and music. When she reaches the age of seven or eight, the women of her family instruct her that the time has come for her to stay out of the *salamlek,* the men's quarters, where her father resides, has his study, and holds his Friday night salons. Ramza stubbornly refuses. Her father is consulted and declares that she does not appear to be the sort of little girl one can "confine to a harem."

When Ramza manifests her passion for writing by scribbling all over the papers on her father's desk one day, he gives her a pen instead of punishing her, to the astonishment and outrage of the harem, excepting her mother and her Aunt Narguiss. And, later, when he allows her to attend his Friday nights hidden behind a curtain, the seeds of rebellion are sown. For Ramza, these concessions represent triumphs against repression that will set the tone for her future actions, and, combined with her spirited nature, will set the stage for her budding feminist consciousness. The outcome, however, will be irreparable conflict between father and daughter, Ramza's separation from her family and the world of her childhood, and searing pain for all concerned.

Ramza's father is unusual in indulging his daughter's desire for education—Ramza is not only taught at home but is also allowed to go to school, a privilege few of her contemporaries would have enjoyed. Farid Pasha, however, is also typical of the enlightened men of his time in adhering to traditional family values and practices.

Ramza's mother and Aunt Narguiss were probably purchased for the harem of Farid Pasha in the late 1870s, the beginning of Out el Kouloub's story. It is important to mention, if only fleetingly, some of the real people and events that surround Ramza's story. They will help to explain Farid Pasha's (and of course Out el Kouloub's) attitudes, which were no doubt based on the dawning awareness of the need to bring women into the mainstream of national development.

The Khedive Ismail, an eminent public figure in *Ramza,* came into power in 1863, a time of economic prosperity for Egypt. During the first part of his reign, the railway system was expanded, and bridges, canals, telegraph lines, and postal services were improved. The Suez Canal was opened in 1869. Educational reforms were also instituted, as was a push on the part of the sovereign to Europeanize Egypt. Hence, young men like Farid Pasha, who would once have been educated in Cairo or Constantinople, were sent to France. Furthermore, Egypt was experimenting with constitutional government in 1866; the first state school for girls opened its doors in 1873, under the patronage of Khedive Ismail's third wife; slavery was abolished in 1877; women began to explore issues surrounding their emancipation in tracts and in journals as early as the 1890s. Qasim Amim, whom Ramza mentions hearing during the course of one of her father's Friday evening gatherings, published *The Liberation of Women* in 1899.

Despite her rebellion against the harem, Ramza remembers the women of her family who loved her and whom she loved with nostalgia and exquisite tenderness. She also recalls only signs of contentment on their faces, reflecting that the freedom she paid so dearly to obtain was not something they seemed to miss. Their needs were met and they lived surrounded by plenty, enjoying a sense of well-being that appeared to fulfill them. "Only rarely," she says, referring to the birth of her own feminist consciousness, "did I come across one who, like me, seemed to require something more."

Until the 1920s—and for many women long after that time—upper- and middle-class Egyptian girls were cloaked and cloistered by the age of ten. They donned the veil, behind which their lives and their emotions transpired. At the same time, they were segregated from the males who, subsequently, would chart and control nearly every detail of their lives.

Out el Kouloub, like the Ramza of her story, experienced not only the harem but the beginnings of the Egyptian feminist movement. *Ramza,* written in 1958, was not only inspired by the birth of that movement but was also based on the climate that preceded and followed it. Feminist leaders like Huda Sharaawi, a little older than Ramza, were taught at home and married off at the age of thirteen or fourteen, as were many contemporaries. Marriage at an early age was customary in Muslim, Christian, and Jewish families, particularly for girls. I recall my grandmother telling me how, in our Coptic family, her eldest sister (born in the 1880s or early 1890s) was betrothed "off of her mother's shoulder." She was married at the age of eleven. "Her husband put her to bed and cared for her like a child until she was old enough to be a wife," my grandmother told me. She had her first child at the age of fourteen and died twelve years later, leaving behind two sons and a daughter, who was educated in France and became a physician in Paris before the Second World War.

In the spring of 1923, Huda Sharaawi and her niece returned to Egypt after attending the International Feminist Congress in Rome. They were welcomed at Cairo station by a crowd of women in veils and long, black cloaks who broke into applause when the two women bared their faces in public for the first time. The final chapter in *Ramza* alludes to this act that dealt a decisive blow to the organization of the harem in Egypt.

The similarities between Huda Sharaawi and Ramza cannot be overlooked. For me they have made *Ramza* a living document, fleshed out with a woman's as well as a family's struggles, emotions, and day-to-day existence. "Being a female became a barrier between me and the freedom for which I yearned," writes Huda. How much like Ramza that sounds!

Out el Kouloub, like Huda Sharaawi, must have known and been deeply affected by the pronouncements of Sheikh Muhammad Abdu, a nineteenth-century Islamic modernist, who pointed out that the development of Egypt as a nation was impeded because Muslims neglected to apply the true spirit of Islam to women's lives, depriving them of the rights that Islam naturally granted them. Qassim Amin asserted that Islam did not require that women be secluded and veiled. Murqus Fahmi, a young Coptic lawyer, wrote that Egypt would remain backward as long as women were not emancipated.

These writings, as well as those by women themselves that analyzed their own conditions, were certainly invaluable sources for Out el Kouloub. They no doubt helped shape the character of Ramza and define the heartbeat of the time in which she lived and loved.

It is therefore essential, when reading *Ramza*, not to lose sight of it as a document and, even more importantly, as an insider's account written by one who experienced the harem first hand. This is certainly not the work of an Orientalist. Rather, it is a heartfelt dramatization of a piece of Egyptian feminine and feminist history set in a time when Egyptian women were struggling to come forward. It is also a record of the life of her time. *Ramza* is a work imbued with astonishingly tender, personal recollections as well as keenly felt social and political views.

Out el Kouloub's work, by and large known only in Francophile circles, deserves greater recognition. She is a writer who combines the skills of an ethnographer, the talent of a good storyteller, and the concerns of an activist. Her novels are fragrant with the drama of daily life in a past time and highly evocative of an Egypt that is today only a memory.

At times Ramza's story has merged with my own recollections of an Egyptian childhood. The book has felt like a second skin. Almost ten years ago I read it and wrote a first translation, which I put away. I felt it had done its work. The process of manipulating the words, of translating a life with a distinct beginning and end, had been therapeutic. I could now go back to collecting and writing oral histories. *Ramza* had pulled and pushed me through a summer of personal difficulties. I sat daily to work at the mammoth dining room table in a friend's house in Alexandria, the sea breezes wafting Ramza's world into my own along with the perfume of Turkish coffee.

How much easier it was to interact with this woman living between the pages of a book than with the men and women whose life stories I collected! In a sense, this time, it was she who played the role of the vessel collecting pain and pleasure, instead of me. If I got tired, I could walk away. If I began to feel endangered by my own empathetic responses, I could close the pages of the book.

This year it occurred to me that I had "cloistered" Ramza, and perhaps even myself on some level, by leaving *Ramza* inert in a drawer. I pulled out the battered manuscript with pages missing, which I had first written by hand, which a friend had then lovingly typed, which I had rearranged by cutting and pasting, and which I had then retyped. I began to enter it on my computer. In the process, the book and I began to grow together once more. We shed dead wood and we sprouted fresher, more vibrant skins. In my East Village study, *Ramza* evoked memories of my own growing up. I remembered our household full of women and better understood my own rebellion, as well as my mother's.

The manuscript of *Ramza* and my worn copy of the novel were some of the few things I had packed in a small duffle bag I took with me when I left Egypt in 1987, not knowing when I would return. During the course of almost a dozen moves in New York City over a period of five years, I lost my copy of the novel; but the manuscript somehow always reappeared. When I finally took it up again with the exquisite pleasure of embracing a beloved friend, I felt that Ramza's story had merged with my own. Her roots and mine had entwined. She had remained a lighthouse that would bring me to safety, and I had a re-sponsibility to bring her back to light in English.

Often, as I translated *Ramza* this second time, I imag-ined my own ear listening to her story, and my pen record-ing it directly. Thus some of my own experiences and emotions have worked themselves into the text. For this reason I must call my rendition of *Ramza* a free translation.

RAMZA

PROLOGUE

We two ladies were alone, as usual, in our corner of the hotel terrace in Aswan. Beneath us the Nile flowed rapidly, licking the giant black boulders along the shore. Across the way, off the tip of Elephantine Island, tourists threw gold coins into the water and watched in amusement as little Nubian boys dove in after them.

My neighbor paid no attention to these games, but looked into the distance at a group of young men and women frolicking among the lush greenery of the Island of the Kings. Their laughter and the timbre of their voices rose up to us and filled the dry evening air with cheerful sound. The group was composed of three girls and two boys. We saw them run through the garden alleys and down to a boat that was waiting for them nearby.

As my companion watched them, I saw her face change. She sat up in her chair, attentive, and her fine features seemed to grow young. Her eyes glowed and her breathing became more rapid. She regained a color and vivacity that made me see clearly how beautiful she must once have been.

Her name was familiar to me, even though I had met her only a few days before at the hotel. We were two lonely old ladies whom chance had brought together, and we found comfort in each other's company. As we conversed she took a red rose from the lapel of her black serge coat and inhaled it deeply. She loved flowers and their perfume, particularly roses, jasmine, and heliotrope. Observing her gesture, I reflected on how graceful the hand that held the flower was, despite dark spots and prominent veins, the heartless legacy of age.

She was about seventy years old. Her name was Ramza. She must have felt my glance and discerned my thought, because suddenly she said, "Yes, I'm an old woman!" She was smiling still, but the brilliance had gone from her eyes, and with it the youthful air I had fleetingly apprehended earlier. I took her hand and squeezed it affectionately. She sighed and motioned with her head toward the sailboat that the young people had boarded now.

"I would like to be their age," she said. She was suddenly very still, as if delving deeply into her thoughts. I said nothing, sensing that she was about to confide something of importance to me. And she was.

She looked again toward the young group on the boat below and began by saying, "I feel I know them all," and then turning to me she observed, "I watch them live, every day, every hour. I try not to miss a moment of laughter, nor a single one of their songs. I can tell you that Soliman is loved by Omria, the little one sitting at the far end of the boat; she doesn't take her eyes off his face. He prefers Fawziyya though, the blond one with the high-pitched laugh who has her back turned to us. Mustafa and Zakiyya, who are sitting side by side, have decided to get married; that's why they look so serious. They're committing themselves. They've been allowed to choose each other!" Then she explained, "If you had told me thirty years ago that this spectacle would one day be possible in Egypt, I would not have believed you!"

She was speaking of Muslim girls, their faces unveiled, accompanied by young men to whom they could give their hearts freely. "That's the first generation to enjoy the fruits of our labors," she said. "Their freedom is our work, my work!"

Ramza's voice was animated and full of warmth as she said this. I looked at her in surprise, and she said, "Do you know why I spend so much time in hotels, drawing rooms, clubs, and on beaches?" I asked, "Why?" She answered, "To see the budding of the seeds I have sown."

I had, of course, heard of Ramza's notorious court case many years earlier. It had shaken the walls of the harem. But I ignored any of the intimate details that produced it. She had rebelled against tradition, against what she considered to be abusive family constraints and religious customs; she had taken her plea before a court of law, not only in an effort to gain justice for herself but to petition for the rights of women and their emancipation.

She had fought publicly like a man. But in her heart, she must have suffered like a woman.

During our sojourn in Aswan, as we sat on the terrace of the hotel, she told me about herself, remembering her struggles and her suffering.

The following is Ramza's story, told in her own voice.

1 · MY FAMILY

I was born in the harem of a rich family. I grew up there among slaves. Some were servants, some were wives, some white and some black, some old and some young. These women had one thing in common: they were either bought on the slave markets or born to slave mothers. Those who were freed lived no differently from anyone else, as their universe was bounded by the harem walls. They suspected little of a world beyond its precincts. The long hours spent looking through the narrow lacework of the *mashrabiyya* windows, designed to protect them from probing outside eyes, revealed only a fraction of what transpired in the neighborhood or on the streets just below. Any new face or unusual activity excited their interest and sent ripples of speculation and comment flittering through the harem.

These women formed a closed circle, a community of females looking inward. Their days were punctuated with folk and religious ritual, the rhythm of habitual domestic activity, and the call to prayer falling like short showers from the minaret of the neighborhood mosque five times daily.

The play of affections, the hatreds, jealousies, intrigues, quarrels and reconciliations, illnesses and grief, feasting and feuding that occupied their time and to which they committed their energies offered as much color to their lives as they seemed to require.

Now, years later, when I look back and think about

these women, I wonder whether their lives, these lives which I saw unfold before me daily, were unhappy ones. I don't think so. Rather, I suspect that they were no less happy than they would have been had they been free. Freedom was not something they missed. They had no sense of what it meant. Their every desire was met; they lived surrounded by plenty and enjoyed an atmosphere of well-being that appeared to satisfy them. Only rarely did I come across one who, like me, seemed to require something more.

When I remember the faces of the women I knew, long since gone, who loved me and whom I loved, I recall nothing but signs of contentment. My mother with her supremely tender eyes; my grandmother, her expression austere beneath the black lace veil she was never without; or my plump aunt, Narguiss, who cajoled me as if I were her own child and attended to my every need even more than my mother; or the proud, magnificent Gaulistan, my father's first wife; or Neemat, the head housekeeper who directed the domestic affairs of the harem with relentless discipline; or this black servant; or that copper colored one—all these women, friends, or adversaries appear before me today, in my mind's eye, with smiling faces.

Present too among them are the expansive Koutchouk and Mabrouk, the head eunuchs who looked after all of that female world.

In that sea of faces, I never remember my mother's without emotion. I never think of her except as a young woman, perhaps because she died before her fortieth year.

My mother had fine blond hair and very white skin, and she was incapable of an ungraceful gesture. She must have been unusually beautiful when she was in good health. Even as an invalid, her eyes enlarged and darkened by fever and her features drawn with pain, her face had such charm and delicacy. She also possessed childlike sweetness and innocence, which were the most prominent features of her character and which she never lost.

Because she herself did not have a trace of malice, she

could never suspect the existence of it in others. I remember, as a little girl, how exasperated I became with her passivity. I screamed at her, telling her that she was stupid when she did not respond to someone who maligned her. But then instantly I regretted my words and threw myself into her arms, sobbing to beg her forgiveness. Before the age of ten I became like an older sister and defended her. No one dared attack my mother in my presence. I acquired the reputation of being fierce, and I was proud of it.

My mother was an exquisite musician. She often beckoned me to her side trying to spark my interest in the piano. She wanted to teach me to play, but I preferred to listen to her. She played beautifully, and I never tired of listening.

But, as illness overtook her, she spent long hours motionless on the divan. The last few years of her life were filled with suffering. My eyes constantly filled with tears at the sound of her coughing. But when she felt well enough to talk, she called me to her side, and I nestled against her. She caressed my head and called me her gazelle.

At that time she also began to tell me the story of her life in bits and pieces. She naïvely sought to entertain me with tales of the splendors of days gone by. How could she possibly have imagined another way of life or wished for a different one for her daughter? She never noticed my hands clench into fists, nor did she realize that she was helping form my rebel's heart as she spun out her life's history, the story of a slave woman.

2 · MY MOTHER

My mother was of Slavic origin, but had been given the Turkish name of Indje. That is how I addressed her when I got older and we became friends.

In the last few weeks of her life, the memories of the

forgotten little girl she had once been came rushing to the surface; and for the first time in her conversations with me, I heard her allude to her native village. She no longer knew its name, but she remembered that it was surrounded with purplish mountains. She recalled playing in a garden next to a cottage that was beside a church. She remembered the church being ablaze with light, and candles flickering in front of images of people with haloes around their faces. A chandelier hung like a fountain of diamonds from a limitless dome. In front of an altar, a priest with blond hair, a beard, and vestments resplendent with gold embroidery, gave a benediction, arms raised. In the memory of the child who became my mother, this man was her father.

Later, in Istanbul, when she heard a servant girl singing in a foreign tongue, she recognized the sounds of the words without understanding their meaning. The girl was born in Serbia.

My mother remembered a man who came toward her along a garden path as she played beside a rosebush near her parents' house. She was not afraid of him because he was familiar to her. Unexpectedly, he sprang upon her, crushed shut her mouth with his hand, and carried her off. Night fell. She heard her mother calling, "Olga . . ." She wanted to cry out, but no sound came through her lips.

That was all she could remember of her abduction. Indje recalled this scene with horror, and throughout her life it was a recurring nightmare.

She was taken to Istanbul, to a school run by nuns, where the sisters continued to call her Olga until she was sold to a woman who became like a mother to her. My mother could not remember how she came to be sold, only that Tewfikeh Hanem, who had lost both her children, lavished affection on her and spoke to her so tenderly that her words were like a caress. My mother often said that her real parents couldn't have been kinder nor more devoted to her. Tewfikeh Hanem referred to her as *kiz*, or my little girl, and the little girl called her *nena*, or mother.

Kiz soon forgot that she had spoken any language other than Turkish, or that she had prayed in any other but the Muslim way. Yet, she continued to attend the Rumeli Hussar School, run by the nuns. There she learned to read and write in Turkish and French. She was taught handwork and music and became as skilled in the art of embroidery as at playing the piano.

Because she was beautiful and quickly learned the social graces, Tewfikeh Hanem assured her that she would marry a prince and changed her name to Indje, meaning pearl. This name she kept for the rest of her life.

Tewfikeh Hanem died before she could find a prince for Indje, however. She left all her possessions to her brother, who was all the family she had. Indje was part of the inheritance. This man, a former janissary with bright red whiskers, was morose and brutal. Indje was afraid of him. Tewfikeh Hanem knew this and had made him promise that if she died he would let the little girl determine her own future.

Indje, who was then thirteen, chose to be put back on the market.

My mother's decision astonished me. I asked her why, if Tewfikeh Hanem loved her so much, she had not freed her in the first place. "What would I have done with freedom? I was not quite fourteen years old. I had no one in the world," she answered.

She was right, of course. In a big city, at that time, freedom would have been a liability for a girl without a family. The slave trader was the safest option.

Indje was at an age when girls dream of adventure. She knew that the education she had received increased her value as human merchandise and dreamed of being purchased for the harem of a prince. She might attract the prince's attention one day. She might become his favorite, maybe even a sultana . . .

As my young mother spun her dreams of glory, Roustoum Agha, a respected slave trader, was making his way to

Istanbul from Cairo. He bought Indje along with twenty other hand-picked slaves, all natives of provinces of the Ottoman Empire. These girls had nothing in common except their status as slaves, their youth, and beauty.

Before long they were sailing for Egypt. The journey was memorable, and my mother spoke about it often. The girls were first locked up in a hold, where there was neither light nor air, and remained there for two days. My mother recalls that the second night was so stormy that the little girls screamed and cried in terror as the boat rolled, heaved, and jolted them.

Finally, when the sea grew calm, they were released and taken up on deck where a sheltered tent was constructed at the stern of the boat to protect them from the curious eyes of the crew. They were treated kindly, well fed, and enjoyed the rest of the voyage like a gaggle of school girls on an outing. My mother always ended her story by saying, "We were little more than children, you know, not much older than you are now!"

During the crossing my mother made friends with a young Circassian named Narguiss, who was her neighbor on the boat. She had been less seasick than Indje during the journey and had cared for and comforted my mother during the storm. They were about the same age, but Narguiss was the taller and stronger of the two.

Soon, they began to exchange life stories. Narguiss told my mother that she was born in the Caucasian Mountains and had known almost all her life that she would be sold into slavery by her parents. They were poor and had many children. As soon as she could understand, they had told her that she would enjoy a much better life elsewhere. They took extra care of her, feeding her well, making sure she was never fatigued or frightened. They kept her away from anyone who was ill and anything that would spoil her perfect complexion. When she reached the age of puberty, they sold her to a merchant who came periodically to the village.

She too dreamed of a brilliant future in the harem of a young, handsome prince!

Narguiss told me that she never regretted leaving her family or her native land.

The voyage from Istanbul to Cairo was to mark the beginning of a lifelong friendship between Narguiss and Indje. They prayed that life would never separate them, and their prayers were answered.

My mother remembered being transported up the Nile to the Port of Boulac in Cairo, aboard a houseboat, a *dahabiyyah,* with few windows and heavy curtains, then by closed carriage to Roustoum Agha's house.

Subsequently, my mother never traveled any other way than in a closed carriage. She never knew anything of the streets through which she passed, nor could she locate the neighborhood in which she lived, even though she knew it by name. Had she wanted to escape, after living in Cairo for twenty years, she would have been as lost as a total stranger.

This cloistered life bred insatiable curiosity in harem women, and questions were heaped upon anyone who stepped outside. Servants, eunuchs, merchants, children, anyone who had been lucky enough to see another aspect of life was asked to describe in detail everything they had seen, smelled, experienced. Thus, when I left the harem walls as a little girl, I took care to record every sight and sound I came across for my mother's benefit. She liked to compare her girlhood impressions of Istanbul with mine of Cairo. The game delighted her, and provided us with many hours of conversation.

My mother was never able to explain to me exactly where Roustoum Agha's house was located. She only knew that it was a large building, with many rooms, where the windows were fitted with thick *mashrabiyya* screens, grills, and solid metal bars. But she spoke about Roustoum Agha without hatred or rancor and even with affection. She said that he was a generous, well-intentioned man. He once had been a slave himself, a *mamluk* who had been manumitted. He ran his business with the help of his wife, Rokeyya, who was also a freed slave. Both were old and respected, trusted by the aristocracy whose harems they furnished. "They even furnished the harem of the Khedive Ismail," Indje used to say proudly.

Roustoum and Rokeyya took good care of their slaves and chose their clients with circumspection. They watched over their wards even after they were sold and visited them regularly. They always included a cautionary clause in the sales contract: if a master mistreated a slave, they had a right to take her back. And Rokeyya had unlimited access to the harems of the best families in Egypt, visiting them regularly.

When a slave was very young, they kept her with them until she came of age, raising her as if she were their own daughter. Roustoum's establishment included a real school in which little girls received instruction in all they needed to know to be good wives or servants. The children called him "father" and Rokeyya "mother."

Over the years the couple legally adopted some of the girls they had bought. When Roustoum and Rokeyya died one year apart, the daughters inherited their fortune. One of them lived in a beautiful villa in the quarter of Abbasiyya and wore the jewelry left her by Rokeyya, splendid enough to befit a princess.

Indje's stay in Roustoum Agha's house was brief, however. One day she and Narguiss were offered as a pair to a fat eunuch wearing a black cap whom Roustoum treated with great deference and who in turn trusted Roustoum implicitly. The girls were expecting to be examined meticulously, but the fat *agha* bought them sight unseen, without even bargaining.

3 · INDJE AND NARGUISS

At first Indje and Narguiss thought that they had been purchased for the harem of the Khedive Ismail, or at least one of his sons. But Roustoum Agha explained that they would be happier where they were going than in the harem of any prince. He told them that the eunuch they had seen was Beshir Agha, chief overseer of the harem of Ismail Pasha, the *mufattish,* a powerful minister of state. Roustoum sang the praises of Ismail Pasha to these two ignorant children, telling them to thank God for their good fortune. The *mufattish* was the richest man in Egypt after the khedive, a most capable finance minister, in fact the only capable one, as well as the most expansive and generous of masters. How lucky Indje and Narguiss were to be destined for his household! They would live in a palace and enjoy endless feasting among splendor that aroused the jealousy of the khedive himself. Roustoum Agha told them all this in a conspiratorial tone.

Indje was dazzled, but Narguiss, who was more wary, wondered if all the praise were not hiding a defect: Was the *mufattish* too old perhaps? Roustoum Agha replied that the *mufattish* was not a young man, but a vigorous man, a man of the world who was a more suitable choice for two young women than an inexperienced youngster. He quickly added that the minister was also very generous, distributing sumptuous gifts when one knew how to please him. He explained that all of his household would gladly give their lives for him, and that all of his harem loved him.

Indje was a little anxious but grateful, at least, to be going with Narguiss. What mattered most to her was that they had been paired and, she hoped, would be sisters for life.

There existed an unwritten rule in this strange world of the harem that respected sisterly bonds between pairs of slaves; these bonds were considered even stronger and more lasting than blood ties. Such slaves were usually never separated and were always bought or sold in pairs. This was the case with Narguiss and my mother, who from the time of their sale to the minister called each other by the tender name of *abla,* or cherished sister. Their devotion to one another never waned, and when I was born, Narguiss automatically embraced me, and I called her "aunt."

When I was a child, the bonds between slave pairs were so firmly established that they carried with them rights of inheritance that were equivalent to those between blood relatives. And I am as much therefore related to Narguiss through my mother as to a descendant of a slave brother of my great grandfather's who had been a *mamluk* belonging to Prince Muhammad Ali, who was himself a former slave. And even though this slave fraternity dated back two generations, we still maintained our ties with his family.

The day after Indje and Narguiss were purchased for the minister's harem, Beshir Agha sent dressmakers to Roustoum Agha's house to measure them for identical pink silk outfits. These consisted of long blouses with full gathered sleeves, matching pantaloons, silver lame belts and vests, and veils intricately worked with tiny pearls. The girls were delighted with the dressmaking sessions and glowed with the happiness of brides preparing for their weddings. They were as coquettish and coy as you would expect anyone to be who saw themselves as human merchandise. They were trained in the art of pleasing. They knew how to perform every task with womanly grace while retaining the freshness of little girls, which, of course, they still were.

Finally, when the day came, Rokeyya took them in a closed carriage to the palace of the minister, which was located in the new quarter of Ismailiyya. On the way she instructed them on how to conduct themselves. It baffles me to think that Rokeyya, who had been as a mother to the little girls, who was tearful at the prospect of losing them, whom they affectionately called *nena,* was the same woman who negotiated their sale and was now handing over her merchandise to a new owner!

Indje and Narguiss were destined for the harem of Zohra Hanem, the first of the minister Ismail Pasha's four wives. They were to be attached to her "house" as two of a group of official concubines. Rokeyya delivered them in person to the *khalfa,* or head housekeeper, an old Ethiopian servant with a severe demeanor. She asked that they be given appropriate accommodations immediately and remained to see that they were comfortably settled and treated well.

The *khalfa* took them to their room, which was outfitted with two beds, two wardrobes, and brand new furniture imported from Paris. When they were ready, Rokeyya took them to the great hall, where they met a dozen young girls who were dressed in identical pink frocks, Zohra Hanem's color. The second, third, and fourth wives had dressed their retinue in green, yellow, and purple. Rokeyya knew most of the girls attached to Ismail Pasha's harem. She spoke with them individually, recommending the newcomers to each one with the tender concern of a mother leaving her daughters among strangers.

"The world of the harem is hostile and competitive," Narguiss explained to me when I was old enough to understand. My mother remembered that newcomers met with critical glances; eyes undressed them, took note of their good features, and assessed the danger they posed in the mercurial hierarchy of favorites.

My mother was afraid, but Narguiss faced her new world without quivering, answering the questions of the curious without hesitation.

When the new girls were asked to sing to show off their musical talents, Narguiss refused. She said that she and her sister would only play before their mistress. She had instinctively understood the subtle manipulations of the harem, navigating with care and extending her protection to Indje. She knew the power of envy and how those who were unable to defend themselves could fall victim to it. Thus, she fended not only for herself but for her sister.

4 · ZOHRA HANEM

When the *khalfa* came to fetch them, the pink-clad bevy followed her into the imposing presence of a tall, haughty woman in her fifties who was heavily made up and covered with jewels. That is how Indje remembered her. Zohra Hanem looked the girls over from head to toe, and remarking on my mother's extreme youth, said, "If you are obedient, you will see nothing but kindness from me." The girls formed a semicircle around the *hanem,* and soon four *aghas,* wearing black morning coats and red fezzes, ushered in Ismail Pasha. When he entered the room, everyone from the lowliest slave to the most respected wife bowed in deference to him, and the girls followed their example. "When I dared to raise my head," my mother said, remembering that first encounter, "I was terribly disappointed; the pasha was small, hunched, older and uglier than I had imagined. He looked deeply worried and tugged at his beard for the duration of the visit."

After the appropriate salutations and formalities, the *hanem* invited her husband to sit down and offered him a cup of coffee. He glanced casually around him, his eye lingering briefly on Narguiss and Indje. The *hanem,* attentive to his slightest mood or gesture, beckoned to the newcomers. They curtsied deeply before the pasha, who only commented, as his wife had done earlier, on how young the girls were. Meanwhile, the rest of the company took up drums, violins, and other string instruments and began to play. The pasha hastily interrupted them and asked Indje, in Arabic, to play something. She did not speak Arabic, and did not understand his request until someone explained that the pasha had said: "You are from Istanbul, you must know some Turkish songs." She then answered, in Turkish, that she did, and he invited her to sing and was pleased with her performance.

When he took leave of the harem, an Italian dance mistress came in to train the girls in the art of dance, teaching them certain figures of ballet designed to enhance the grace of their movements. This took place under the watchful eye of the *hanem*. Indje and Narguiss performed reasonably well, and after the lessons, the afternoon was spent in leisure activities and more music making.

That first night the *aghas* came to fetch Indje and Narguiss and conducted them through a series of narrow passageways and secret staircases to a large hall where other women were gathered. This hall hung above large reception rooms used for elegant festivities. The women could watch, without being observed, hidden behind the latticed *mashrabiyya* windows. My mother remembered her first glimpse of the minister's guests; they were clad in black evening dress, or highly decorated military uniforms and other formal attire. Orchestras played, servants offered trays laden with refreshments, and one special attraction was promised that night: the famous singer Almaz, or Diamond, who was then at the height of her glory. She sang for male gatherings, but always hidden behind a curtain. My mother recalled her songs long after as having swept her into a land of enchanted dreams.

The following day a celebration was planned on the palace grounds. Indje described this event with childlike wonder. It was one of her most treasured memories; yet often, in telling me about it, she wondered if it had indeed been real or a figment of her imagination. This event, which delighted her, horrified me!

In the afternoon the girls put on their dresses and seamstresses fixed gauzy, silk wings stretched on light frames on their backs. Each of the pasha's four wives had her following of young girls dressed in the pastel shade representing her house with wings to match. Outfitted in this way, the girls fluttered down to the garden, where every opening had been carefully sealed to protect them from prying eyes. The *aghas* stood vigilantly guarding the gates. The broad alleys of the park were lined with royal palms, the opulent flower beds were in full bloom, and the scent of roses and carnations permeated the air. Whimsical gazebos, trimmed with low, sculptured hedges, were scattered throughout the immense park, at the end of which stood the palace, resplendent with a façade of golden columns glinting in the afternoon sun. Each gazebo had an orchestra of female musicians who played in turns. The girls, under the direction of the ballet mistress, criss-crossed each other in a choreographed pattern of light, graceful movements leading toward the front steps of the palace where the pasha, his wives, and children sat. This fairyland setting enchanted my mother, and she never forgot it.

At four o'clock the pasha invited his wives for a stroll around the park and then joined his children under the wide porch of the palace to watch an astonishing spectacle. This entertainment was so unbelievable that I would have doubted my mother's description of it had Narguiss not confirmed it. I found it hard to conceive of such diversions being organized to distract a powerful man from his daily worries!

In the garden four lightweight chariots waited side by side along one of the alleys. All were trimmed with pink, green, yellow, and purple silk to match the dresses of the girls and decorated with the name of a season in gold letters on the side. The young slaves were then attached to the chariots with ribbons and streamers, and each wife took her place in the vehicle bearing her color. When a signal was sounded, the girls began to pull the chariots in a mad race across the garden while the orchestras played a lively rhythm to cheer them on. They ran shouting, laughing, their wings fluttering, and their veils flying behind them. The wife whose chariot won the race received a diamond brooch, and her team a scattering of gold coins tossed at random.

My mother bubbled with mirth when she recounted the events of the afternoon to me. Her only regret had been not winning the race. The green team had come first that time.

Even as a very young child, I blushed with embarrassment at the thought of her being used in this way, and I felt deeply humiliated on her behalf. She was astonished at my reaction. She remembered the race only as a delightfully happy game.

After my mother's death, Narguiss spoke to me of these festivities, adding that they were staged every week. The sight of the girls pulling the chariots, their cheeks flushed, their eyes bright with excitement, seemed to give the minister much pleasure.

When one of the girls particularly attracted his attention, he let her know it by paying her a compliment. The wife to whom the slave belonged understood the meaning of this and responded accordingly. That night she dressed the girl elaborately, perfumed her, and even lent her her own jewels, then sent her to the pasha's apartments. His degree of satisfaction with the girl was always expressed by a more-or-less sumptuous gift to the wife whose slave had given him pleasure. Children born of these moments of passing fancy automatically belonged to the mistress of the slave. They were brought up alongside her own children, according to her wishes.

In Narguiss' opinion only this last practice was objectionable. She felt a mother should bring up her own child.

As to the rest, she saw nothing wrong with the rituals and amusements of the harem. She considered them quite natural. She was surprised at my indignation and did not understand that these stories watered the seeds of revolt in my young heart even before I began to learn to read.

5 · ISMAIL PASHA

Soon after my mother and Narguiss entered Ismail Pasha's harem, the minister fell from grace. He was banished, and my mother was never again attached to a chariot, nor was she ever accompanied to his apartments at night. Narguiss, however, saw him on the eve of his demise and recounted the incident to me in detail.

Although the pasha was much too preoccupied by the time Narguiss and Indje were purchased to ask for their company at night, Zohra Hanem, thinking to relieve his anxiety, sent him my aunt Narguiss, who was a virgin. She chose Narguiss over Indje because she was better formed and seemed older. Narguiss was prepared and decked out, and the *khalfa* was summoned to accompany her to the pasha's apartments.

They sat a long time in an antechamber, my aunt remembered. They heard voices, furniture being moved, paper being shuffled, and all sorts of noise coming from the minister's study. When the door opened abruptly and the pasha emerged, he was furious to see the company and shouted for them to leave at once.

As they turned to leave, he noticed Narguiss, and his voice softened at the sight of the young girl. He stopped then and conversed with her for a moment, asking kindly about her country of birth, her age, and about the slave trader who sold her. He also asked after her sister, and after returning to his room, came back with two diamonds, which he handed to Narguiss saying, "For you and for your sister." Before she could thank him or kiss his hand as would have been proper, and as she had wanted to do, he was gone. He appeared burdened and seemed older than she had remembered him.

Narguiss did not know whether to be flattered or humiliated by the brief encounter, which as it turned out, was their last.

The following day the minister did not visit any of his wives for the customary cup of coffee with his families. This put the harem in a state of complete bewilderment, causing endless speculation. Women went back and forth, chattering and seeking out Narguiss, who had been the last to see the minister. The *aghas* were also questioned, but refused to talk. Narguiss said that she had only had a passing glimpse of Ismail Pasha, and she took good care not to mention the diamonds he had given her.

It was said that after Narguiss returned to the harem, Ismail Pasha had remained closeted in his study with Beshir Agha and his secretaries and had not slept all night.

That afternoon another chariot race was scheduled. The girls put on their costumes and waited, but the vast park remained silent. Briefly, an orchestra struck up a tune but was soon discouraged by the gloom that seemed to settle on everyone. After an hour of waiting, word was circulated that there would be no race. The seamstresses removed the gauzy wings from the backs of the dresses and the chariots were put away.

Late that night Beshir Agha came to Zohra Hanem's apartments and took Narguiss and Indje away. He told them to gather their personal effects and follow him and then escorted them out of the palace. On a warm autumn night, they were returned in a closed carriage to Roustoum Agha's house.

The story went that the day before, the minister had had

a violent quarrel with the khedive. He feared that he would be arrested and deposed and therefore spent the night putting his house in order and instructing his staff. He was conferring with Beshir Agha when the *khalfa* had brought Narguiss to him. After she left it seems that the pasha had said to his head eunuch, "Beshir, I like this little one. Don't leave her with Zohra. Take her back to Roustoum's tonight, where I know she will be well cared for." Beshir Agha asked about Indje and was instructed to return her as well until such time as Ismail Pasha could send for them both.

Beshir Agha did as he was told, but in his heart he felt sure that his master had overestimated the danger he was in. He was sure that the minister would be in the khedive's good graces again in no time. Had not the khedive come to the minister's palace of his own accord the following day to reconcile the differences between them? Had he not heard with his own ears his master saying, "The khedive has come to see me. I know I am indispensable to him!" Beshir reported that Ismail Pasha had hastened to the *salamlek,* the men's guest quarters, to greet the khedive, and they had shaken hands cordially and left the palace together. They had stepped into Khedive Ismail's carriage, which had been waiting for them at the foot of the steps of the palace, and had driven off in the direction of Kasr el Nil bridge.

Beshir Agha was certain their destination was the khedivial palace on Gezira. But, as it turned out, it was Beshir Agha who had underestimated the danger his master was in.

6 · THE HOUSE ON THE KHALIG

Thirty years ago I could still have shown you the house where I was born, where Indje and Narguiss lived, and where the turbulent little person that I was spent most of her childhood. This was the house of my father, Farid Pasha.

It had first belonged to a Mamluk Bey from the household of Ali Bey el Kebir, who fell victim to the janissaries of Muhammad Ali during the massacre that took place at the Cairo Citadel. When Ali Bey died, Muhammad Ali offered the house as a gift to my grandfather along with an impressive estate north of the city. When I was born, the house was already over one hundred years old.

Although it was not a palace, the house on the Khalig was a huge residence. It was made up of many rambling old buildings that were attached to each other by stairs, passageways, and incidental rooms that had been added over the years. The windows looked out on a narrow street on one side, and on the canal, which flowed directly beneath it, on the other. Later, the Khalig would be filled to make room for the noisy Cairo streetcar lines.

On both sides of the house, there were solid, high walls erected for privacy. When I was growing up, the palm trees in the neighbors' gardens had shot up past the top of these walls. I loved gazing at them balancing gently in the wind, but enjoyed even more watching the gardener who tended them. I was curious about the activities beyond that wall, no doubt because they were out of my reach.

I never missed a chance to observe the spectacle that unfolded above the wall. I discovered that palm trees were male and female and that, in order for their fruit to be edible, a delicate operation had to be performed to pollinate the females. In March or April, the gardener came to do this. I watched him as he cut long, heavy, green pods bursting with fragrant pollen from the tops of the male trees, then climbed down, out of my sight. Next, he went up the female trees and inserted cream-colored strands he had taken out of the male pods into the female pods containing the fruit. He secured each of the ten or fifteen clusters on each female with palm leaves to keep the pollen from flying, and repeated the operation until all of the clusters on each female were served.

After he was gone, I watched the pods swell as the weather grew warm and the dates break out in cascading clusters of golden fruit. The gardener came back to harvest them when they were ripe in August or September.

Despite his agility in climbing the trees, my heart beat fast when I saw him. I watched open-mouthed, trembling with fear, as his calloused feet scrambled up the trunk, notch by notch. I would have given anything, though, to have been in his place!

He supported himself with a belt made of rough, reddish palm fibers that girded both his loins and the slender palm trunk in a fascinating marriage of man and tree. He secured it with a knot on one side, and leaning his back against the stiffened hoop, he started up the first rung. With his hands grasping each side of the rope, he flicked himself skyward.

In winter, I listened for the rustle and thud of the fronds falling away in dusty splendor, as the gardener pruned the palms. And, at harvest time, I watched eagerly as gigantic, circular trays were hoisted to the tops of the trees, heaped with dates, and lowered into the garden, out of my sight.

By some mutual agreement between neighbors, on days when the gardener climbed the trees, the gardens were off-limits to the women, which included me as soon as I reached the age of seven or eight. I would not be deprived of the wonderful spectacle, however, and continued to watch from a window on the top floor of the house.

You see, in the life of a cloistered child, every ritual, every fluctuation in the rhythm of a day, every change of season was an event. Still today, when I think of these moments, I am filled with a memory whose charm has remained vivid and indescribably sweet.

In that house where I spent my childhood and adolescence, only one opening led out to the street. It was secured by a massive door studded with hobnails and topped by a narrow slit protected with a grillwork of iron bars. The lock and key to this door were a source of wonder to my brothers and me because of their enormous proportions, or so they seemed to our childish eyes. The door was guarded at all times by a very tall, blue-eyed Albanian, Abdallah. Watching that door, monitoring who came in and out, was his only occupation. He was fierce looking with his giant, silver mustache and a full beard. He wore billowing black trousers cinched at the ankles, a black vest trimmed in silver, and a monumental turban that he was never without. But it was the pistols hanging from both sides of his wide belt that greatly piqued our curiosity. And on the rare occasion when we could charm our way into his old heart, he spoke about them. He told us stories of his exploits and took us into his little room beside the gate to see his sabre and to admire the shotguns lined up on a rack. We begged him to explain to us how these were used and asked him if he had ever killed anyone with them. This was the question, if any, we knew would lead him to telling us tales of battles he had known.

Abdallah had been one of my grandfather's slaves, and had gone with Fawzy Bey on all his campaigns. His favorite story of that time was about the assault they had made on the walls of Acra. He was still very young then and was attached to a battalion of soldiers who besieged a fortress he referred to as Kapou Bourgou. Abdallah described engaging in hand-to-hand combat with Albanians like himself and brought to dramatic life those long forgotten times. As we sat transfixed, listening intently, he laid out the corpses of his enemies before our avid young eyes, then reenacted his own bloody collapse.

I relished his stories. And, I must confess, I dreamed of disguising myself as a man when I grew up in order to go into battle as the captain of a fleet or as a general. The women who were the models for what I was intended to become seemed pale by comparison. Their lives appeared insignificant and bland when held up against the glare of my daydreams. All they were interested in was eating and dressing, while I imagined myself going forth on great adventures, performing extraordinary feats of valor from which I would emerge victorious. The main entrance of the house, with its beautiful double doors, was only used occasionally by the time I was born. It was on the canal side of the house and had two wide steps leading directly down to the water. The heavy doors were elaborately decorated with metal work and were flanked by fluted columns that must have been pillaged from an ancient Roman temple or even a church. On the ground floor there were slits through the thick walls meant to accommodate rifle barrels, rather than give light. Jutting out over the canal was a huge, airy stone balcony surrounded by *mashrabiyya* screens. This was part of the *mandara,* which you reached by a set of steep, narrow stairs. It was a roomy, elegant hall with high ceilings that was considered the most beautiful in the house. The *mandara,* paved with big slabs of sandstone, was raised into platforms on either side to form sitting alcoves as well as on a third side, which was the balcony. These platforms were covered with rugs and cushions. In the middle of the hall was a carved stone fountain that my father turned on whenever he wished to please us. I remember trembling with excitement as I poked my little hands and feet beneath the feathery jets at the first sign of warm weather. Light from colored glass windows glowed down on this fountain tinting the drops of water and devising fleeting patterns on the pale floors. In the afternoon, the ceilings retreated in cool, mysterious shadow.

On festive occasions, the two enormous chandeliers that hung in the *mandara* were lighted with hundreds of candles. The ceilings then came to life. The massive support beams were intricately carved, painted in red and gold, and glinted in the warm radiance of the candlelight. The walls were almost entirely lined with little cupboards and niches filled with my father's books. The woodwork was quite ornate, and as children we followed the decorative contours as part of a game in which we imagined animals and plants of all sorts emerging from the geometric patterns.

My father owned a collection of manuscripts of Arabic poetry that were illuminated and had soft leather bindings that I longed to touch. It was their beauty that attracted my attention as a child, although later I would appreciate their contents. My father, however, forbade me from coming near them, and only rarely showed them to me himself because they were extremely valuable.

7 · MY FATHER

As soon as I stopped being a very little girl, the women tried to keep me from going into the men's quarters. I stubbornly refused to cooperate, and my father ultimately declared that I did not seem to be a little girl one could confine to a harem. This pleased me, of course!

I had favorite corners in my father's part of the house. In winter, I liked to sit in a cozy niche between two cupboards; in summer, I chose a breezy corner of the big balcony overlooking the canal.

At first, as long as I didn't get in the way, he put up with my presence in his study the way one puts up with a small, capricious pet curled up quietly on a divan, or on the corner of a rug. Then, I suspect, he got used to my company and seemed pleased to have me with him. He never said anything about it, but sometimes I caught a look of delight on his face that he tried unsuccessfully to conceal.

Although I was nicknamed "Whirlwind" by my grandmother and consistently misbehaved when I was in the harem, my behavior changed radically when I was with my father. In the *salamlek* I was beyond reproach. I sat for hours motionless with a book on my lap, reading or daydreaming.

Eventually, my father began to guide my readings, and when I was able to understand French, he offered me a book of poetry that he particularly loved. It was in a little niche, above the canal, that I first read *Légende des Siècles,* the poetry of Leconte de Lisle, *Hérédia,* Sully Prudhomme, and many others in volumes bound in fragrant, red leather. These books were printed on thick paper, the bindings were sewn by hand, and the covers were decorated with a vignette: a naked man, hoeing in a sunrise landscape.

My father took pleasure in molding my tastes according to his own. I was subtle enough to understand him. Without ever asking him for anything, I felt he gave me a great deal.

He was a very cultured man. I was told that my grandfather, whom I never saw, could neither read nor write and had suffered because of his ignorance.

When my father was born, my grandfather named him Farid, the "Unique," and resolved to give him the best education he could. As soon as it was time, he sent my father to study with the best teachers, the *ulama,* at the Azhar University. They taught him the Qur'an and all that an educated and pious Muslim should know. Later, Fawzy Bey sent his son to Constantinople to one of the sultan's schools, where he spent three years learning Turkish and Persian. My father acquired a real love for the Persian language and especially for its poetry. He learned hundreds of verses by heart, and it was said that ие willingly recited poetry to anyone who would listen.

By the time he was ready to go out into the world and make his way as an adult, the governors of Egypt were looking for support from European educated scholars, engineers, and jurists. An old-fashioned education, such as the one my father had received, was no longer valued.

My grandfather, who was sensitive to the climate of the times, transferred my father from Constantinople to Paris. My father was ordered to study law, but apparently this prospect did not appeal to him. He did go, however; and as he was an obedient son and also a man curious about the world, he made the best of his circumstances. He learned French fluently, joined literary clubs, and wrote poetry. Some of his poems would have appeared in a Parisian periodical, *La Revue du Progrès,* had that issue not been banned from publication by the censors of Napoleon III.

Farid remained in Paris four years. When his father became seriously ill, he called him back to Cairo and had just enough time, before he died, to introduce him to the Khedive Ismail and to get him appointed to his cabinet as a translator.

My father translated all sorts of books, but his favorites remained those of the French poets. He received the work of contemporaries he had known in Paris and read his translations at his Friday night gatherings in the house overlooking the canal.

Of course, I was strictly forbidden to attend, but as my father and I grew closer, he finally agreed to let me stay behind the door of his room to listen, hidden by a heavy velvet curtain.

Oh, the joy of those Friday nights! The musicians, singers, journalists, philosophers, and playwrights who came . . . I heard Hafez Ibrahim and Sami el Baroodi reading their first works there. There were interesting conversations about literature, heated discussions and commentaries on the ideas of Gamal ed Din el Afghani, Abou Naddara, and Sheikh Muhammad Abdu on the emancipation of women and their role as nationalists.

I listened hungrily and sometimes, when I could not stand the isolation, I ventured out from behind the door, lifted a corner of the crimson curtain, and tried to make out the faces of the guests. Often, I was so drunk with the

words or the rhythms I was hearing that I forgot myself
until I was startled out of my reverie by my father's imperious voice. If he caught me, he ordered me back to the
harem. I went. But I had heard enough to understand that I
would one day do everything I could to bring about its
downfall.

8 · THE PURCHASE OF SLAVES

Despite my escapades into my father's world, the harem
was where I spent most of my time. The building was
composed of many full-sized rooms, as well as abbreviated
spaces that passed for rooms. No two rooms were on the
same level, nor alike, but every nook and cranny echoed
with the history of generations of women who had lived
there or just passed through.

The harem was a jumble of hallways, stairs, niches
where servants slept, corners, bedrooms, reception rooms,
baths, and a mosque.

In the center of this complex was the *kaa,* a large hall
that occupied the entire first floor. Extending out from it
was a spacious, covered balcony, protected on all sides by
mashrabiyya windows. On the other side was a second, open
veranda that extruded over the gardens that were strictly
reserved for the use of the women of the family. This balcony faced north and was always swept by cool breezes.
The women kept their long-necked, pear-shaped water bottles on the stone balustrades among the pungent, white jasmine that blossomed there all year long. Because the bottles
were made of porous clay, they sweated. In this way, the
breezes wafting around them cooled their contents.

I remember with what meticulous care the women prepared these *ollas,* as they were called, before filling them. A

new bottle was carefully washed, left to dry, then turned upside down over a burning piece of incense until it filled with fragrant smoke. The incense permeated the pores and not only purified the interior but also gave the water an ineffably sweet taste. Hidden in the wide necks of the *ollas,* a little below the lip, were exquisitely perforated filters decorated with pinprick geometric designs, sometimes of animals or plants. Each woman topped her bottle with an ornamental cone made of hand-hammered silver. Indje's was adorned on top with a little golden dove in flight, and Narguiss' with three pointed leaves.

Although the *kaa* was a very beautiful room, it was dark. Sunlight entered only at noon from the adjacent balcony overlooking the gardens. The floors were made of pink marble, and the walls and ceilings were decorated with elaborate woodwork. The floors were slightly raised on the sides, as they were in the *mandara,* and were spread with carpets and cushions. That is where the women sat.

At night, only two candles lighted this great room; and despite its elegance, I found it gloomy. I further disliked it because that is where my grandmother presided and received her visitors. I was often obliged to be in attendance. I found the conversations boring and the restrictions put on me intolerable. The hours spent in that room were a supreme torture and colored my feelings about it.

Often, when I left my father's quarters to get back to Narguiss' part of the house where I lived, I had to follow a dark passageway that was between my grandmother's apartments and those of her daughters-in-law. This hallway led into the *kaa.* I took great care to avoid it when it was full of people, making a long detour. But I was not always able to escape.

My grandmother, Gaulizar, ruled over the harem and the entire household with a stern hand. She was heavy, and her ankles were swollen, which made it difficult for her to get around as much as she would have liked. She never missed going into her son's rooms, however, to ensure that they had been perfectly aired, cleaned, and ordered. The rest of the time, she sat in the *kaa;* but her imperious voice reached to the far corners of the house, striking terror in the hearts of every one, especially the servants.

Every morning her staff gathered around her. First in command was my father's first wife, Gaulistan; then Nee-mat, the *khalfa,* or head housekeeper; third was Tahasin, the *khalfa's* right hand; and last but not least were the two *aghas,* Koutchouk and Mabrouk, who transmitted her orders to some thirty household slaves. Most of these slaves were Ne-groes, and their service guaranteed the efficient running of the entire household.

Gaulistan kept daily accounts; and together with my grandmother, she decided whether a cow or sheep should be slaughtered for the kitchens of the house and what provisions were needed from the shops or from the family farms. They decided on the menus for my father's dinners, which were prepared by his private cook for himself and any possible guests who might drop in. He rarely ate lunch at home. Gaulistan always added certain delicacies, which she prepared herself and sent to him after every meal: dainty sweets such as "lookooms," turkish delight, baklava, and ladies' fingers, among others. Sometimes, the harem received savory dishes from the men's kitchens after there had been a big party.

Gaulizar and Gaulistan lived in perfect harmony. They were both Circassians and had belonged to the harem of the palace before their marriages. The great *wali,* Muhammad Ali Pasha, had given Gaulizar to my grandfather; Gaulistan was a gift from the Khedive Ismail to my father when he returned from Paris.

On feast days Gaulizar and Gaulistan, loyal to their first home, went to pay their respects to the members of the household that had once been their own. They wrapped themselves from head to foot in their opaque *habaras,* care-

fully veiled their faces, and were driven to the palace in a
closed carriage, which returned to pick them up at the end
of the day. They were proud of their connection to the nation's leading house and considered their access to it an
honor. Gaulizar and Gaulistan took care to bring back a
flood of details about the visit that regaled their fellow in-
mates at home and provided them all with hours and days
of conversation.

Only one cloud cast a shadow over the otherwise perfect accord between Gaulistan and my grandmother: Gaulistan was barren. After ten years of marriage to my father,
endless attempts to conceive, multiple visits to tombs of
saints, and resorting to black magic as well as assiduous
prayer, she had to admit that she could not have children.

Although Farid Bey had not raised the issue or complained about Gaulistan's childless state, both Gaulistan and
Gaulizar knew that, one day, he would choose a second
wife. Both women wanted to guard against someone in
their midst who could be a painful source of discord. They
decided to take the initiative and choose a mate for my father, thus increasing the chances of having an ally rather
than a rival.

9 · INDJE AND NARGUISS

Gaulizar sent Koutchouk Agha to Roustoum Agha asking him to look out for two virgins: one Circassian
and one Ethiopian. Roustoum had furnished their harem for
years, and Gaulizar knew she could count on him.

The old trader was disconcerted when Koutchouk con-
veyed Gaulizar's request to him, however. Slavery had recently been abolished, and the police were vigilant, looking
for anyone plying his trade in secret. Only the night before,

soldiers had come knocking at his door to inspect. The cunning Roustoum had taken precautions in plenty of time, however, and had disposed of all but a few of his slaves. Indje, Narguiss, and three other women were left, along with a number of household servants. The officers questioned the five women, who affirmed that they were visiting their relative, Rokeyya, at her house in Bab el Shereyya.

The servants corroborated Roustoum's statement that they had chosen to remain with him of their own free will. But the officers insisted on reading out the decree before all the members of the household in order, they said, to apprise them of their rights. Only one young Sudanese male decided to leave. Roustoum did not try to dissuade him but handed him a small sum of money, saying, "May God bless you," and wished him farewell. Later, he said to Indje and Narguiss that he felt the man was stupid to abandon the security he had enjoyed for the unknown.

Roustoum Agha complained bitterly about this new decree. He had savings, and asserted that he was not motivated by financial need. Rather, he said, he was heartbroken to see the demolition of the most refined and civilized of societies. Of course, someone who had been a slave before becoming a slave trader could conceive of no other universe but one inhabited by slaves and masters.

He repeated endlessly, "Why do we have to change? Because some foreigners living in our country want to impose their customs on us?" He maintained that since the fall of Ismail Pasha, the *mufattish,* strangers had ruled Egypt, and he was persuaded that they had put the khedive up to this.

"What business was it of theirs, whether or not we have slaves," he griped. "Did the slaves complain?" He could see no reason for this disruption of a perfectly good system. Didn't the slaves become favorites of the harem? Weren't the *mamluks* pampered by their masters? Didn't some even become rulers of Egypt? Didn't this system provide people with the most enviable of lives? They were fed, dressed, sheltered, well married, given generous dowries, and eventually, even their freedom when they had earned it, and if they wished it! Were the Negroes who served in these rich houses not more fortunate than their brothers in the wilderness of the Sudan or Ethiopia?

Roustoum Agha complained that European servants who were free were subjected to insufferable abuse. "They have the freedom to be fired, to be reduced to penury on the most insignificant of pretexts," he ranted. "These intruders howl about the cruelty of slave merchants! But am I cruel? Do I treat my slaves any differently than I do my children?" he growled.

Roustoum and Rokeyya spent hours lamenting the unfairness of being condemned because of the excesses of a few irresponsible characters in the trade. He could not abide the reasoning behind the suppression of a whole way of life. Indje and Narguiss agreed with him, and neither of them ever changed their minds. They considered the slave-master relationship natural, and I came to realize, finally, that this concept was hardest to uproot from the hearts of slaves, especially those who had been treated kindly.

When Gaulizar's word reached Roustoum, he found himself faced with a genuine dilemma. He would have refused outright to consider her petition had it not been for his high esteem of Farid Bey. How was he going to satisfy a client he venerated and avoid trouble with the law? . . . He knew where to find a young Ethiopian . . . Transacting a sale was a risk . . . As to Circassians, he only had Indje and Narguiss left . . . They were virgins . . . He could perhaps send Narguiss . . . She was the more mature of the two . . .

When Indje and Narguiss found out that Roustoum was not only thinking of selling them but that they might be separated, they burst into tears; their friendship had deepened during the months they lived side by side in his house. Rokeyya, seeing their pain, began to weep herself, and reproached her husband. She had become very attached to the two young girls.

Because of his wife's indignation, Roustoum nearly sent

word to Gaulizar that he had no more slaves to sell, but
changed his mind. He understood the workings of the
harem intimately and could easily guess the reasons for
Gaulizar and Gaulistan's appeal to him. A slave who would
give the master a son would become a wife, be cherished,
and be treated with respect. He could no more deprive Indje
or Narguiss of this chance than stand in the way of a good
marriage for one of his daughters. He put the problem before them, and asked them to decide. The sisters each
lovingly offered the other for this privileged opportunity
until Rokeyya proposed another solution: she would take
them both to Gaulizar, arguing that the old woman could
most certainly be persuaded to buy the pair. Roustoum,
wishing to ensure the success of his wife's mission, told her
that he would sell Indje and Narguiss at a price that Gaulizar
would find difficult to turn down.

He could afford to be generous! He had reclaimed most
of his former slaves when the *mufattish*'s household was broken and had paid nothing to get them back.

Roustoum Agha's house was close to my father's house.
One foggy morning, heavily shrouded, Rokeyya took the
sisters and went on foot to see Gaulizar and Gaulistan.
Nothing in their appearance betrayed who they were, nor
could anyone have guessed that Rokeyya was a merchant on
her way to dispose of a pair of slaves.

My mother clearly remembered the walk to the house
on the Khalig. She told me that it had been the only time
she had gone anywhere on foot since being brought to
Egypt. She recalled glimpsing an old mosque with a fountain burbling nearby, smelling oil from what must have
been a working oil press, crossing a bridge, and then feeling
a surge of intense anxiety when she heard the heavy gate of
Farid Bey's house close behind her.

What fate awaited her and her sister Narguiss?

The three women followed Abdallah up a set of complicated stairs, and Koutchouk led them through a labyrinth of
hallways into the wing of the house inhabited by my grand-

mother. Gaulizar was in the kitchens. Someone was sent to fetch her. She came promptly with the *khalfa,* Neemat.

Once they were in the house, Indje and Narguiss removed their street clothes and veils. Beneath the dark layers, they were elegantly dressed in identical costumes appropriate for their ages and station in life. They wore *yaleks,* short jackets of deep blue taffeta, pale blue blouses and full silk skirts cinched at the waist by silver lamé belts. The *yashmaks* that covered their heads and faces were made of matching blue georgette, bordered with silk fringe. They wore jewelry given to them by Roustoum and Rokeyya and little red leather slippers, open at the back.

They must have looked breathtakingly beautiful.

Narguiss had quick black eyes, set in an oval face without a blemish, and opulent dark hair. Her nose was slightly arched and her mouth full and sensuous. She was tall, well-developed, and vibrantly healthy. My mother had a delicate kind of beauty and was more fragile. She had a small, round face with a very straight nose, a tiny mouth and dimpled cheeks, a creamy complexion, and fine blond hair. Her blue eyes were meltingly sweet and never lost their childlike candor. She was short and a little plump.

Rokeyya had told the sisters what to expect from Gaulizar and Gaulistan. They knew that they would be rigorously examined. Farid Bey's wife and mother would not miss a chance to disparage the merchandise as part of the bargaining game. "Don't take any of what you hear or see too much to heart," Rokeyya cautioned Indje and Narguiss.

If Gaulizar and Gaulistan agreed, the girls would take up residence in the harem for a trial period that lasted as long as the two women required: one month or longer.

Rokeyya then warned them, "Farid Bey's household is run by two discerning women, who keep a sharp eye on every detail!" She emphasized that the house on the Khalig was not a palace, like the *mufattish*'s, run by the *aghas.* Here the women were in charge!

It was important for Indje and Narguiss to make an

equally good impression so that Gaulizar would find it hard to choose between them and buy them both. That was Rokeyya's strategy. The girls had to prove that they were even tempered, modest, reserved, submissive, and capable of strict obedience while not appearing servile. Rokeyya promised to stay with them day and night to prompt them and begged them to follow her instructions to the letter.

During the first interview, Gaulizar and Gaulistan asked the sisters about their origins, ages, skills, and tastes. They pretended not to attach too much importance to their beauty.

Rokeyya did her part by introducing them as sisters who would languish and die of grief if they were separated. She recounted the story of their meeting, and spoke convincingly of the affinity between them and of their tender allegiance to one another. The merchant's words did not fall on unsympathetic ears. Gaulizar and Gaulistan had been slaves and understood these feelings. Gaulistan still had such a sister in the khedivial palace whom she visited frequently.

When it was decided that Indje and Narguiss would remain for a trial period, the *khalfa* was sent to collect their personal effects, and they were taken on a tour of the buildings and gardens. Gaulistan gave special attention to showing them the kitchens and the bakery. She was especially proud of how well run they were, and Rokeyya did not fail to express her admiration with the prevailing order in both.

After the tour, it was time to eat lunch. For Indje and Narguiss this provided a first opportunity to display their grace and some of their skills. They rose every time a servant brought in a dish, took it smoothly from her hands, served Gaulizar first, then presented it to Gaulistan, and finally to Rokeyya before helping themselves. They knew they were being watched, and carried out these rituals with just the right amount of humility and pride. They moved with poise around the little circular tables, and they took care never to turn their backs to any of the women seated on the cushions on the floors. They showed their agility by getting up and sitting down frequently without ever using their hands, a lesson in grace they had been taught since becoming slaves.

At the end of the meal, Narguiss prepared an orange syrup drink in an elegant pitcher, filled thin, matching glasses to the brim, and served the refreshment without ever spilling a drop.

Next, Indje made the coffee by expertly fanning the embers in the charcoal brazier, heating water in a small, brilliantly polished copper pot, adding just the right amount of coffee and sugar, and pouring the thick, fragrant brew into Gaulizar's coffee service. This service consisted of a dozen miniscule pink porcelain cups, which were so fragile that she trembled at the thought of breaking one.

My grandmother was very fond of this Japanese coffee service, and prized it even though it was not particularly valuable. Coffee was served in it daily until I broke it on my eighth birthday. I don't know what devil of vanity took hold of me; I wanted to act grown up and insisted on serving the coffee. My mother tried to dissuade me, but I obstinately refused to listen. The coffee cups were barely bigger than a thimble, nestled inside little silver filigree holders, sitting on tiny, unsteady stems. I started to fill the first one, upset it, and watched in horror as it fell and broke. Gaulizar was furious. She told the *khalfa* to catch me and give me a spanking right then and there. The public slight was too much for my proud nature; I ran to the tray holding the remaining eleven cups and trampled them to pieces in a fit of wrath!

I was punished again, of course, and locked in a dark closet under the stairs. My grandmother refused to see me for fifteen days, and my sensitive mother fell ill with shock, pain, and humiliation. My Aunt Narguiss, and even the haughty Gaulistan, however, brought me sweets in secret to console me.

My father never interfered in matters of discipline in the harem, and I don't believe he was ever told about my temper tantrum or the damage I had done.

The young Narguiss and Indje were far more dexterous when they joined Farid Bey's household than I ever was and they never put a scratch or a nick in the treasured coffee service. But even so, Gaulizar and Gaulistan did not hesitate to embarrass them at the least sign of clumsiness. Every movement, every activity was a test. In peeling an egg or an orange, for example, they had to remove the shell, or the skin, meticulously so that the egg or fruit emerged whole and pristine.

Their culinary skills were also examined. Narguiss told me they did well enough to pass, but not so well that they risked arousing Gaulistan's jealousy.

The tests, Narguiss later told me, were not limited to their performance skills, but covered their most intimate personal attributes. The first night, while they took a bath, the door was opened and Gaulistan came in. She sat down and chatted easily with them for a few minutes, then left. Another day she offered, in the friendliest of manners, to trim and polish Indje's fingernails. Indje understood that she was testing their quality, and knew she had to concede. A third time, Gaulizar caressed my mother's head, and tugged playfully at her hair to see that it was healthy and make sure that she was not wearing a wig.

One morning, my grandmother gaily thrust a piece of caramel candy into Indje's mouth to see if her teeth were solid, and sniffed her breath on the sly to ascertain that it was sweet. She instructed Narguiss to cook something that required her to stand for a long time over a hot stove, making her sweat. This was an experiment to sample her natural body odors and determine whether or not they were tolerable.

Narguiss, who was generally very good natured, jovially recounted this incident to me, adding that these tests were performed in an atmosphere of fun and games. I never could hold my tongue, however, and lashed out with indignation, "But Auntie, you were being picked over like fruit!" Narguiss made a point of avoiding an argument with me. Instead, she told me another story in an effort to lighten my mood.

"One day," she began, "your mother was in the kitchens downstairs when she heard Gaulistan calling her urgently from the roof terrace; Indje was credulous and rushed up, arriving out of breath!" I can still hear Narguiss' chuckle as she added affectionately, "Your mother was quite plump at that time; Gaulistan was testing the soundness of her lungs!" It seems that upon seeing Indje flushed and panting, Gaulistan pretended to feel sorry for the little girl, and stroking her comfortingly, she took advantage of yet another opportunity to sample the merchandise.

My mother was terrified at the thought of being rejected. The following day, Gaulizar played the same trick on her, but this time Indje had grown wary and she did not hurry too much! When the old lady examined her at the top of the stairs, she appeared satisfied.

Among other things, Indje and Narguiss' linen, bedding, and underclothing were frequently inspected, either while they slept or when they were out of their room. Gaulizar and Gaulistan wanted to be certain that they were clean and fresh. Although Gaulistan made no disobliging remarks, Gaulizar always found cause to grumble about the carelessness of the new generation.

One washday, the sisters were conducted to a pile of clothes and linens that had been washed and dried under the brilliant morning sun on the terrace. The servants had collected the laundry, and while it was still warm, Indje and Narguiss were invited to stretch, fold, and iron it. Woe to them if a crease was out of place in Gaulistan's *yashmak,* or Gaulizar's *yalek!*

When they found themselves before Farid Bey's *gebba,*

kaftan, and shawls, however, they were stumped. They were totally unfamiliar with men's clothing and did not know what to make of the broadcloth trousers or how to handle the silk lapels on the morning coats.

Gaulizar and Gaulistan remarked on this, and reproached Rokeyya for giving the girls an incomplete education.

Narguiss was truly despondent about their failure; but it did not take her long to find out that neither Gaulistan nor Gaulizar could do better and that caring for Farid Bey's wardrobe was not women's work, anyway. Gaulistan and Gaulizar's indignation had been feigned. They were, in fact, quite relieved to find the girls wanting in this respect and quickly recognized their deftness at folding and organizing clothes and perfuming and storing linen in coffers.

When they were asked to show their skills at sewing and embroidery, they performed passably. Once again their examiners were relieved because they were not too talented at needlework. They certainly did not wish to be outshone.

Indje had hoped to distinguish herself through a display of her musical talents and her education. No one was interested in these, however, and she soon discovered that neither Gaulizar nor Gaulistan could read or write.

One day, in an unusual moment of quiet in the harem, when no one was around, Indje found an old string instrument hanging in one of the rooms. It had been neglected, and was out of tune. She repaired and tuned it and asked Rokeyya whether she should perform for the harem. Rokeyya cautioned her to keep her talent well hidden and to reserve her delicate accomplishments for the ears of Farid Bey only, adding knowingly: "He will know how to appreciate these treasures!"

Indje, however, could not resist taking down the instrument and strumming it. She played some popular songs, an unpretentious diversion, for which she was applauded warmly. By the time they discovered the full extent of her talents, it was too late. Farid Bey had already fallen in love with her.

I never found out how much Ismail Pasha had paid for my mother and Narguiss, but Gaulizar and Gaulistan made no secret of the bargain they had struck. They were proud to let everyone know that a mere 1,200 Egyptian pounds had been paid to Roustoum Agha for their purchase. Normally, one virgin of my mother's beauty, age, and education brought no less than 800 to 1,000 Egyptian pounds at that time. They had acquired two for little more than the price of one!

An unwritten code governed the selling and buying of slaves. Although no contract was ever drawn up for the sale of Indje and Narguiss, the rules applied. The agreed upon sum was to be paid in gold coins, half at the time of purchase and the rest at the end of the first year; Rokeyya would have visitation rights once a month for that period to ensure that the girls were not only treated well but were happy. Either party could rescind the agreement during that time. If Indje and Narguiss were returned for any reason, Roustoum and Rokeyya would have to reimburse the full price of their purchase provided they were still virgins and in good condition. Otherwise, the first installment was retained. In either case, the slaves were restored to the merchants with only the personal effects they had brought with them during their probation. Any clothing or jewelry they had received during their stay had to be returned.

There was a time when I could not think of my mother being sold without bitter tears of rage, and years passed before I was able to forgive my grandmother and Gaulistan. But my resentment was particularly acrimonious toward my grandmother, Gaulizar, whom I held responsible for what I considered to be the supreme indignity inflicted on my mother. But of course Gaulizar and Gaulistan were acting in good faith, in accordance with the customs of their time. It never entered their minds to question the system that sustained them and had looked after women like them for generations, nor did they think of slavery as an abomination.

Who was guilty then?

Was it Roustoum Agha and traders like him? . . . Was it men like my father? . . .

They were all persuaded that they acted in the best interest of everyone involved, that they did so honorably, honestly, and with great goodwill. They respected the rules and traditions that governed their world and felt, in all good conscience, that they were God-given and that they executed them thoughtfully.

Who was then to blame? . . .

10 · THE MASTER

Indje and Narguiss were introduced to their master only forty days after they came to the house on the Khalig. They shared a room in the remotest corner of the harem, a precaution against his accidentally seeing them. But there was no danger of that really because he never went further than the *kaa* when he visited the harem, and he never came unannounced.

My mother claimed that she saw my father for the first time only on the day when she was introduced to him formally. When I refused to believe this, she was angry with me. Narguiss, on the other hand, smiled mysteriously. She had had a glimpse of Farid Bey the day after Rokeyya had brought them to his house. She had questioned the *khalfa* about him, and when Neemat told her that he was as handsome as the prophet Joseph himself, Narguiss was intrigued. She had charmed a servant into taking her to a window hidden in a small closet that overlooked the men's gardens, and standing there, she saw my father walking with a friend. She claimed to have liked him instantly!

My father was a very handsome man. He was tall, erect, and always well dressed. His auburn hair, moustache, and beard had golden highlights, his nose was beaked, his eyes bright and intelligent, his hands slender and lively, and his carriage proud. As I was growing up, and especially as an adolescent, to me, he personified the ideal of masculine beauty.

One day, as I looked through one of my father's picture albums, I found the photograph of a young woman with a serious, melancholy face. She was dressed in a long, gathered skirt, her hair pulled back tightly under a hat that must have been in fashion in the Paris of my father's student days. At the back was an inscription which read: "To Farid, always yours." It was signed Marguerite and dated May 1, 1867, in Saint Cloud.

That picture set me dreaming. I took it out often and gazed at the face of this Parisian woman who must have been my father's first love. I thought I detected a resemblance between her and my mother and conjectured that my father had fallen in love with Indje for that reason.

It was my father's habit to come to the harem every morning for a cup of coffee with his mother and Gaulistan. This morning coffee was a ritual. My grandmother always took her place in a window seat, on a wide divan, sitting with her legs tucked under her. The enormous mass of her body was even more imposing at rest than when she was moving, and her huge face was very white and looked like a full moon. This effect was further exaggerated by the huge white wool turban she wrapped around her head. Gaulistan sat a little below her, on the left, on a cushion. My father had an easy chair on his mother's right.

The *khalfa,* Neemat, came in as soon as my father appeared. She was usually accompanied by an Ethiopian slave. Both were dressed formally in long, blue silk dresses with wide, vertical yellow stripes, a brocade corselet worked with gold thread, and with their heads always covered. The servant brought a large silver tray laden with cups and brightly polished coffee servers, *kanakas,* which she set down on a low ebony table inlaid with mother of pearl. On her head, Neemat carried a small rug, fringed and heavily embroidered with silk and gold thread. She flicked it with a studied movement on to the servant's shoulder, and the servant spread it on a small table placed in front of my father. The *khalfa* then poured the steaming coffee from each kanaka, and presented the first cup to my father, the second to my grandmother, and the third to Gaulistan. She then squatted in a corner of the room and waited.

My father chatted about one thing and another with his mother and his wife, then taking his leave of them, he walked out tossing a few silver coins to the *khalfa* and the servant. Much later, my mother, Narguiss, and I were granted permission to serve coffee and then allowed to sit beside Gaulistan as my father drank it.

Although my mother was my father's property, he knew nothing of her existence in his household until Gaulizar and Gaulistan decided it was time to reveal their secret.

The day Indje was introduced to Farid Bey, she took the place of the Ethiopian servant for the coffee ceremony. Her hand trembled so much that she spilled a drop on the embroidered rug. She was mortified and blushed furiously. She must have looked delectable! My father was puzzled by the appearance of a face he didn't know under his roof and asked about the young girl. Gaulistan, smiling mysteriously, explained. It was clear he found Indje attractive, and as she felt his eyes resting on her from time to time, the little slave averted hers modestly.

That night, Indje did not lay out her mattress beside Narguiss'. She was taken alone to a richly furnished room, in a different wing of the harem, which henceforth became her own. An Ethiopian slave was attached to her service and attended to her personal needs. The servant helped her dress, arrange her hair, bathe, and perfume herself.

When Indje appeared among the womenfolk the next morning, she had a valuable square-cut emerald on her finger which she wore until she died.

There was no formal marriage ceremony, no festivities celebrating their union, and household rituals were carried out as usual. Six months later, Narguiss became my father's wife, and my mother was already pregnant with a child who did not survive.

In all the years I watched my mother and Narguiss, I never once noticed the slightest hint of jealousy between the two sisters. The sharing of a man did not alter in any way the tender affection that united them.

11 · THE REBELLIOUS CHILD

I was born at noon on the first day of spring, the feast of *Sham el Nessim*. My arrival was greeted with warm breezes, bird song, resplendent sunshine, drumming, flutes, and the sound of fire crackers. I was told that I responded by squawking loudly, which my grandmother would later explain by saying, "She was already showing signs of her notorious bad temper!"

My mother did not have enough milk, and so a wet nurse had to be found; but until then, my grandmother bought a goat and a cow to meet my needs, and someone was hired to milk them. I have no recollection of the cow, but the goat was around all the time I was growing up and lived to a ripe old age in a corner of the garden. When I could walk, I went there to pet and feed it. This was a daily ritual.

When Gaulizar sent word to my father's village to say that we were looking for a nursing mother, a *fellaha,* the wife of a peasant, was sent to us. I was put on the breast along with her baby daughter. My nurse's name was Amina and her daughter was Fatma. Amina was short and plump and had a round face that grew rounder the longer she stayed in our house. Nothing she asked for was ever denied. She gorged on candies and cakes to such an extent that it resulted, I am persuaded, in my lasting distaste for sweets. If anyone tried to curb Amina's excesses, she complained to the midwife who came to the house to examine her once a week. This woman forbade anyone from interfering with Amina's whims if we wanted her milk to remain abundant.

Amina had been thoroughly examined when she first came to the harem; my grandmother and Gaulistan had scrutinized her, and the midwife had to verify that she and her baby were healthy and clean and that her milk was good. My grandmother ordered that the clothes the mother and baby had come with be removed. Amina was bathed, her body scrubbed with a new *loofa,* her feet with a pumice stone and disinfectant soap, and her hair was washed and combed with a fine-tooth comb to make sure it was not infested. Her baby was also thoroughly bathed and given a new layette. Amina's new clothes included long, ample cotton dresses, white cotton underclothing, head scarves, handkerchiefs, slippers, and a heavy black velvet overdress for street wear.

As time went on, Amina's neck, wrists, and fingers glistened with gold. She loved jewelry and was offered a piece to celebrate every event that punctuated my childhood: my first smile, my first tooth, my first word, my first step, my first birthday, my weaning, not to mention all the other occasions she fabricated in between when she wanted something.

Narguiss told me that when I started to walk, my grandmother threw five gold coins on the floor of the *kaa,* a short distance from where I stood. I was expected to cover that distance without help and toddle into her open arms. My success would be a happy omen, a sign of my future good fortune, and also Amina's, of course, because she would be rewarded with the coins. Amina had gone through this little exercise with me, and could already hear them jingling in her pockets! But that day, I fancied going in the opposite direction, stumbled, and fell flat on my face. My mother fainted, Narguiss ran to pick me up, and my grandmother raged at "this unruly child of whom we shall never be able to make anything" and took back her five gold coins. I don't think my nurse ever forgave me their loss! Narguiss laughed whenever she told this story. She said, "It was the open door that had attracted your attention, you rascal! You were already looking to escape."

Amina loved to go out for rambles in the streets of the city. She never hesitated to ask the coachman to harness the horses and take her for rides. She would settle back triumphantly in the plush seat and stay out as long as she wished. She took me along, but I was rarely alone with her. My milk sister, Fatma, was always with us. She was a big baby whose plump arms, legs, and full cheeks drew the admiration of all the harem women and accentuated my mother's distress. Indje lamented the fact that I remained thin and wiry while Fatma flourished. But Fatma died at the age of seven or eight after Amina left our house, and I survived.

My earliest memory dates back to a time when we visited my father's family village. I remember our house was big and square. The mud houses of the peasants abutted like nests against the rear wall, while the façade looked out over brilliant, green fields. I remember the hum of activity when peasant women came to bake. This was done in a room surrounded by orange and lemon trees, whose pungent blossoms permeated the air, especially in the early morning. This room was a little ways from the house, at the end of a grape trellis. I remember distinctly a sweet smell of smoke from the oven fires, the women with their sleeves hiked up above their elbows, kneading, and the bread being taken out with long, wooden paddles and scattered on mats to cool.

My father, for some reason, was absent that summer. My mother was already ailing and had been sick since my birth. My grandmother and Gaulistan ran the house in the village as they did the one in the city, and their authority was unquestioned. My mother languished all day on a divan, Narguiss always at her side. The wives and mothers of the peasants who cultivated my father's land lived in the houses nestled against ours and visited regularly, sitting cross-legged on the floor beside my mother.

This house full of women is my first memory.

In the fall of that same year, Narguiss gave birth to her second son, Hassan. Her first child was born dead, and Hassan lived only to the age of ten. Narguiss had three more children, a boy and two girls, who also died young. Hassan's nurse had a daughter. For her, for Fatma, and for me, Hassan became a living toy.

Often, in the late afternoon, when the sun was not too hot, Hassan's nurse and Amina took us into the village, escorted by guards, to show us off. They rode on mules and were self-important. We children rode donkeys, led by young boys. I remember screaming because I wanted to ride by myself, and these boys would not let go of my little grey donkey's bridle.

As you know, it is rare to find a wet nurse who does not finish her days in the family of the child she has nursed and raised. These women are spoiled rotten, and get lazy.

This was not to be the case for Amina. She had become so vain and quarrelsome, loud and demanding, as to make her presence intolerable. She bickered constantly with the servants and accused them of lacking respect for her. Her voice was so shrill that you could almost drill holes in the walls with it. Neemat and the *aghas* repeatedly tried to quiet her, but nothing worked. If they interfered, she screamed louder, and even Gaulizar and Gaulistan couldn't make her stop.

Sometimes, when the sound of her tantrums reached the men's quarters and my startled father appeared on his balcony, the floodgates of Amina's interminable laments were thrown wide open. As soon as she saw him, she wailed more persistently, complained that she was abused, threw her arms up, looked beseechingly to the heavens, pointed to the sky, gestured, and made desperate pleas for divine intervention, sobbing all the while. My father, like everyone else, was helpless before her, and quickly escaped to his study.

One day, after an unusually violent confrontation with my grandmother, Amina grabbed her daughter by the hand and left, the sound of her protests echoing all the way down the street. My father ordered her belongings sent to her in the village with explicit instructions that she never set foot in our house again. Later, when her husband came to ask my father to forgive Amina and take her back, my father refused. He gave him some money and sent him away. This man, Abu Salem, had stopped working when he saw that he could depend entirely on his wife's wages. He opened a little grocery store in the village but soon went bankrupt, and he and his family survived mostly on what money he begged from my father and later from me.

Meeting Amina was always a painful experience. Not only did she not spare me her recriminations, bemoaning our ingratitude, but she loomed large in my grandmother's vindictive remarks when Gaulizar was ever angry with me. "Oh, you are truly Amina's daughter!" she would shout, "You drank her foul character along with her milk!"

After Amina left in a huff, taking Fatma with her, I was given a new playmate. Zakeyya was a few years older than me, a little Sudanese girl, and the daughter of one of Gaulizar's slaves. We took to each other instantly, and she remained a devoted friend until her death ten years ago.

12 · MAGIC

My grandmother, Gaulistan, Narguiss, my nurse, and all the women in the household believed in spirits with the exception of my mother, who because of her education perhaps, was not only skeptical but never took part in the ceremonies surrounding them.

My childhood was peopled by djinni, phantoms of one kind or another. I will always remember how, at any hour of the day or night, in some remote corner of the harem, one could run into secret gatherings of one sort or another. These consisted of household members and visitors, whose faces were quite familiar to me because they came so frequently, performing some magic to dispel the evil eye of envy and exorcising or protecting against some malevolent spirit. The visitors were *sheikhas* and *codias,* "wise women" who had the gift to commune with the spirits and the world of the invisible.

Because she was so afraid of phantoms, my grandmother never allowed me to sleep alone. She believed that there was protection in numbers; Amina, my milk sister, Fatma, and later Zakeyya always shared my room.

Every morning, an old woman, Sheikha Zahira, came to read the protective *Surat el Falak* (Of the Dawn) for my benefit. She held a copy of the Holy Qur'an over my head, saying: "In the name of God, the Most Gracious, the Most Merciful,

> Say: I seek refuge
> With the Lord of the Dawn,
> From the mischief
> Of created things;
> From the mischief
> Of Darkness as it spreads;

From the mischief
of those who practice
Secret Arts;
And from the mischief
Of the envious one
As he practices envy.

Then, she scattered seven pinches of coarse salt in a circle around my head, gathered them up again, put half in the
fire and threw the rest in water. Again, at night, someone
tossed salt and incense on the live coals in the brazier in my
bedroom to chase away any evil spirits that might be lurk-
ing in corners ready to harm me. As the salt popped and
crackled, I had visions of little men and strange animals undulating in fragrant folds of smoke then beating a hasty retreat. Even now, the crackling of a fire evokes this scene
from my childhood.

If I ever sickened or even became slightly indisposed, it
was always owing to someone's having cast a spell on me.
Amina was rigorously questioned, and so was I: Had someone looked at me too long? Who had spoken to me that
day? Had anyone complimented me? Compliments were
particularly suspect because it was believed that they were
born of envy, and could never be well meant. If the culprit
could be identified, the *sheikha* roughly twisted a piece of
paper into the shape of a doll, and saying the person's name,
she put out the "eyes" with a needle, threw the doll on the
fire, and circled the brazier murmuring incantations to exorcise the evil eye.

If no individual could be blamed, Amina was called on
to list those who had seen me on a given day. As she rattled
off the names of possible mischief-makers, the *sheikha*
pierced the doll's head twice with a hat pin. Or, sometimes,
a piece of alum was tossed on the live coals and, depending
on the shape it took as it melted, the women decided who it
was and whether it was male or female. Between them all,

they rarely failed to find a guilty party, whom the *sheikha* then punished. She stabbed the alum with a needle and threw it, along with the evil person it represented, into the canal below our house. I was always made to attend and participate in these ceremonies. I wonder now how I ever stopped believing in the evil eye and the magic used to dispel it because these practices had had such a powerful impact on me as a child.

As I grew older, magic practices began to lose their charm and, eventually, their hold on me. I must have been influenced by my mother who abhorred them, my father who condemned them, and whom I often heard admonishing Gaulistan for her superstitions, even though he dared not say anything to his mother. Also, as I began to read, the last vestiges of my grandmother's legacy lost the power to move me. The practices, however, decreased only after my grandmother's death. By then I was an adolescent.

If Gaulizar had lived long enough to witness the troubles life had reserved for me, she would certainly have insisted that they were born of my incredulous neglect to use the protective measures she had taken so many pains to teach me. And, at times, I must confess that I am given to wondering if she might not have been right!

13 · EDUCATION AND ESCAPADE

My grandmother was the first person in the household to consider the question of my formal education. I was assigned a teacher, Sheikh Hefny Soliman, whom we called Ustaz, or Master, Hefny. He was a trained reciter of the Qur'an and other sacred texts. He was a short, wiry old man with a white beard, always dressed in a white *kaftan,* who was a permanent resident of our household, as was his father before him. I remembered hearing the beautiful timbre of his voice, chanting in our mosque, long before I was ready to learn to read or write. He lived in the *salamlek,* the men's quarters, and had a daughter who chanted the Qur'an in the harem. He had trained her. His father had been my own father's teacher. And so it was quite natural that my grandmother thought of him when she was looking for a teacher for me and for Zakeyya, my little playmate.

Aside from his duties to our family, Ustaz Hefny ran a small *kouttab,* a school where he taught the children of the neighborhood to read, write, and recite the Qur'an. He received donations from his pupils' parents in addition to the support he had from us.

Every afternoon he waited for Zakeyya and me in a small room near the entrance hall of the house. When we first started taking lessons, Koutchouk, our old *agha,* was present. He sat in a corner of the room patiently counting his worry beads, but after a time, we were left to our own devices.

My father had a special table built for our lessons. It was made of polished hardwood and smelled deliciously of beeswax. A chair for the master was placed in front of it, but most of the time master and pupils preferred sitting on a Persian carpet on the flagstone floor.

Zakeyya and I each had a little slate on which Ustaz Hefny outlined the letters we were expected to copy and learn. We were each provided with a damp rag to erase our first awkward attempts at writing. Zakeyya and I mischievously took turns hiding the rags, and delighted in watching Ustaz Hefny search for them. If he did not find them, he would pull out a huge cotton handkerchief from his *kaftan* to do the job. Sometimes he even licked the slate clean, and we took pleasure in imitating the master.

When the great day came to show off what we had learned, my father, mother, Narguiss, Gaulizar, Gaulistan, and many others gathered in the mosque to hear us recite the opening verses of the Qur'an. Zakeyya and I were warmly congratulated when we performed successfully, and Ustaz Hefny was rewarded by my grandmother with a beautiful new robe, a *gebba* made of white wool, and two full measures of wheat for his family. Afterwards, we went to the *kaa* with the women and gorged on sweets and pastries.

When the sheikh found an opportunity to show my grandmother the slate where I had already written my name followed by "Bism Illah el Rahman el Rahim," In the name of God, Most Gracious, Most Merciful, he was further rewarded with a white silk *kaftan,* which he put on right away.

I received my share of compliments, but without pleasure. I knew full well that my little hand had held the chalk to write, but that Ustaz Hefny's had guided it. As my shame stimulated my pride, however, I soon learned to write the formula by myself.

When I grew dissatisfied with writing on a slate, I persuaded my teacher to bring me paper, pen, and ink. He obliged me. A few days later, he came to our lessons with a long brass box that was a portable inkwell on one end and a quill holder on the other. In the space of a few short moments, Zakeyya and I had our hands, faces and clothing, and the paper, covered with ink spots. We were scolded, and Ustaz Hefny was sternly reprimanded by Gaulizar and Gaulistan for listening to me.

One morning I went with my grandmother on her daily inspection tour of my father's rooms. In his study, I spied a pen holder made of glass with a metal pen nib. The temptation was too great to resist! While my grandmother supervised the servants in the bedroom, I approached the desk cautiously. I took the long penholder in my hand, fingered it, looked at the nib, at the inkwell, at a pile of papers on the desk, and began. In the center of each page was a column of tightly fitted lines, written in small, even script. On either side of the writing were wide, blank margins. These unused spaces attracted my attention, and I began to fill them with my name and the words I had mastered during my lessons. But, as I only knew a few words, I could not fill all the blank spaces and began to scribble lines, meant as decorations. As I ran out of space on each page, I turned to another, and another, and another. All these efforts were, of course, accompanied by copious ink splotching. There were spots all over the table, my hands, and my clothes. I also left my eager fingerprints on all the pages.

When my grandmother saw what I had done, she screamed in horror and would have beaten me if I had not run away. Her heavy legs could not carry her fast enough to catch a little girl as quick and lively as a sparrow! I escaped and hid on the terrace in a raised alcove I knew she couldn't reach. I could hear her imprecations from a distance, accompanied by threats of the sort of punishment I could expect when my father came home. Nothing persuaded me to leave my hideout, however. Zakeyya, who knew where I was, brought me some cakes she had stolen from the kitchens, and I devoured them in my cramped space. I heard voices on and off all day, calling me.

It was hardest for me not to respond to my mother and Narguiss pleading with me to come out.

When it started to get dark, Zakeyya warned me that my father was home and had been told everything. My scandalous behavior had caused a tremendous stir; everyone in the house was talking about me.

Finally, Zakeyya showed Narguiss where I was, and my aunt succeeded in catching me. I fought like a devil to get away, but she held fast and carried me to the *kaa,* where my poor mother stood in tears. My grandmother was livid with anger, Gaulistan was stern and impassive, while the *khalfa* and servants trembled with fear at the prospect of what would happen to me. Narguiss pleaded with my grandmother to let her clean me up before taking me to my father, but Gaulizar refused. She said he had to see me as I was. I saw my mother give Narguiss an imploring look, and Narguiss wink back at her empathetically. She would have changed me had not Gaulistan followed us to enforce my grandmother's orders. I was as afraid of her as I was of my grandmother.

Narguiss only released me when we were in front of my father's desk. "Here is the pretty bird," she said, planting me firmly on the ground in front of him.

"A real demon!" Gaulistan shouted.

Even though I was furious, I managed to avert my eyes in my father's presence. I ground my teeth, clenched my fists, and watched him remove the shade from his desk lamp to get a better look at me.

He saw a dishevelled little girl, covered with ink, not to speak of dust from the alcove, and he burst out laughing. Narguiss followed suit, but Gaulistan was clearly taken aback. She tried to explain the enormity of what I had done, but her words fell on deaf ears. My father just fixed his eyes on me and continued laughing.

I believe that night was the first time my father looked at me with some degree of interest. I was only a girl, and my birth had no doubt disappointed him. He might even have held me a little responsible for my mother's illness, or perhaps he was just not interested in children. He had never been very attentive, in any case. That day, however, he and I became friends. Had he scolded, punished, or hit me, I would have certainly grown even more rebellious than I was already and would have harbored the same hostility toward him as I felt toward my grandmother and Gaulistan. His laughter disarmed me, although I remained a little doubtful about his motives. Was he just making fun of me? No. His voice held neither anger nor mockery when he said, "Come, Ramza. Come closer. Come show me your hands. So, you are interested in writing too! But, my daughter, if you wish to publish your work, it should not be at the expense of one of your colleagues. This poor Khalil. . . . Look at the state to which you've reduced his poems! His verses have totally disappeared under yours! You've destroyed them! Of course, they may not deserve better, but the author would not think so. He will certainly not be pleased at the sight of his masterwork scribbled over in this way. I will have to tell him the truth, and you will have to bear the consequences!"

My father smiled at me and added, "From now on when you wish to write, come here. Do you see these beautiful pencils? I will lend them to you. And this pen can become yours as soon as you learn to use it properly."

I looked at my father, my eyes wide with wonder, and he handed me a penholder made of ivory in the shape of a goose feather. It had a small glass inset in the stem. By putting your eye to the lens, you could see a magnificent palace shimmering with light. On the side it bore an inscription in French: "Paris Worlds Fair, 1867." I kept it a very long time.

Even though the pen was heavy and awkward, I was so pleased to be holding it that my father didn't have the heart to take it from me. He removed the metal nib and let me keep it.

I returned to the *kaa,* brandishing my penholder triumphantly for all to see, and ran to show it to my mother. I can still remember her look of relief at the unexpected outcome of my misdeed. She got up and dragged me off to her room followed by Narguiss, who bathed and changed me while merrily giving my mother a detailed description of the events.

My grandmother took the matter very badly. She cursed her son's weakness and predicted that he would live to regret having condoned my disobedience and encouraged my whims.

14 · ILLNESS AND RECOVERY

A round that time, I fell seriously ill. Amina, who came to visit me, spread the rumor that I was sick with grief at having lost her. She held Gaulistan and my grandmother responsible and, hypocritical to the end, showered my mother and me with concern.

What I had was typhoid!

My life was in danger and, despite my grandmother's cries and objections, my father consulted a European doctor who had an established reputation even though he was still young. His name was Doctor Comanos.

My grandmother had summoned Sheikha Zahira at the first sign of fever, and Sheikha Zahira multiplied her prayers and rituals.

One night I woke up, startled, feeling something warm and sticky trickling down my face. She had killed a pigeon and, while it fluttered in the last throes of life, the old witch held it over my head, letting its curative blood drip down on me. This was meant to exorcise the demon who was the source of my sickness. I only got worse!

A *codia* was summoned next, who claimed that I was possessed by a female djinni in love with my father and jealous of my mother, who was trying to kill me out of spite. She recommended a *zar,* an exorcism ceremony. As my father had strictly forbidden these, it had to be performed secretly and in silence. There was none of the drumming or chanting ordinarily associated with the *zar.* But, in my delirium I was aware of movement: people twirling, feet stamping, huffing, puffing, and heavy breathing. Several goats, sheep, and calves were slaughtered to appease the jealous djinni, and once more I was smeared with blood. The carcasses of the animals were given to the *codia,* who it was said, would throw them out to the dogs, and my illness with them. I wondered!

A talisman was fashioned from bits of hair cut off the hides of the sacrificed animals and kept religiously under my pillow until the day my grandmother died.

Dr. Comanos prescribed ice-cold baths. Not a single woman in the house would take charge of this operation, not even Narguiss. My mother was certain the doctor was a madman and dragged herself at my father's feet, crying and imploring him to spare me. She was absolutely persuaded I would die. My father would not listen. Finally, he had to give me these baths himself. It was not until much later that I understood the anguish this operation had caused him and the relief that came as my fever subsided and he was assured of having made the right decision.

Strangely enough, I have delicious memories of my convalescence. When I started to feel myself coming back to life, I was moved to a large, sunny room, cheerfully decorated with flowered wallpaper, and a bright blue wool rug on the floor. It was smartly furnished in the latest styles from Paris. It had an enormous Louis XV bed, into which I gratefully sank, an armoire with mirrored doors, in which I could watch everyone's comings and goings, and a round table with gracefully curved golden legs. A deep *bergère,* upholstered in pink silk, was placed under a window, near the bed, and that is where my mother reclined during the long hours she spent at my side.

The room was in the *salamlek* and was normally reserved for my father's house guests. The door opened out to a landing, near the stairs leading to his quarters. He had decided to put me there so that Doctor Comanos could call at any time without having to wait for the *aghas* to clear his passage of womenfolk.

At night, Narguiss slept at the foot of my bed on a mattress, and looked after me as she would have her own child. During the day a lot of visitors came, and Zakeyya, in particular, remained vigilant at my side. But the hours I relished most were those when both my parents were with me. To have both my father and my mother together at my side was a rare occurrence. My mother sat quietly on the pink daybed, saying little, but the smiles she gave me were suffused with love. My father brought me a doll or a toy of some sort every day and sat on a chair near my mother. Their long, leisurely conversations must have drawn them closer and deepened their affection in ways that might otherwise have been difficult in households such as ours.

I believe it was then that Gaulistan began to feel jealous of my mother. No particular incident stands out in my memory to illustrate this, but I seem to recollect a visit she and my grandmother made to my room while my mother was there. All three were ill at ease, and I sensed then both Gaulistan's and Gaulizar's veiled hostility toward her.

I did not enjoy these visits, even though both women spoiled me; and as soon as I could eat normally, Gaulistan even prepared delicious treats for me with her own hands. But somehow, I felt that I too had entered into the circle of their jealousy.

Strangely enough, it seemed to me that it was I they resented, almost more than my mother!

One day my father brought me a book of fairy tales, the *Contes de Perrault*. I asked him a thousand and one questions about the pictures and made him tell me the stories twenty times over.

I knew no French and yet wanted to learn to read. I wanted to know the meaning of the big, strange looking letters and words underneath the pictures. Finally, I made my father read to me. I did not understand a word, but he patiently taught me until I could repeat whole sentences by heart. Little by little I began to recognize the words I heard, and match them with those on the page.

When my father was not there, I made my mother read to me whether she wanted to or not. But when I was alone with Zakeyya, it was I who played the role of teacher. I taught her to read "Little Red Riding Hood" in chorus with me. We made the new syllables ring and showed off in front of visitors. Narguiss laughed, Gaulistan and my grandmother shrugged their shoulders and said we were a pair of crazy girls, and Sheikh Hefny understood nothing at all of our antics and looked perplexed.

Those dear, dear fairy tales! It was thanks to them that I learned my first words of French while playing.

My recollections of that time include three animals I adored that had been given to me by my father: A turtle, a parrot, and a baby donkey. The turtle lived only a short time, but I can still remember it moving slowly on the carpet, and even on my bed. My grandmother's superstitious imagination took flight at the sight of this little animal. Even though I was not at all afraid of the turtle, she pretended I was terrified and fainted in horror whenever it stuck its head out of the shell. She also maintained that my fever subsided because the turtle appropriated my illness. She swore this was true, invoking her favorite saints, Sayyed el Badawy and Fatma el Nabawiyya, but to me it was nothing but old wives' tales!

The turtle was a wonderful live toy for Zakeyya and me. When it was found dead under the wardrobe one morning, we were both heartbroken. This was my first encounter with death.

I bombarded Narguiss and my mother with questions about what it all meant, but they simply answered, "She's dead," which did not further enlighten me.

That same day my father brought me a parrot I named Sadek, and the turtle was forgotten. I gave Sadek rose water to drink, stuffed him with almonds, and would not be parted from him. I taught him to say, "bonjour" but when he learned nothing else, I gave him away to one of the servants because his monotonous repetition finally exasperated me.

When I was well enough to leave the room, my father had a surprise waiting in the garden: A little grey donkey, newly saddled and bridled, ready for me to ride. I not only took him on rambles in the alleys of the garden, but he served to transport me to all the mosques of Cairo later that year. My grandmother had made a vow that if I were cured we would visit them one by one and give alms to the poor. I'm not sure we went to every one, but for a whole year we visited many I have never seen since.

Although we sometimes used my father's carriage to get there, my grandmother preferred going on donkey back. I trotted beside her on my new beast, three or four women from our household accompanied us, and we were surrounded by donkey boys and servants on foot, brandishing sticks to make way for our party.

My grandmother knew which saints to invoke and which of their tombs to visit when someone needed a cure for an ailment. She liked to talk about their virtues with the women of the harem, who never lost interest in this subject. They compared stories on which was most helpful to those with eye troubles, who to appeal to if someone wanted a male child, or the return of an unfaithful husband . . .

I was not interested in any of that.

What fascinated me was the street life in front of the doors of certain mosques, where there seemed to be a perpetual fair: Merchants selling goods, restaurants on wheels with ambulatory cooks offering pancakes and rice cakes, jugglers, monkey trainers, puppet shows, shadow plays, dancers, singers, magicians, acrobats . . . It all made me dizzy with pleasure, and my grandmother couldn't keep me from taking it all in. I had a sharp ear and a reliable memory and retained the words of popular songs that were not meant to be heard by little girls like me:

> My handsome love is decked out in gold
> He lives in the most beautiful of palaces
> His mother holds him prisoner there
> to keep him from loving me.

At dawn he escapes, richly dressed,
his sword at his side, his heart bold.
My love comes fearlessly toward me
He places a kiss on my forehead
and puts candied almonds in my hand.
But, that was forty days ago:
I have saved the box full of almonds
and the imprint of his kiss on my brow.

The words of the song fired my imagination. I could see the costume of the handsome prince, his sword, and picture the escape from the palace, but I never understood why the singer hadn't eaten the candied almonds. I asked around me for an explanation, but no one knew.

The singer intrigued and fascinated me. She was a fat courtesan. I admired her prominent features, thick makeup, and eyes, swimming with black kohl, almost devouring the upper part of her face. Her bright red lips entranced me, and her hands, orange with henna, made my heart leap with delight as she played her castanets. I would have thrown all the change in my pockets to her if my grandmother were not watching.

My favorite spectacle was the "Magic Box." I rushed forward to put my piaster in the slot, riveting my eyes on the peephole where the show unfolded. The pictures were so pretty! And the tales were always love stories! Younes and Aziza who lived in the time of the Sultan Qalaoun . . . Aziza's escape to the mountains—which one I never knew—to avoid the marriage her father had arranged for her against her wishes. Aziza's love for the handsome Younes . . .

That tale puzzled and filled me with wonder. I questioned Narguiss about it at night. I couldn't get enough of it and made her tell it to me over and over again before I would go to sleep. I never tired of the story of Younes and Aziza, and Narguiss never refused my request for a story.

15 · MADEMOISELLE

My infatuation with the French language decided my father to engage a French governess to oversee my education. That is how Mademoiselle Hortense joined our household.

When the carriage went to fetch her from the train station, the entire harem crowded around the *mashrabiyya* windows waiting for a glimpse of the Frenchwoman. Mabrouk Agha had traveled to Alexandria to meet her boat and escort her back to Cairo. Mademoiselle had no idea who Mabrouk was and had assumed that an old friend of the family had courteously offered to accompany her. When they arrived at the house, she thanked him and gave him one of her most ingratiating smiles. She then asked my mother who this "charming gentleman" was, and on learning that she had spent an entire day in the company of a eunuch, she turned scarlet with embarrassment. The harem tittered about Mademoiselle's innocence, and the rumor went from mouth to mouth that she had dreamed of marrying Mabrouk.

Mademoiselle was far from beautiful, which must have come as a relief to Gaulistan and perhaps even to Narguiss and my mother. Nothing about her was likely to attract my father's attention. She had a long, misshapen nose, huge myopic eyes, hair that was stiffly arranged in a bun at the nape of her neck, and she was very poorly dressed.

I was shocked when I saw this homely apparition! She was nothing like the smart young woman I had imagined in my dreams, and for a long time, I couldn't help holding a grudge against her for having disappointed me.

My father had renovated and furnished a few rooms in a secluded wing of the harem as an apartment for Mademoiselle and me. They were above some storage rooms, higher than the *kaa,* but lower than the terrace; I couldn't really say what floor they were on exactly because of the peculiar architecture of our old house. They were convenient, however, and gave us easy access both to the garden and to the terrace. Mademoiselle's room communicated with mine and Zakeyya's. That first night, I obstinately refused to have anything to do with her, much less sleep in the new room next to hers. I ran and hid in the folds of Narguiss' skirts, and she was only too pleased to give me refuge. The next day I continued to sulk, pretending not to understand a word Mademoiselle was saying to me. My father was advised, but said to leave me alone and let Zakeyya start lessons without me.

Hidden behind a window, I watched, feeling humiliated, as Zakeyya and Mademoiselle strolled hand in hand in the garden, laughing. During lunch my mother spoke French with Mademoiselle. I refused to open my mouth, much to the gratification of Gaulistan and my grandmother, who did not approve of the newcomer. Their attitude increased my frustration, however, and I was furious with myself.

The next day I stood with my nose pressed against the window of Narguiss' room feeling useless and lonely, when someone took me gently by the shoulders. I stiffened angrily, but Mademoiselle's poor, sad voice said, "You really don't want to love me, then?" Tears rolled down her cheeks.

My heart instantly melted, but I was too proud to let her know she had won. I quickly found a way of saving face by asking her point blank if she knew how to read. She was staggered by my question, but answered, "Yes, I read French." I ordered her to pick up a book and read me "Little Red Riding Hood." Willingly, she obeyed.

When she closed the book, I deigned to offer her a compliment: "You read well," I said, then brought out all my toys, put them in her lap, and asked her to name each one in French. That was my first lesson with Mademoiselle Hortense.

From that moment on, we became fast friends, and the terms of our relationship were settled: I gave orders, and she obeyed.

My mother tried timidly to curb my arrogance and encourage Mademoiselle to get a grip on me that she herself lacked. But she failed. Narguiss laughed heartily at the sight of the teacher subdued by her pupil, while Gaulistan and my grandmother found no end of amusement in watching us. Mademoiselle, who was incapable of asserting herself, lost all her prestige in their eyes. In exchange, however, she gained my devoted protection. If she needed anything, if she were not properly served, or if someone slighted her, she appealed to me rather than to my mother. I would speak to the *khalfa,* to the *aghas,* to my grandmother or, if it were necessary, to my father himself. I always got her what she wanted, and she was always effusive in her thanks.

Mademoiselle grew very attached to me. She was a patient and attentive teacher, and I rapidly learned French. Zakeyya, who was incredibly intelligent, stimulated me too because she could learn faster than I. My pride egged me on to keep up with her. She had shared all my lessons, gone every step of the way through my education with me, and when I stopped, she continued. She had to persevere extraordinarily in a society where women, much less slaves, were not encouraged to study or go to the university. Yet, she succeeded and became a very good teacher, one of the first women formally to join the profession in Egypt.

Mademoiselle Hortense's family name betrayed her aristocratic roots, and the consideration with which my father treated her confirmed it. One day she showed me an album of sketches of her native Limousin, pictures of a château with a high, pointed roof and turrets, courtyards, and a park with a river running nearby. Another album had pictures, in silhouette, of nuns and their pupils standing in front of the convent where Mademoiselle had spent eight years of her adolescence. She showed me photographs of her parents, an elderly couple, and told me stories about her father's diplomatic mission to a northern state at the time of Napoleon III. Her father was bald and had white mutton chops; her mother had a strikingly sad face and was shown wearing a black silk dress with a high collar and a big cross like the ones worn by nuns.

Mademoiselle was born when they were quite old already and had a brother much older than herself who was a gambler. He became head of the family after her father died and lived in Paris while Hortense and her mother lived in their château in the Limousin. The women spent their time doing charitable work and praying, and they saw only priests, nuns, and other "pious" individuals. Their lives were strictly disciplined, and they knew nothing whatsoever of profane pleasures or entertainments.

The summer Mademoiselle turned twenty-five, her brother came home with a friend who courted Hortense and, before leaving, asked for her hand in marriage—she had a portrait of him which she cherished as if it were a relic! He was in military costume, handsome, and had a face with what people then called "regular" features; his manners and conversation easily charmed Mademoiselle Hortense. She became hopelessly smitten with him, and lived all summer dreaming of love and marriage. But the marriage was never to take place.

Hortense's brother, who gambled in casinos as well as on the stock market, ruined them. They had to sell the house in Paris and the château to pay off his debts; and the bridegroom, who was a captain of the Dragoons, requested a mission to Algeria and was never again heard from.

Mademoiselle was heartbroken. She followed her mother into a convent, where the dowager spent the last two years of her life ill in bed under her daughter's care. When her mother died, Hortense decided to take the veil as a Carmelite but discovered this was not so easy. She needed to clear her heart of any worldly attachments; to destroy the letters she had received from her fiancé, his portrait, and any memory of him which lingered in her mind. She could not do it. Alone, with no resources, she knew she would have to earn a living. The last thing in the world she wanted was to become a governess in a French family, which would have been the only profession open to her. She chose instead to go into exile. Having made up her mind, she went to see an old friend of her father's who recommended her to the Turkish Consulate in Paris—Egypt was then under Ottoman rule—and that is how she landed in our house on the Khalig.

Mademoiselle's misfortune left me cold. I looked at this face without charm, at the prematurely aged body, and found her ridiculous for having thought anyone could fall in love with her! Should I blame myself today for my unsympathetic heart? Can I attribute my ruthlessness to childish inexperience? Had I not felt protective toward her from the beginning, I would have made fun of her repeatedly. How far I was from knowing then that fortune had in store for me a fate not so unlike her own! It was only after I had loved and lost that I understood fully what Mademoiselle had suffered.

Mademoiselle died one summer night, in Cairo, long after I became an adult. I was at her side when she took to bed and went myself to fetch a priest when the end was near. When she saw me crying, she told me that I should not grieve for her because she was happy to be going to heaven.

I am certain that Mademoiselle remained faithful to her first and only love until her last breath. I saw her tears when I came into her room one morning without warning and caught her hastily closing a drawer. I knew it contained letters, photos, tokens of her brief and unfruitful romance.

I feel I owe her a great deal. Although she was never able to discipline me, her company and conversation considerably widened my horizons. She taught me a language, drawing, music, embroidery, manners, and bequeathed to me all the trappings of her genteel European upbringing.

Like me, she had been brought up in a world of women, even though hers was an altogether different one, which otherwise I might never have known.

Although Mademoiselle was the opposite of a rebel, her example paradoxically helped me formulate my ideas and strengthen my will. In a negative way, she contributed to my thinking about women's emancipation and the role I wanted to play in it. I was determined not to be vanquished, and certainly not to surrender without a struggle as she had done.

16 · LESSONS

After I recovered from typhoid, my father, who had been strict before my illness, became an indulgent parent. When he had visitors now, he allowed me to stay in my favorite alcove, or corner of the balcony, with a picture book open on my lap. In this way I heard newspaper readings, political discussions, and learned the names of potentates such as Sultan Abd el Hamid and Queen Victoria. I pictured them dressed like the kings and queens in my book of fairy tales. But what I enjoyed best was listening to poetry.

One day, a guest left an Arabic newspaper on the divan in my father's study. I picked it up and said to my father, "I really want to learn to read and also to write poetry."

My father smiled and answered, "You are certainly ambitious, Ramza! How old are you?" I answered that I was eight and a half years old and that I had three new teeth.

He said, "I'll look for a teacher to give you Arabic lessons."

Not long after, a student from the Azhar University was hired to teach me and Zakeyya. Sheikh Nassif was not so young because he had a wife and children; he wore round, wire-rimmed glasses, and never smiled. I didn't like him, but he taught us well.

I soon found out that he was not to be trifled with. If I was not attentive, he smacked my fingers dryly with a ruler. It was clear that, unlike Ustaz Hefny, he would not put up with my pranks.

Koutchouk Agha attended all our lessons, dozing in a corner of the room, while Zakeyya and I applied ourselves and learned Arabic grammar, composition, and arithmetic.

When I turned nine, I asked my father if Sheikh Nassif could also teach us geography. The word *sea* had set me dreaming, and when I was alone, I would repeat out loud to myself the names of cities I knew: Paris, London, Rome . . . Even Alexandria, where I had never been although it was only a day's journey from us, excited my imagination. It was a city by the sea, boats left from there to go to far away places . . . I had only been to Tanta with my grandmother, my mother, and my aunts to visit the tomb of the holy man, Sayyed el Badawy . . . Had I been able to hide, I would have gone all the way to Alexandria . . . This port city was a gate to the world.

One day I expressed my desire to see Alexandria, and my father promised to take me there the following summer. Thereafter, I mercilessly bombarded him with questions to which he did not always have answers.

Two months went by, yet Sheikh Nassif had still not begun our geography lessons. My father was surprised and asked why. It appeared that my grandmother had stopped in to see my teacher and told him that all I needed to learn was arithmetic to keep household accounts and the Qur'an in order to bring up my children in the Islamic faith. Being a true conservative, Sheikh Nassif couldn't agree more.

"You know, Sheikh Nassif," my father reasoned with

him, "the study of geography is intended to make us better appreciate God's creation. Even the Qur'an relies on geography when it says that Allah is Lord of the Orient and the Occident. I wish for Ramza to understand the meaning of these terms. You will teach her geography."

The sheikh had to agree, but he did so without grace. He bought two elementary atlases for me and Zakeyya but limited his instruction to showing us where the cities of Egypt were located. It was Mademoiselle who introduced us to a greater world picture. As soon as I was able to read French well enough, my father lent me many of his own travel books, which I devoured hungrily.

If we had some free time after lessons, I asked Sheikh Nassif to recite poetry for us. He did so gladly, as he knew thousands of verses by heart. And even though his voice was on the cold side, it certainly had resonance. My eyes grew wide with interest whenever he recited the richly nuanced verses of Arabic poetry or explained an obscure passage, which he did well. At such times I admired Sheikh Nassif.

One morning, when I had been on my best behavior, I took my courage in my hands, got up, and said, "I know a poem," and recited the following verse to him: "Even though I wear the veil, I am educated . . . " The rest was about the virtues of instruction for women.

"Where did you learn this?" he asked, his face deadpan.

"I heard the verses recited at my father's last night by the poetess, Aysha el Taymouriyya," I answered.

"That's fine," said the sheikh.

I then repeated "Even though I wear the veil, I am educated . . . " and parroted an opinion I had heard from one of the guests the night before: "Why doesn't she take off the veil and have the courage to show her face if she is so educated?"

The color went out of Sheikh Nassif's face and he glared at me from behind his glasses.

"Perverse creature!" he cried "You only retain evil opinions! That's where the education they are giving you is leading! I have two daughters, and I swear that they will never be allowed to learn to read! I shall go straight to your grandmother and advise her to keep an eye on you. You are in great danger!"

"I will not remain with my grandmother," I retorted, looking him straight in the eye, "I'm learning French, and I will go to Paris."

Sheikh Nassif was stunned. He must have thought I was informing him of my father's intentions for me, and so remained silent. Our relations after that day were less than cordial, and the following autumn I entered the Sanieh School and never saw him again.

The project of sending me to school was discussed in the harem almost daily for an entire year. My grandmother was firmly opposed to it. She said that it was immoral to give girls too much education. My mother and Mademoiselle suggested a school run by nuns as a compromise. They had picked the Mère de Dieu, which was then located in the new quarter called Ismailiyya. It was on the road to Boulac, quite a distance from our house.

According to some letters I later found, my father had at first agreed to this plan but in the end changed his mind.

Sheikh Muhammad Abdu, who was not yet mufti at that time, was my father's friend and a firm believer in educating girls in Egyptian, rather than foreign, schools. He was also known to chide all who claimed that women were inferior or that they had to be cloistered. He proclaimed that as future mothers, they were the cornerstones of the nation and had to receive a good education to prepare them for the responsibility of raising generations of Egyptians of sound mind and body. To prove that he had the courage of his convictions, he sent his own daughters to the Sanieh School, the best Egyptian school of the time.

My father was very much under the influence of Sheikh

Muhammad Abdu, who easily persuaded him to send me there. That is how Zakeyya and I ended up going to the Sanieh instead of the Mère de Dieu.

I was absolutely enchanted with this change in my life, and so was Zakeyya. I must have been about ten years old at the time, and she twelve or thirteen when we started. We were to remain in that school for five full years.

The Sanieh was quite close to our house, and every morning we walked to school accompanied by Mademoiselle, followed by the aging Koutchouk. When Koutchouk Agha died, Mabrouk, who was not much younger, took his place and tottered along behind us in the morning and came to fetch us at the end of the day.

I felt extraordinarily elated when I saw the joyless walls of our old house quite a distance behind me, and particularly so because I knew that, for a time at least, I was escaping my grandmother's jurisdiction. She had become entirely immobilized because of her weight and her rheumatism and even more quarrelsome than before.

There was strict discipline at the Sanieh, and although I was unruly at home, at school I became a model pupil. To my father's surprise, no one ever once complained about me in all the time I was there. We had a British headmistress whom we feared; Italian teachers for music, art, and singing; a robust young Swede taught us gymnastics; and a Swiss lady initiated us into the art of home economics. The students gave receptions for each other, where we invited our teachers and served cakes and cookies we had baked ourselves. We were taught French, Turkish, and English. English was new to me, but I learned it quickly.

At recess I often played the piano, which I had mastered tolerably well thanks to my mother's lessons. My heart was filled with joy when my teachers and fellow students complimented me on my playing. This little talent won me some popularity, as did my ability to recite poetry.

One day, I joined a group of older girls who were in the

habit of strolling around the courtyard of the school, de-
claiming. I gave them a rendition of a poem by Baroodi.
They had never heard of it, and as a result, I got the reputation of being precocious and an intellectual. I was very
pleased with this and ritually went to my father's study to
copy poems in Arabic, French, or Turkish to share with my
schoolmates the next day.

I was admitted to a sort of literary club—I say sort of
because it was in part recognized by the school, and in part
clandestine. It was largely made up of girls from the upper
grades. We met most often in the library, where we leafed
through all the journals and magazines we could get our
hands on. We also wrote reports on articles that interested
us or were relevant to issues we were discussing. Most of
the publications we consulted were written in English.

When we were alone, out of earshot of the staff, we
discussed politics and social change. Sometimes, I sum-
marized books I borrowed from my father in preparation.
Other times I brought books to school, camouflaged in the
regulation blue paper used to cover our textbooks and man-
uals, and read entire passages out loud to my schoolmates.
One of my great successes was John Stuart Mill's book on
the subjugation of women, which caused such a stir of en-
thusiasm among my companions that they became ardent
feminists like myself.

On the very first day of school, I was assigned to sit
next to a girl who was slightly older than I, although less
advanced in her studies. Her name was Bahiga. She and I
were different in every possible way: I was quicksilver, and
she was phlegmatic. I responded aggressively to frustration,
she cried. Yet, we became inseparable. She was my shadow,
following me even to literary meetings, which held no real
interest for her. When I played the piano, however, she
took up her oud, and we improvised. We even had little
musicales for our schoolmates and teachers.

Bahiga, who trusted me blindly, had been unhappy

since the death of her mother, a year before she came to the Sanieh. Her father, a wealthy wood merchant in the quarter of Shoubra, remarried a woman who was glad to be rid of a cumbersome stepdaughter. It was she who encouraged Bahiga's father to place her as a boarder at school. Bahiga hated this woman and felt betrayed by her father. She used any excuse to avoid going home, which was not difficult because her father and stepmother were not insistent on her visits anyway. She missed the big, beautiful garden of her childhood, however, and talked longingly of her brother, Maher, to whom she was deeply attached. He had been sent to a military school.

I asked my father about inviting Bahiga to spend school holidays with us, and he gladly agreed. Her sweet, serious nature appealed to him. Bahiga's father was flattered by our invitations because of my family's status, and raised no objections; but he insisted on reciprocating. And so to please Bahiga and to satisfy her father's pride, I went occasionally to her house in Shoubra. I never lingered, though, because I thoroughly disliked her stepmother.

It was during one of these visits that I met Bahiga's brother, Maher. This meeting was to change my life.

At the end of our first year in school, Bahiga gave a party in Shoubra for her schoolmates and teachers. I had arrived a little early to help her get ready, and chattering happily with Bahiga, I ran into the kitchen to get something. I bumped into a young man coming out. I jumped back. I froze. I was caught without my veil. He took a few steps back, making way for me to get by, but I was dumbstruck and couldn't move. We stood face to face, like a pair of wooden dolls, not uttering a word, not knowing what to do. I noticed that he was handsome. At long last, I regained my wits, and with eyes glued to the floor, I darted into the kitchen, giving the young man a little curtsy on the way.

When I told Bahiga about my little adventure, all she said was, "Oh, that was my brother, Maher!" I found sev-

eral excuses to return to the kitchen in hopes of seeing him
again, but Maher was not there. As the evening drew to a
close, I lingered after the others. Zakeyya, Mademoiselle
Hortense, and I were last to leave. As our carriage turned
out into the street, we came across a young military cadet,
looking trim in his black uniform. It was obvious that he
was looking in my direction and that he had made a point of
coming out in search of me. I felt so proud!

The summer holidays began. I wrote Bahiga to come
and see me, discreetly making some mention of her family.
She answered, came, and talked to me about her brother.

"He is so intelligent and considerate, Ramza," she said,
"You have no idea how kind and affectionate he has been
since our mother died!" And, smiling, she added, "Maher
said that he thought you were very pretty, and that you
couldn't be a day younger than fifteen!"

I started blushing furiously and stood up. Then all at
once, to hide my embarrassment, I jostled Bahiga, grabbed
her hand, and dragged her off on a mad race across the garden.

17 · THE ANGEL OF DEATH

I was growing up. On my fourteenth birthday, my family
no longer allowed me to go out of the harem without a
veil. I was forbidden to enter the *salamlek,* even my father's
rooms there, without first sending the *agha* ahead to clear
the way of men. This caused me great frustration because it
was precisely at that time that my father's library attracted
me most. I was reading extensively, and I longed more than
ever to listen to the discussions and readings that continued
to take place there. I refused to give them up and had to
resort to my old habit of hiding behind doors to listen.
From the snippets of discussions which I heard, I would

attempt to reconstruct a context. I knew that the voices I
strained to make out were in the process of making history.
Sheikh Muhammad Abdu had become grand mufti, shaking
the Muslim world with talk of women's emancipation and
reforming the Azhar; the poet Shawki, and another poet Ismail Sabri were regulars; young Prince Haidar Ali, whose
sonorous laughter I learned to recognize and delight in, was
a frequent visitor. How I longed to be in their midst!

One night, on my sixteenth birthday, a particularly animated discussion took place in the library. I will never forget it. It was so revolutionary that I had to crack the door to
better make out what was being said. I knew that if I were
caught, I would instantly be chased out, but I had to take
that chance. I heard enough to be sure that the passionate
speaker, whose young-sounding voice only partially
reached me, was defending ideas that were already very dear
to my heart: the necessity of educating women, giving them
the same rights as men, of liberating them from the veil, of
reforming the unfair personal status laws concerning them,
and protecting them from being married against their will
and divorced without reason or recourse . . .

The next day, I ran to the library in search of some indi-
cation of who had been there the night before. My eyes fell
on a book entitled *Tahrir el Mar'ah,* or *The Liberation of
Women.* I knew right away that the author of that book had
been the speaker. His name was Kassem Amin, a name I
would never forget. The book on the table was dedicated to
my father in the author's own hand. I felt as proud of that
dedication as if it had been addressed to me personally and
set out to read the book hungrily, as if my very life de-
pended on it. Later, when I shared *Tahrir el Mar'ah* with my
schoolmates who had never heard of Kassem Amin, all of
them bought the book, and some of them memorized it
from cover to cover.

Not all of my readings were that serious, however. I
must confess, I wondered about my father's wisdom in not
better supervising them! I read novels. I devoured any work

of fiction I could lay my hands on, in English or in French, and my imagination took flight. I remember *Clarissa, The Portrait of Dorian Gray,* and *Les Vièrges Fortes,* among others. I read and daydreamed. I pictured myself strolling under trees, along rivers with a lover. I saw myself dancing what I imagined to be a quadrille or a waltz in salons shimmering with candlelight, like the European and English heroines of the stories.

At that time, when I most needed the guidance of a mother, I lost mine. Poor Indje never took hold of the influence that my affection gave her leave to exercise on me! By the time I was eleven or twelve, she hardly ever left her room. She liked my company, though, and I spent hours sitting at her side listening to her reminiscences. It was then that she told me all about her cloistered life. Nothing she said inspired me to emulate her, even though she insisted that she had been happy. I did not envy her that happiness, and would have refused it at any price.

I was fourteen when she died. Gaulistan died a month later, followed by my grandmother. It was as if that particular year had been marked by the angel of death.

My grandmother and I made up our differences before she died, and curious as this may seem, it was into my care that she commended her son, my father. She chose to pass on to me the responsibility that had been hers and that, even as an old and crippled woman, she had never relinquished. She instructed me to be attentive to my father's needs, to supervise personally the preparation of his meals and the care of his clothes, and to be vigilant and make sure that he was always comfortable.

I had just turned fifteen and assumed my new responsibilities in a new home. That year, we left the house on the Khalig forever.

The family had decided to move a few years earlier—the water had stopped running in the canal, the house needed costly repairs, and the neighborhood had deteriorated.

My father, who was then chamberlain to the Khedive Abbas Helmy II, also wanted to be closer to the palace. To that end he bought a huge plot in Koubba, surrounded by fields, and built a pleasant, modern house and a huge garden. The garden was divided as it had been in our old house. Half was for men and the other for women. The same was true of the house, where the distinction between the *haramlek,* the women's quarters, and the *salamlek,* the men's quarters, remained.

We moved to the new house a year after my grandmother's death. We took with us all our furniture and personal belongings, as well as our traditions, which remained intact. Although the new house was very pleasant, I could not forget the old one, where the walls echoed with history and where my childhood unfolded.

Of all my father's wives, only Narguiss remained. My aunt was her big, loud, and jovial self. We quarreled constantly but always made up quickly and loved each other too much to let differences come between us.

Mademoiselle Hortense had a dual devotion, to God and to me. Whenever she was not in church, she was attending to my needs, and I did as I pleased with her.

With only Narguiss and Mademoiselle setting limits in our household, there were even fewer restraints on my tempestuous nature than before. I took full advantage of the relative freedom that was mine, almost by default.

18 · THE TRAP

My friend, Bahiga, was married a short time before my grandmother's death. Perhaps I should say, she was handed over, by her father, to a rich merchant from Alexandria.

I was in Bahiga's room along with all of the women of her family the day of *Katb el Kitab*. As was customary, two witnesses had to ask my friend if she was consenting before her father and groom could sign the marriage certificate. They had stood outside Bahiga's door, repeatedly clapping their hands. No one heard them. We were making too much noise. Suddenly, two men were upon us, and not one woman was veiled.

The first one to see them let out a scream. Everyone followed, grabbing whatever they could get their hands on to cover their faces, or covering their faces with their hands. I ducked beside Bahiga's bed. When I looked up, my eyes met those of a young cadet in black. It was Maher. I blushed and was disgusted at being seen in this absolutely ridiculous position! I was furious with myself and promptly stood up, my face uncovered, defying all the rules of decorum. But Maher and the other witness were gone, taking with them Bahiga's reluctant consent.

This was the second time I had seen Maher, and it was even more awkward than the first. The incident left me disgruntled all evening long, particularly with myself.

Poor Bahiga needed solace that evening. She told me that she was sick to death at the thought of this marriage, yet she had to go through with it. She had no real choice. She knew nothing at all about the groom, having never seen him, and the reluctant description she got from her brother left her more worried than before.

"He must be old, pot-bellied, bald, and disagreeable!" she cried to me.

"Why did you accept? Why didn't you say no to the witnesses when they came to ask you?" I piped up naïvely.

"You don't know my father!" she answered.

"Couldn't your brother have intervened on your behalf?" I persisted.

"He wasn't asked his opinion," she answered, sadly. "In any case, had he dared to speak, my father would have beaten or even killed him!"

I gazed at her for a long moment without saying a word. There she was, in her beautiful white silk dress, cowering in her chair, dabbing her streaming eyes with a handkerchief, resigned. Like her mother before her and like all the women of Egypt, she was submitting.

I was upset. I wanted her to do something. I had a strong urge to insult her when I saw her so passive in the face of her destiny. But like the others, there was nothing I could do to help her, and I resolved to hold my tongue. I was overcome with pity for Bahiga. It would have been useless to add my invective to her pain!

I then remembered going to see an adaptation of *Romeo and Juliet* with Mademoiselle on my twelfth birthday. It was performed in Arabic at the Sheikh Salama Hegazy Theater. We sat in the loge reserved for women behind a tightly latticed screen, and although we could hardly see the actors, we had heard them clearly. Watching Bahiga that night, a helpless puppet in her father's hands, the plot of *Romeo and Juliet* came back to me. I determined that I would kill myself, as Juliet had done, rather than be chained for life to a man I did not love. Not much later, however, I was nearly trapped in the same way!

After my grandmother died, my father started taking breakfast in his own sitting room, and it was I who served him coffee. He woke up at seven o'clock, prayed, washed, read a few pages from the Qur'an, and at eight o'clock on the dot, he walked out to the little salon where his breakfast was laid out on a big tray covered with small silver dishes containing cream, stewed fruit, jam, honey, cheese, and bread. I was always there before him. I poured out the coffee for him, and he invited me to sit down. We always shared this first meal of the day, and spent a wonderful hour together. He leafed through newspapers and magazines to which he subscribed, read to me, or asked me to read to him.

I remember vividly my father's rapture when, at his request, I read him Boustani's translation of the *Iliad*. I remember also his pleasure at explaining verses from the poetry of Yazgi, or others, to me. He enriched my knowledge of history and literature in this way. And, as we grew closer, our affection for one another deepened.

My father went to work at nine o'clock sharp every day. I will never forget how he would look at his watch, and sometimes in midsentence, would get up and leave. I stayed to put away his clothes and supervise the cleaning of his rooms. Narguiss came in to make sure this was done properly and always said to me, "We learn many things at school, but we only learn how to run a house at home."

One morning, as I was busying myself in my father's rooms, a servant came to tell me that my aunt wanted me. I said I had to finish my chores first, but Neemat, our old *khalfa,* dragged me off to my room saying that someone was waiting to see me right away. She made me put on a new dress and carefully combed my hair, then accompanied me to the *kaa,* where Narguiss was sitting with a fat, middle-aged woman, Sitt Khadiga. The visitor examined me from head to foot without saying a word. I knew the customs of the harem. This was a matchmaker, a widow I had heard about who earned her living as a go-between for families with marriageable children. I sat speechless as I felt her undressing me, estimating my weight, evaluating me like a horse trader. I was certain she already knew how much my father was worth, if my fortune was comparable to that of a prospective bridegroom, how much her share—10 percent of my dowry—would be, what gifts she would receive, what privileges a lifelong association with the two families would entitle her to! I saw gold coins dancing in her eyes, the gifts she could expect on feast days, and even, if all went well, a retirement pension she could count on if she succeeded in concluding a deal.

When she was gone I confronted Narguiss. I had always been blunt with my aunt, and I was not ready to spare her that time!

"What do you take me for, Auntie?" I said. "Do you think that I'm just going to let myself be married off to the first comer? What's the meaning of this circus?"

"You will do as you are told, my girl!" she retorted. "Don't think that because you went to school you're any different than all the others! Your education doesn't give you the right to trample over our traditions! I'm responsible for you, smart aleck! If you give me any trouble, you'll have to answer to your father!"

"My father? I'll speak to him myself!" I retorted, "I'm certain he has no intention of marrying me off! I'm not a slave!"

Narguiss and I had a good fight, and as usual, we ended up laughing, then kissed and made up.

"Listen to me," Narguiss said finally, "I have heard great things about this young man. Look, I'm not trying to marry you off to make you miserable! I'll do my best to find out all I can about him and his family. I'll even try to get you a photograph of him, Ramza."

Then, almost as an afterthought, she said, "I'm not backward, you know!"

I was only sixteen years old, and Narguiss could be quite persuasive.

"I'll do all I can to make this easy, but in exchange you need to cooperate with me, keep your temper in check, and let me guide you through the formalities." Then, gently, she added, "Don't count too much on your father's European ideals, Ramza. I know him much better than you do in certain respects, and I can tell you without a doubt that he is very attached to our traditions when it comes to family life.

"Besides, if the young man appeals to you, would you find it so unpleasant to be married? Wouldn't you like to have a home of your own, run it the way you want, dress as you like, go out when you wish?

"Just let me take care of this," she concluded, "I'll know

how to stop the process in plenty of time if we don't like what we see."

Even though she had not fooled me entirely, I began to feel excited. I started day dreaming.

Narguiss made me promise to act as if I knew nothing and especially not breathe a word of our discussion to my father. She cautioned me that this would be calamitous.

"Girls are supposed to be ignorant," she said, "Your father must not suspect that you understand what's going on, or even that you have noticed that anything is happening."

But, curious though I was, I wanted to know about marriage. I searched for explanations in books. What I found in my father's library was Molière's comedy on marriage, *L'Ecole des Femmes*. I read it avidly, laughing at Agnes' stupidity, raving at Arnolphe's pedantic maxims, and vowing once more that I would only marry a man I liked.

I intentionally left the book open on the divan in my father's study hoping he would notice it and bring up the subject. He never did.

The following day, about eleven o'clock in the morning, I was again summoned to the *kaa*. This time Sitt Khadiga had come with four other women. Their eyes instantly turned on me the minute I walked in the door, and the matchmaker smiled triumphantly. As for me, I had agreed to play the role of Agnes. I came forward timidly, kissed my aunt's hand respectfully, and gave each of the ladies present my politest curtsy. Only then did I take a seat keeping my eyes modestly downcast and my hands crossed in my lap as became a well-bred girl. I avoided looking at Narguiss for fear that if our eyes met, I would burst out laughing. I felt quite superior and was enjoying my little act.

When a servant came in with coffee on a tray, Narguiss said, "Serve the coffee, Ramza."

"Yes, my aunt," I answered demurely.

I served the coffee with the skill and grace expected of a

proper young woman then sat down, tall and poised in my chair.

Narguiss then said, "You can leave now, Ramza."

I answered obediently, "Yes, my aunt."

On the way out, I curtsied again to the ladies who, this time, answered my curtsies with smiles.

I found Neemat behind the door, and in a fit of mirth, I grabbed her by the shoulders and spun her around. She did not dare cry out for fear of attracting attention, but only raised her fists at me as I ran away. Actually, Neemat was quite fond of me despite her churlish airs. Five minutes later, when I returned on tiptoe to watch the ladies leaving, I caught Neemat igniting a whole box of matches, and tossing a handful of salt in the flames to ensure the return of the visitors. I burst out laughing, ran to the kitchens, and came back with three more boxes and a bag of salt.

When I set them blazing, Narguiss and Neemat could no longer keep a straight face, and peals of laughter rang out in the *kaa*.

19 · WEDDING PREPARATIONS

Eight days later, Narguiss gave a photograph of the bridegroom to Mademoiselle Hortense who, of course, promptly gave it to me. All of this was done secretly, and Narguiss could not admit that she was in any way involved. Medhat was handsome. He had a black mustache tapered at the ends, a style fashionable at that time. He must have been about thirty-five years old. His full name was Medhat Safwat, an unusual name which I repeated over and over to myself. Sitt Khadiga did not fail to tell us that his family was prominent and that some of his relatives were cabinet ministers. He had studied engineering in Paris, received his degree from the Ecole Centrale, and it was rumored that he was assigned to build the first bridge linking Giza to Old Cairo.

I was delighted to find out that he intended to travel extensively—to the Orient, Europe, and perhaps even America—and that he had asked for a bride who was. educated and could hold her own in the world. I bombarded Narguiss with all sorts of questions: Would I have European furniture? A grand piano? Did Medhat like music? Was he interested in art? In books? Would we have our own house, or would we live with his family?

One morning I returned from the *salamlek,* after breakfast with my father, to find the *haramlek* in a frenzy. The activities in the kitchens had doubled, the *khalfa* and the servants were setting a very long table, and everyone was being mysterious. If I stopped near any group of women, conversations ceased; even Mademoiselle was acting strangely. Finally, I demanded to know what was happening but only got evasive answers. It was clear that the party had something to do with me. I stood behind a *mashrabiyya* window and watched, determined to find out who was expected.

Soon, clusters of veiled women began to arrive. I had no trouble recognizing the visitors of a few days ago among a crowd of figures of all shapes and sizes. The members of the harem of the bridegroom's family had come to give their opinion of the future bride.

I was not invited to attend the lunch, but at around four o'clock, Neemat came to fetch me. When I walked into the *kaa,* my Aunt Narguiss kissed me, took me by the hand, and introduced me to a tiny, dignified lady who got up and fastened a feather-shaped diamond brooch to my dress.

This was Medhat's mother.

When she kissed me on the forehead, all the other women got up, crowded around me, and offered me their congratulations.

I had been accepted . . . bought! The diamond brooch bound me, from that day forward, to the woman who had pinned it on my dress. Our families were now united.

I experienced such a panoply of feelings that day! On the one hand, I was angry at having been trapped like everyone else; on the other hand, I was thrilled with the attention and excitement centered around me. I was both curious and afraid. Yet, despite all my high ideals, I started to do what every young woman in my position had always done. I began to prepare my trousseau.

Mademoiselle bought a Singer sewing machine with an attachment for embroidering, and we went to work. Under her expert supervision, I embroidered sheets, sachets, towels, napkins, handkerchief and stocking holders, pockets for candies . . . Heaven knows what else! While working, Mademoiselle and I merrily discussed my fiancé and made plans for the future.

One day, Mademoiselle saw Medhat and spoke with him. She was bursting with excitement to get home and tell me all about him.

"He's tall and handsome. He has blue eyes and beautiful auburn hair. He asked a lot of questions about you, especially about your tastes. He told me he was very eager to see you, even though he knew this was not possible before the *Katb el Kitab* . . . "

When I found out that Medhat planned to court me in the "French" way as soon as the marriage contract was signed, I was delirious with excitement and pleasure. Getting to know my bridegroom before our marriage was consummated was something I had not even dreamed of! Was I dreaming, or would we be allowed to have tea together in the presence of a chaperone? Mademoiselle, for example?

"Medhat told me he is going to visit your father tomorrow and will be wearing a red rose on his lapel."

The next afternoon, eyes glued to the *mashrabiyya* window, I waited breathlessly and was rewarded with a glimpse of the man who, God willing, would become my husband. He was just as Mademoiselle Hortense had described him.

Given my father's European education and his liberal views, I expected him to break with tradition and discuss my marriage with me. He did nothing of the sort. I had to admit that Narguiss had understood him better than I. There was not even a hint that he knew what was happening or any mention of where we would live after my wedding. It was only through Narguiss that I discovered that he wanted me to live in the neighborhood so that he could see me easily every day.

"Your father is in no hurry for the wedding to take place," she said in passing. Neither was I. I was beginning to have a wonderful time!

"The longer the engagement is, the greater the merriment, and the more presents we will get!" I thought, just like a child.

I remember receiving, among other gifts, a red silk dress from Pascal's, a stylish sport jacket from Le Dé Rouge, and a white linen parasol lined and trimmed in purple from Omar Effendi. These were gifts from Medhat's mother to me. They came from the department stores that had just begun to open in Cairo. I had never been in one but had seen them on those very rare occasions when I was driven in our carriage to the Mousky, Ezbekiyya, or Wagh el Birka, a short distance from our house. No woman or girl of any consequence would have been allowed to go into a store at that time! Special salesladies came to the harem with samples of merchandise. They took orders, and the merchandise was delivered to the house.

At the time when my family was preparing my trousseau, these salesladies came to our house daily. Normally, I would have had no choice in what was purchased for me, but as a special favor and contrary to custom, my father gave me a chance to express my likes and dislikes. This was always done indirectly. He was supposed to know nothing.

I would find catalogs casually left open on a couch and I marked what I liked.

Among the more spectacular preparations that took place at home was the work of the mattress, cushion, and quilt makers. I remember watching them labor for days on end on one of the terraces. They fluffed cotton, carded wool, and stuffed and sewed no less than fifty mattresses and twice as many pillows and quilts. A girl of my standing had to bring at least that many to her new home! And, of course, it was necessary to prepare as many sets of bed sheets, pillow cases, bedspreads, quilt covers . . . Ten of the quilts were always covered in gold embroidered silk, and put aside for special occasions while the rest, for daily use, were covered with percale or satinette, in soft pastel colors.

Narguiss and I had daily arguments about every detail because we had such different tastes. Finally, we ended up agreeing; that is, she always backed down.

The excitement in the harem doubled as the date for *Katb el Kitab* approached. It was time to choose a wedding dress, which the harem would customarily have done without consulting me. But I got around that by letting Mademoiselle know about my preferences. My dress was thus entrusted to a couturière from Paris, hired and brought to work in Cairo by the merchant Mohardi. Mademoiselle reminded her explicitly to make an orange blossom sprig, in the French manner, for my bridal tiara.

The month of Moharram flew by amid all the activity.

On a beautiful March day, Mademoiselle and I sat on the balcony of the *kaa* embroidering a tablecloth, talking, and keeping an eye on the courtyard. We caught sight of the *agha* and the servants, dressed in formal attire, cashmere shawls gracefully draped over their shoulders. When he gave the order, they lined up facing each other, the length of a broad walkway leading to the main gate of the house.

Like the ceremonial gate of the house on the Khalig, this big gate, with its heavy double doors, was rarely used. That day the doors were flung wide open, and a horse drawn cart drove through. The harness and the flatbed were decorated with flowers, and on top were two huge fish, each no less than a meter long. We heard the clatter of feet rushing in every direction, the clamor of voices, and I saw a hand emerge from the *mashrabiyya* across the way. It was Narguiss, tossing down silver coins in celebration to everyone gathered in the courtyard. A second cart then followed, also decorated with flowers, then a third and fourth until ten carts were standing side by side in the courtyard.

Mademoiselle and I dropped our work and ran to find Narguiss. "Where does all this fish come from?" I asked breathlessly.

"These are the first of your wedding gifts, my girl," she answered.

"The first," I cried in alarm, "We'll be eating fish morning, noon, and night!"

"The other offerings will be fruit," Narguiss answered reassuringly, adding, "That's the tradition."

The gifts were taken into the harem kitchens, and soon the appetizing fragrance of onion and garlic frying began to waft up to us. There would be enough fish to feed our household and to send to every family in the neighborhood. By way of sharing our joy, the servants took heaping trays full of fried fish to all our friends, and even to the harem of the khedive, where a few of my grandmother's "relatives" still lived. The trays were returned with reciprocal gifts of sweets and pastries, and the servants were congratulated on my good fortune with a gold coin each.

As I was the first girl in my family to get married, mothers of marriageable girls were especially likely to keep the bones from my wedding fish as tokens of good luck.

Next, baskets full of fruit arrived. They were decorated with flowers and tied with gold ribbon. Every basket contained a different kind of fruit: Jaffa oranges, strawberries from Gezira, and cherries, which were extraordinarily exotic and little known to any of us. We all wanted to taste them, and soon every finger and cheek was smeared with the red juice.

How we laughed and joked that morning! All of these activities delighted Narguiss, Mademoiselle, and me.

20 · THE OTHER BRIDE

The smell of fish still hovered in the house, and there were a few cherries left in the fruit bowls when my father came home one day, glanced worriedly in my direction, and went straight to his rooms. A half hour later, Mabrouk Agha was sent to fetch Narguiss, and within moments we saw them both climb into the carriage, accompanied by Neemat. They left without a word of explanation, while Mademoiselle and I sat face to face wondering what the strange behavior could mean.

At lunch we ate more fish and cherries, but without Narguiss, we felt cheerless. As the afternoon wore on, we wandered aimlessly through the house. I went to my father's apartments, but he had not returned, and no one came home for dinner.

The next morning while serving my father his coffee, I was overcome with curiosity. I wanted to say something, ask him to tell me what was happening, what all the mysterious goings on were about, but he was so gloomy that I did not dare open my mouth. We ate lunch in complete silence.

When I went to Narguiss' room after lunch, I surprised Neemat pulling out my aunt's black *yashmak* and the grey dress she had worn for my grandmother's funeral.

"Neemat, for God's sake tell me what's going on? Who is dead?" I asked urgently.

Instead of answering my question, the *khalfa* suddenly took me in her arms, embraced me, and started to moan.

"For God's sake, Neemat, tell me who's dead. We have no relatives! Where have Narguiss and my father gone?"

Finally, Neemat broke down: "It's your bridegroom, Medhat," she said, weeping.

It is hard for me to explain the feeling I had at that moment. The closest I can come to describing it is to say that it was a brutal shock. Although I had never met Medhat, I had become accustomed to the idea of living with him. In the face of his sudden death, I was shaken and saw my future crumble around me. No more gaiety, no more happiness! I burst into tears. Neemat, having spoken, felt compelled to tell me what she knew. It seems Medhat had suffered sudden stomach cramps that no herbs, teas, or poultices could relieve. By the time the doctors realized that he was suffering an acute attack of appendicitis, it was too late. They operated, but the operation was fatal.

Three days later, my father summoned Mademoiselle, told her about Medhat's death, and instructed her to store my trousseau away in coffers. She reported that my father was very anxious about me because I was now considered a widow and would not be able to envision another marriage for at least one full year.

"I don't care a hoot about marriage. I'm in no hurry. As to comporting myself like a widow without ever having been married, never!" I cried indignantly.

I felt genuine grief at the death of the man who had been destined to be my husband, but I also experienced something quite unexpected, a feeling of relief and deliverance. I think I realized at that moment that I had been carried away and had talked myself into accepting that a husband found through a matchmaker was really not much different than one I would have chosen, as long as I liked him. I had dug a hole, buried my ideals, compromised my pride, and violated my principles. I had duped myself and taken the path of least resistance.

Yet, despite all my rationalization, the roaring inside me had not ceased. When Medhat died, I knew I had escaped. I felt like a hunted animal released from a trap. I saw myself standing on the threshold of limitless open spaces, and an almost savage joy filled my heart.

Narguiss had been absent for a week. When she came home, still dressed in full mourning gear—grey dress and black *yashmak*—she put my nerves on edge by loudly lamenting my loss. She extolled the virtues of my late husband to be, and I was obliged to listen to these words of "consolation" as well as descriptions of Medhat's death and funeral. She didn't spare me a single detail.

I was informed that his bereft mother had dressed him in his wedding suit. She had given him a wedding feast to bid him farewell with such dishes and delicacies as one served on joyful occasions. There had been roast lamb, turkey, stuffed pigeons . . . Narguiss could not suppress a little gurgle of pleasure as she confided to me that the glazed spice cake and the petits fours that she adored were so delicious that she had to restrain herself from eating too many for fear of appearing inadequately grieved.

"Medhat's relatives from Alexandria and the Fayyoum were not so discreet! They ate their fill and stuffed their pockets!" Narguiss reported.

I burned with rage. I felt suffocated. These stories killed the least shred of compassion or empathy I might have had. I could only see the horror and indecency of these rituals organized around a corpse. And when Narguiss began to describe how the body was covered with flowers and how Medhat's mother continuously sprinkled her dead son with bottle after bottle of eau de cologne, I exploded.

"That's enough! Enough!" I cried, "So you've married Medhat to the angel of death? I refuse to be jealous of his new bride!" And, saying this, I flung open my wardrobe, pulled out all the jewelry I had received from his mother and flung it at Narguiss' feet.

"Here, take these! Take them to Medhat! Let him give

them to his new bride! I don't want them! I don't want them! I'm free! I'm free!"

After this outburst, I collapsed on my bed in tears. Utterly astonished, Narguiss, the *khalfa,* Mademoiselle, and other women who were within earshot, rushed to my side.

"Poor child! Poor child! She's lost her head! The shock was too much for her! Look how she's suffering! Who would have believed that she had already fallen in love with her bridegroom? . . . "

Of course, they had understood nothing. I was exasperated with their stupidity, and when I couldn't stand to hear another word they were babbling, I hurled myself at them, beat them with my clenched fists, and chased them out of my room.

That night I conceived the wildest plans. I thought of running away from my family, of escaping to a foreign land, of working to earn a living . . . . I just wanted to be away from the stifling atmosphere of the harem, its servility and hypocrisy, but I did nothing of the sort. The time had not come to escape yet, and the following morning, I served my father his coffee as usual as if nothing at all had happened. Neither of us mentioned Medhat Safwat. It was as if he had never existed.

21 · MAHER

One winter, my father was absent for several weeks. He had accompanied the Khedive Abbas to Aswan for the dedication of a new dam. They had continued on to the Sudan, stopping in Khartoum. My father returned with all sorts of stories and anecdotes that he had collected along the way. He also kept a diary and illustrated it with photographs for my benefit. Photography had become his new hobby.

During his absence, I spent long evening hours reading in his library. I felt a need for absolute silence, and Mademoiselle was the only person I would allow to join me. Poor Mademoiselle! Her health had begun to fail by then, and despite her fatigue, she had the patience of a saint, especially with me. She sat quietly, making herself as unobtrusive as possible. I did not hesitate to interrupt her to read to her or to comment on passages I found interesting. The dynamics between us had been established long before, with me becoming more tyrannical the more devoted Mademoiselle was. But I sincerely loved her!

A few days after my father's return home, we were having breakfast together when he showed me the pictures he had taken on his trip. In the midst of a group of young officers, I recognized Maher, Bahiga's brother. I blushed without realizing why, but my father took no notice. Although I had neither seen nor thought of Maher since Bahiga's wedding, his face, his bright eyes looking out from the brownish photograph, stirred me.

That same afternoon, as if destiny was beginning to weave her web around me, Bahiga dropped in for a visit. Seeing Bahiga so unexpectedly was a real pleasure for me. We no longer met regularly because she had moved to Alexandria, although when she came to Cairo, she often stayed several days with us.

My father liked Bahiga, and Mademoiselle and Narguiss welcomed her visits because they brought a breath of fresh air into the house. We organized musical evenings, which my father attended, and I went out more often. As a married woman, Bahiga was a trusted chaperone. We went together to Gezira, to Shoubra, and even to the theater.

This time, Bahiga had come to attend a military parade in which her brother would take part. When she invited me to come along, my heart leapt even though I had teased her previously about her interest in such inane entertainments.

"Maher is now a member of the khedivial guard," she said, "Don't you want to come and watch him?"

Before I could answer, Bahiga was asking me if I remembered her brother.

"You saw him the day of my wedding!" she said.

Did I remember him? How could I forget him! When I
saw him in the photograph my father showed me, the stir-
rings I had felt on the two occasions we had run into each
other were revived. Over and over again, I saw in my
mind's eye the young, slender cadet in his close-fitting black
uniform, with his dark, trim moustache, and audacious look
in his eyes . . .

"Do you know that Maher often saw your father in the
Sudan?" Bahiga said innocently. "He wrote telling me that
he thought you looked a lot like him, and asked me if you
still had blue eyes?"

I blushed and, to hide my confusion, I shrugged my
shoulders and laughed.

"How can he remember the color of my eyes," I said to
Bahiga, "He had a mere glimpse of me, and it was so long ago!"

"Well, you see that he does remember! My cousin
Nafissa has an apartment which overlooks Abdin Square.
But of course if you'd rather not come to the parade, I'll go
alone."

Finally, I got up the courage to ask my father if I could
go. To my surprise he raised no objection, but encouraged
me to go. I did not breathe a word about Maher, of course!

At eight o'clock the next morning, Bahiga and I, Mademoiselle, and the *agha* piled into the carriage and headed for
Abdin. We were welcomed by Bahiga's cousin and were
comfortably settled on a large balcony surrounded by *mashrabiyya* windows, overlooking the square. We moved the
shutters right and left all morning trying to get a better
glimpse of the activity below. There were passersby, police
officers, coffeehouse owners who came and went, renting
chairs and tables to parade watchers and serving tea and coffee. The windows and terraces around us began to fill with
spectators.

Soon, we heard the sounds of a military brass band; the

musicians had assembled on the bandstand in front of the palace. Bahiga and I kept thinking that we saw the khedivial guard, but Nafissa, who was the daughter of an officer and knew the uniforms, told us that was not so.

I was disappointed in having to wait so long to see Maher who was in the mounted guard, according to Bahiga. The cavalry was on the opposite side of the square along with the *Meharis,* frontier guards mounted on white camels. We searched for Maher in that distant crowd, and even with the help of Nafissa's binoculars, we did not see him.

At eleven o'clock the rostrum began to fill. It had been set up for dignitaries who filed in dressed in gold-embroidered uniforms. Down below officers pressed against the barriers.

"Are these officers the khedivial guard?" Bahiga and I asked eagerly. Nafissa answered impatiently that these officers were not even participating in the parade. She then explained that the khedivial guard were dressed in blue trousers and gold sashes with white stripes on the side.

Just as I aimed my binoculars at a group of officers, the band struck up the khedivial anthem, and a cannon salute and orders rang out amid the blinding glitter of swords. We heard the sounds of galloping hoofs: It was the khedivial guard gathering in the palace courtyard. The officers, dressed in white tunics, were mounted on white horses and carried banners raised above their heads on lances. It was a dazzling spectacle!

Suddenly Nafissa cried, "Here is the khedive!"

I don't think I took any notice of the khedive. I had eyes only for a young officer in the second company, wearing a gold sash across his breast, poised and proud in his saddle. His waist was tightly cinched in a gold belt, and he looked elegant in the snug-fitting white *dolman,* the dress uniform, decorated with gold bullion and a spray of highly polished buttons. The braided epaulets that hung in spirals on his sleeves, all the way to his elbows, made his shoulders look very broad. With one hand he held the reins short and low, and with the other he flourished his saber, which glittered like a flame in the morning sun. The combination of his brown skin, white uniform, and crimson fez was striking. He was breathtakingly handsome!

All of a sudden, Bahiga shouted, "It's Maher, it's him!" and handed me the binoculars. I was startled to see Maher's face so close to me. I recognized the high cheekbones, the aquiline nose, the moustache trimmed to perfection, and those dark eyes with their velvety look beneath heavy eyebrows, which had so impressed me the first time I caught a glimpse of him.

Maher was just as I had remembered him, perhaps even more handsome. Erect on his horse, he looked like a noble centaur, and I no longer needed binoculars to pick him out of the crowd.

When the troops had gone past, we left the balcony. Nafissa invited us to stay for lunch, and we discussed Maher. The cousins were certain he was on his way to becoming a general. Nafissa's father had been an army man stationed in Khartoum. She told us stories about how exciting and full of adventure that life was. She was sure Maher would enjoy great success in the military.

Mademoiselle joined in the discussion with stories of members of her family who had been officers. She believed that there were only two great careers for a man: the army and the diplomatic corps.

By the time we left Nafissa's house, my head was spinning with what I had seen and the intense emotions I had experienced.

When we went back to our house in Koubba, I felt I had undergone a transformation. I had fallen in love with Maher. I could think of nothing else all day, and dreamed of him at night. Had I not seen Maher again, I suppose I might have forgotten him. But fate had a surprise in store for me. I was not only to see Maher but to speak to him a few days later.

This meeting was to change the course of my life.

22 · EGYPTOLOGY

My father had become very interested in Egyptology after his trip to Upper Egypt and the Sudan. He had made a detour to visit Luxor and had gathered sacks full of ancient statuettes and scarabs he had found in the sand. Had he found a mummy, he probably would have brought it home as well.

Back in Cairo, he met with Mr. Maspero, the director of the Museum of Antiquities, and frequently consulted him on what books to read on the history of the pharaohs. Many of the books I found on his desk at that time were on the subject, and most of them were in French. I shared his readings, and this provided us with new topics of conversation.

Two days after my visit to Koubba with Bahiga, to watch the parade, my father spoke to me enthusiastically about going to the museum. It had recently been moved to its new quarters in Kasr el Nil, where Maspero proudly became its first director.

"You must absolutely see it, Ramza," he said, "A young, cultured woman should give herself a chance to admire this miraculous legacy of our ancestors. They had a prodigious civilization!"

"I've already seen the collection," I answered. "Our school teachers took us on field trips to the museum when it was in Giza."

"There has been quite a change," my father said, "In Giza, the museum was poorly organized. You should see it now. When would you like to go?"

To be quite honest, I had no interest in going. Typical of Egyptians of my generation, I felt indifferent to the civilization of "our ancestors," as my father called them. All I remembered of the field trips we had made to the old museum was that it had been a chance to get out and that we had enjoyed the beautiful Arabic-style palace that housed the collection, and in summer particularly, I had liked the gardens. I had better memories of the museum when it was in Boulac, right on the river, when my grandmother took me there, accompanied by Gaulistan and a whole troop of servants. I delighted in the white sphinxes sprawled like a pair of giant cats facing each other under the trees and never forgot a sphinx made of red granite in front of which I stood open-mouthed, in admiration.

My grandmother certainly did not have my education in mind when she took me to the museum, though, but because she believed in the magic power of old stones and ancient objects. I think I had a fever and a rash, and she wanted me to touch a stone scarab, a representation of the sacred dung beetle, which was believed to have curative powers.

When my father suggested a date for a visit to the new museum, I pretended to be busy with chores, saying that the museum would be there a long time. Yet, an hour later, I had changed my mind and was pacing back and forth impatiently, waiting for a chance to see my father and to ask his permission to go.

What had happened was simply this. An hour or two after the discussion with my father, Bahiga came to say good-bye to me. She was leaving for Alexandria the following day. We talked lightly of one thing and another and said how much we looked forward to seeing each other during the summer months—my father's new duties as chamberlain to the khedive took us to Alexandria where the court summered. As I walked her to the door, she said, "I'll be going to the museum in the morning before taking the train, and . . . "

"You too!" I burst out.

"I didn't suggest you come with me, Ramza," she said shyly, "because I was afraid you would just make fun of me."

"Make fun of you? On the contrary, I think it's wonderful that you are interested in our ancient civilization, that you want to broaden your perspectives . . . "

"See, you are teasing me," Bahiga said, shrugging her shoulders, "You know that I'm not going to the museum for my education! My mother-in-law insisted I visit the mummies there to make me fertile. My husband's family is reproaching me for not giving them children after four years of marriage!"

"And you, Bahiga," I said, "Do you believe in these things?"

She just said, "I promised to do it, so I'll go. Maher will come with me."

At the mention of Maher's name, I felt the blood rush to my face and my heart pump faster. All I could think of was how to see Maher.

"Listen," I said to Bahiga, "I might be of service to you. My father knows Mr. Maspero, the museum's director. I can ask him for a letter of introduction and perhaps come with you. This would give me the chance to see Ramses the Great in his new home!"

I made this comment in as offhand a manner as I could muster and bantered lightly with Bahiga while my conscience prodded me.

"Liar," it said, "Ramses, indeed!"

That night I spoke to my father. He looked at me strangely and said, "Aren't you becoming capricious, Ramza? You didn't seem in a hurry to go in the morning! I'm not free to take you tomorrow, but we could go the next day."

I had to explain that I had agreed to go with Bahiga and that she was leaving in the afternoon. My father agreed to write a letter to Mr. Maspero, which was delivered that same evening.

Needless to say, I didn't sleep a wink that night. And even though I had agreed to meet Bahiga at ten o'clock in the morning, I was up at dawn. I pulled everything out of my closets trying to choose my most becoming outfit. I was fully dressed by eight o'clock, when I went to have breakfast with my father.

He looked me over with an amused smile and said, "Do you mean to dazzle Mr. Maspero, Ramza?"

To this day, I remember what I wore. I had on a white silk blouse with very full sleeves and a lace dickie around my neck; a long, wool skirt of some rich plaid with a ruffled taffeta petticoat rustling alluringly underneath and cinched at the waist with a silver belt; and my best pair of kid booties with high heels.

Unfortunately, I had to cover all of this with my black *habara*. It is interesting, though, to note all the little tricks which a veiled woman devises to appear enticing beneath the black mountain of clothes she has to wear in public!

I remember planting my white buckram *yashmak* a little off center so that a swatch of the stylish plaid lining, matching my skirt, would show. The thick, white face veil I had to wear obscured my features, but I knew my blue eyes, whose color Maher had remembered, were free to express my thoughts. At least I did not have to cover them, and as they were said to be one of my best features, I would use them to advantage.

When it was time to go, Mademoiselle and I were packed into the Berlin used for transporting the harem. Mabrouk Agha was in front, on the high seat, with the coachman. That morning I took care not to tease him as usual by moving aside a curtain or being indiscreet in any way. I was too afraid he would turn around take me home.

We arrived a little ahead of time. I worried that Mr. Maspero would enthusiastically rush us into an exhibition hall, and I would miss my chance to see Maher. I walked very slowly, stopped to look, and dallied in admiration before this sarcophagus and that sphinx, closest to the door.

Finally, Bahiga arrived with her aunts and Maher,

dressed in uniform. My heart beat so wildly I thought it would burst. My lips quivered, I trembled, and my face flushed behind my veil.

For some reason, I pretended to have run into Bahiga instead of letting Mr. Maspero know that I was expecting a guest. I don't really know why I did this. Bahiga introduced her aunt and her brother, and we followed the director into the main exhibition halls which were still mostly empty. Maher walked discreetly behind us, but I could feel him looking at me and, several times, I met his gaze.

At home, before my mirror, I had studied how to lift my *habara* just enough to show off a swatch of the rich plaid of my skirt, and even a little of my fine kid booties. But, in front of Maher, I found I was incapable of carrying out this coquettish display.

I was startled out of my reveries by a call from Bahiga's aunt, who had gone ahead of us with purpose. She had found the statuette she was looking for. It was carved of green stone, representing the Egyptian Goddess of Fertility with her hippopotamus head and great, pendulous breasts. She instructed Bahiga to look intently at this deity and to walk around her seven times. As for Mademoiselle, she was too absorbed in Mr. Maspero's explanations to notice either Bahiga or me.

Maher and I were left alone. Even though we could find nothing to say to each other, our eyes sent a volley of messages back and forth. In Maher's eyes I clearly read a declaration of love. His fiery gaze forced me to avert my eyes, but my agitation was meaningful. He could not have missed it.

At one point, I lingered beside a monument where, folklore had it, the priests stood hidden in order to hear the Gods speak and to render oracles. Suddenly, I was startled to hear a voice coming out of the stone.

"Ramza, I am very happy to see you," said the voice, then Maher emerged from his hiding place and smiled at me.

We felt so inexorably drawn to each other that everything around us became a pretext for a silent lovers' dialogue. When Mr. Maspero praised the beauty of Princess Nefrit, Maher's eyes said, "You are far more beautiful!"

When he showed us the remains of some blue eye shadow, still brilliant in an ancient cosmetic dish, Maher glanced at me.

"Your eyes need no such embellishments," his eyes said.

Mine answered, "They are aglow with pleasing you."

Bahiga visited all the mummies at the museum. When her aunt made a veiled comment on the beneficial results this visit would have, Maher looked at me and gave me a meaningful smile. I lowered my eyes and blushed hotly under my veil.

When it was time to go, I wished I could have openly said good-bye to Maher or have had him be able to kiss my hand in the European fashion . . . But we were in the Orient. Not only was this impossible, but to respect our traditions, Maher had to pretend he was not even aware of my existence.

"See you in Alexandria!" Bahiga said.

"See you in Alexandria, darling," I responded remembering that Maher, as an officer of the khedivial guard, would also be there.

Maher stole a fleeting last glance at me, I looked back at him intently for a second, then we went our separate ways.

23 · ALEXANDRIA

As soon as I could, I reminded my father of his promise to let us spend all summer in Alexandria. I was so insistent that he suggested I write to Bahiga and ask her to find us a villa to rent.

"Look for something near to you, darling, so that we can see each other every day," I wrote.

Bahiga succeeded beyond my wildest hopes. The house my father rented was in Bacos, right next door to Bahiga's, with only a hedge between our gardens. My heart told me that Maher would be spending the summer with his sister, and I could hardly contain my excitement at the prospect of having him so near.

Love is above all an orgy of the imagination. From the moment Bahiga wrote to tell us about the house next door, I lived mostly in the land of my daydreams. I envisioned a summer full of possibilities. I was in ecstasy at the thought of having Maher just a few steps away.

Needless to say, the weeks before our departure were spent in feverish anticipation. I fantasized endlessly about Maher. I pictured him on horseback, the way I had seen him at the parade, because I knew little else about him. I tried to imagine what it would be like to touch the handle of his sword, to experience the warmth of his hand still on it. I dreamed of caressing his horse, of having this animal he loved love me, and I started searching my father's library for books on military life. I played a game where I substituted Maher for the heroes of the stories and made my father repeat his recollections of his mission to Upper Egypt and the Sudan because Maher had been there. And I even went so far as to look for a place where I could find the solitude I needed to daydream.

We had kept our old house on the Khalig—I still called it that even though the canal had long ago been filled in. We were accustomed to going back there only on certain holidays, but now it served as a refuge where I could be alone with my imagination. I took a box of water colors and had myself driven there on the pretext that I wanted to paint.

I wandered around the empty rooms, the deserted garden, and the old plot at the far end where we used to grow vegetables. The ancient well was still there. The harem called this well the "responder" because if you spoke into it, it sent back your voice in echo. As a child, I was forbidden to go near it for fear I would fall in, which made the well doubly enticing.

On my solitary visits to the old house, I liked to push aside the old boards covering the well and whisper Maher's name. I trembled to hear it repeated, and asked the dark water far below all sorts of questions. I pretended that the well could give me answers about what the future had in store for me. It was certainly a childish game! But then love often makes children of us and, sometimes, even fools.

When summer came, my father went ahead of us to Alexandria. He traveled with the khedive. I expected we would soon follow, but Narguiss took two full weeks to get ready. I don't think I ever hated my poor aunt quite so much!

This daughter of the Caucasian Mountains, transplanted to Cairo, who was now sole mistress of our harem, had turned into a veritable Egyptian matron. In the forty-some years that Narguiss lived in Egypt, she had never taken a train. For her this trip to Alexandria was a momentous event. She felt she had to visit the tombs of all the holy men and women of Islam in Cairo before undertaking the journey to Alexandria. God knows, they are numerous!

But that was not all!

The house my father rented belonged to a Maltese stockbroker. It was entirely furnished. I explained to Narguiss that we needed to take only our bedding and clothes, but she would not hear of it. She insisted on packing all our silverware, dishes, towels, sheets, stoves, kitchen utensils, cooking pots, and mattresses to be sent ahead.

One day, when I thought we were finally ready to go, a neighborhood gossip told Narguiss that there was nothing good to eat in Alexandria except fish. This set my aunt packing more provisions. She had dozens of hampers filled with flour, rice, beans, and enough dry goods to feed an army.

Only then our turn came.

The morning of our departure we forgot our quarrels over all these delays. I kissed Narguiss, Mademoiselle, the *khalfa,* and the servants, who of course, were all coming with us. We all felt exuberant and happy, and in this frame of mind, our journey was a delight. I dragged Narguiss off to the club car and teased her because she suspected pork in every dish and refused to eat anything. We were as happy as children. We watched the countryside fly by, and when we stopped laughing and chattering, I listened to the rhythm of the wheels on the track. To my ears they were singing Maher's name and bringing me ever closer to him.

When we arrived at Sidi Gaber Station, my father was waiting for us along with Bahiga's husband, who turned out to be a portly, amiable man. Bahiga herself was standing on the threshold of our new house as we drove up. She had devotedly looked after my father in our absence. He could not say enough to praise her, and I could not be more pleased to find that the summer had begun on such good neighborly terms with Maher's family.

I immediately liked the garden around the house. It had a huge, undulating lawn; luxuriant, rain-washed trees; and many flowering bushes. The house itself was perched on a hillock and looked as if it had been draped in greenery. The old bougainvillea climbers were full of bright pink blossoms. They were trained on the columns supporting the balconies, and fell cascading to the ground under the arcades.

My room was located above one of these arcades and had French doors that opened out to a veranda shielded by greenery.

"I chose this room for you myself, so that I could have you right across from me," Bahiga told me.

She parted the curtain of greenery and showed me her

room, some twenty or thirty meters away, pointing to a house identical to ours.

"That's my house," Bahiga said, "We will easily be able to signal to each other from the verandas."

Of course, I burned with the desire to ask her if Maher was with her but had to restrain myself.

Soon, she told me what I wanted to know.

"My apartments are on the left and my brother's room is on the right of the little family room whose windows you can see there," Bahiga said, pointing. I quickly turned aside to hide my excitement and pleasure, almost expecting to hear my friend say that her brother had been asking after me, that he loved me, and wanted to marry me. She did nothing of the sort, of course, but moved on to other topics and quickly dragged me off to see the rest of the house and the garden.

We walked first along the hedge that separated the twin houses, and I noted with pleasure that it was neither thick nor high. At the very back was a small gate with a padlock on it that opened into a vegetable garden on Bahiga's side. Nothing could be easier to cross! I had to resist the impulse to try the gate, but my imagination ran wild. I could already see a young officer climbing over it to meet me.

For a girl in those days, such a thought alone was shameful, and dreaming of romance would have been considered immoral. I had thoroughly frightened myself with my own daring, and I turned my back and left the little gate as fast as my legs would carry me.

The first night in Alexandria was magical. I went out on my balcony and stood hidden behind the bougainvillea. I looked out across the darkness at Bahiga's house, and saw a light in Maher's room. He was there. I watched and hoped he would come out on his balcony. When I saw a shadow on the wall, I wanted to believe, of course, that Maher was there because he had sensed my presence. Perhaps he, too, was thinking about me and hoping to see me. I stood still, as he paced back and forth briefly. I strained to see his face, but there was no moon that night and I could only make out a figure. Finally, he went back in, and pulled close his shutters.

As soon as I woke up the next morning, I ran out on my veranda, but the one across the way was empty. Bahiga came out a little later and shouted something I did not understand, but there was no sign of Maher.

The following day I was up at dawn and was doubly rewarded with a beautiful sunrise and the sight of Maher on his balcony. He looked both surprised and pleased to see me and quickly Salaam-aleked, bowing deeply and touching his hand to his heart, his forehead, and his mouth. I answered him likewise. I hoped my gestures would convey the full meaning of the greeting which signifies, "You are in my thoughts, my heart, my words." I was not wearing my veil, in fact I had completely forgotten it. We both smiled broadly at each other, and Maher blew me a kiss. I knew instantly that I should flee, particularly because my face was uncovered, but I was afraid Maher would think he had displeased me.

We stood gazing at each other, as if under a spell. I saw Maher's face framed by the bougainvillea blossoms, sparkling with pearls of morning dew. I felt my heart singing, but the creaking of a shutter startled me back to reality. I flew into my room, but I had captured my ration of happiness for the day!

During the first few weeks in Alexandria, Maher and I exchanged greetings from a distance. I can still picture us standing on our balconies on opposite sides of the garden, at dawn and in the evening, when the light was soft as a caress!

I saw Bahiga almost daily but never came close to Maher. In any case he was rarely at home. Bahiga was far from suspecting the romance developing between her brother and me, and in any case, I would not have dreamed of burdening her with a confession. I knew that if I did, she would feel duty-bound to put obstacles in our way for fear of becoming an accomplice.

Our lives had taken a different rhythm in this new city. Alexandria was more European, freer, more relaxed than Cairo. My father and I had breakfast together as usual, but he was gone most of the day. Our conversations had such a lightness to them! I remember thinking how much they reflected the way Alexandria was. He told me stories about the court and even repeated some of the gossip he had heard. This was uncharacteristic of him but encouraged me to open up as well.

One day I talked to him about the khediva, the khedive's mother, who had just returned from Istanbul.

"I'm told she brought back a wardrobe of the latest fashions, and that the ladies of the court and the ladies in town are all scrambling to copy her."

I had heard that the lavish receptions the khediva gave at Hazina, her palace at Sidi Bishr, created quite a stir.

"I'm a little surprised," I said, testing my father, "that she doesn't hold a salon, like her sister Princess Nazli Hanem, where men and women meet openly and discuss literature and politics. I understand that women attend unveiled! Why doesn't the khediva do the same and set the example for the rest of the nation? She has a reputation for being intelligent and open minded."

"Well," my father answered, "I don't think the khediva is likely to do anything that might cause a scandal. I don't think she approves of drastic changes. She's really quite traditional."

I felt I had scored a point when my father added, "But the old customs are on their way out, Ramza. In time they will dissipate."

After my father left for the day and my household responsibilities were over, I usually met new French friends for a visit or an outing. Camille and Isabelle were the daughters of members of the fairly large expatriate community that lived in Alexandria in those days. I had met them with their mother, Madame Henriette, at a neighborhood tea party. Mademoiselle Hortense and Madame Henriette had been pleased to discover they were both from the Limousin and spent that entire first afternoon reminiscing about their homeland.

Isabelle, who was about my age, and Camille, who was a little younger, played an influential role in my life that summer. For the first time, I could talk to someone about love. We shared an interest in French literature and in music that I could never discuss with the women of our harem. My father had been, until then, my only source of intellectual companionship. And Bahiga, who was really the only friend I had other than my childhood playmate Zakeyya, conversed mostly on homemaking. Even though she had been in school with me, she was not a reader or a thinker, and when it came to music, she leaned more toward the popular than the classical.

Even though, among my schoolmates, I had always been the leader, that summer Isabelle and Camille had the upper hand. They were less sheltered than I was, and their musical education was much broader than mine. They took it upon themselves to teach me what they knew. I found that whereas I had not gone much beyond my mother's beloved Chopin, even though I knew a little Beethoven and some Wagner, the serious Isabelle could initiate me to Bach, and the playful Camille, to Debussy.

We experienced such deep pleasure in each other's company that from the start we were inseparable. Luckily, my father approved of my association with them, and we did everything together. Of course, there was no question of going out with my face uncovered as they did. In this I had to obey my father's strict orders, but I envied them and stubbornly used only my thinnest white veils, even to go out. I resented not being able to feel the full force of the wind on my face.

Isabelle and Camille were in the habit of bathing in the sea at Glymonopolou. They went in the early morning, the hour the beach was reserved for the use of women. I enjoyed going along with them but hated having to sit covered from head to toe in their bathhouse while they frolicked in the sea. One day I took my courage in my hands and asked my father if I could also go bathing—actually, sea baths were becoming quite acceptable for women at that time, and were even recommended by doctors. They were prescribed for tuberculosis, eye diseases, and to help people lose or gain weight; and sea water was used as a popular gargle. Even the ladies of the court indulged, and the khediva herself took sea baths daily at her private beach in Sidi Bishr.

Narguiss, who was concerned about my health, talked to my father. She was worried that I seemed pale and more subdued than usual. She pleaded with him to let me take baths to invigorate me, and finally, he agreed. Unfortunately, this experience was not at all what I had looked forward to. I was only allowed to frequent the special establishment reserved for women at the beach of San Stefano, where the atmosphere was stifling.

I tried hard to convince my father to let me go to Glymonopolou; I took him to see how secluded the beach was, explained that the bathing costume I would wear would cover my entire body, and pointed out that the beach at that early hour was heavily guarded. But he was intractable. "Since you need these baths for your health, Ramza, you will take them at San Stefano," he declared.

What a disagreeable place that was! The sea was like a pond there. The beach had been closed off, and completely surrounded by cabins that blocked off the sun. I envied my friends the brisk open air, the waves, the early morning sun, and the quiet of the beach at Glymonopoluo. San Stefano was crowded with women who came to meet their friends, show off their clothes, their jewelry, prattle, share the latest gossip, and display their daughters before the ever-present matchmakers or mothers of marriageable boys.

Narguiss was in her element at San Stefano. This was an extension of the harem and felt like home to her. She relished the fresh gossip and the new faces. I hated the crowds, the women dabbling in clumps in the murky water under the probing gaze of hundreds of curious eyes, and I longed for the open sea. From time to time when I could get someone to come with me, I went to San Stefano early enough to avoid the throngs. I enjoyed a blissful hour of peace during which I could dream of Maher's morning kiss to my heart's content, and enjoy the cool caress of the water. I rarely found anyone to come with me at that hour, though, and Isabelle and Camille, who came a few times to please me, found it so stifling that they refused to return. I soon gave up going myself and followed my friends instead. How much bluer the sea was there! How much more exhilarating and fresh the air and the open vistas! As an obedient daughter, I had to stay covered. Still, I enjoyed the pungent smell of the sea, the feeling of the wind catching up my veil as I sat on the sand. I loved watching the waves quiver and crest while thinking of Maher.

I did not tell Isabelle and Camille about my secret love until they confided in me. I had noticed that, after bathing on certain mornings, one or the other of the two sisters took the streetcar downtown on some mysterious errand. One day when I did not have to be home for lunch as usual, I went with Camille. Her destination was the post office, where she picked up two letters. She opened one and pulled out a photograph which she handed to me very naturally, and said, "His name is Raymond. He's the man I love."

I stared at her in astonishment and asked, "Are you engaged?"

"Not yet," she responded. "Not officially. We met in Vichy. He's a colonial administrator in the Senegal."

"Do your parents know about him?"

"They saw us walking together, but they don't know that we're in love. He has not asked for my hand yet because he's not rich, and he's not a high-ranking official. He's afraid if he spoke to my father now, my father would refuse him; but I'm determined to marry him no matter what."

Camille had said this in a perfectly quiet voice.

I was surprised and asked, "How can you marry him if your parents don't agree?"

She answered, "I'll wait until I reach my majority, and then I'll be free to make my own decisions."

Isabelle then told me about her secret love, insisting that she too would follow her heart.

"I'm very attached to my parents, especially my mother. But if my parents force me to choose between them and Etiènne, I will elope," she confessed.

I could not believe my ears, and asked, "You would really do that?"

She looked at me without answering, but the set of her little square chin, and the look in her green eyes told me that she meant what she said. This conversation made me thoughtful. Camille and Isabelle's behavior was beyond reproach. They were devout Catholics. They were very proper. I was truly puzzled by what they had just told me. I asked them how far they had allowed their amorous adventures to go, and they answered that both their lovers had not gone beyond hand kissing.

Their confessions had endeared them to me and encouraged me to tell them my secret.

That same day, as we were coming back from their house, we ran into Maher at an intersection. He recognized me. I squeezed Isabelle's hand excitedly, and whispered, "It's him!" In those few instants, I had seen such a look of love in Maher's eyes that it put me in a tender trance the rest of the evening.

24 · FIRST ENCOUNTER

A few days later Bahiga's husband was out of town. She invited us all to dinner. Camille, Isabelle, and I were fond of Bahiga but could not tell her any of our secrets. She had gone from the domination of a father to that of a husband, and we felt she would not understand.

That evening my two friends stopped by to pick me up, and as we started across the garden together, Isabelle gave me a mysterious little smile and handed me an envelope. It was blank. I was puzzled and looked at her for an explanation, but all she said was, "Open it, open it! It might be from your Prince Charming!"

At first I thought the letter might be a prank, but it was indeed a note from Maher. He had found a way of meeting my friends at the streetcar station in Ramla, and had discreetly slipped one of them the note. He was asking me to meet him. He knew that I was having dinner at his sister's house that night and told me that, after dinner, he would wait for me under the big tree near the kitchen garden. I knew the tree he meant. It was a giant weeping willow, close to the garden gate. I had imagined such a meeting on the very first day that Bahiga took me on a tour of the garden. My first impulse was to jump for joy, and my second was to recoil in horror. I felt like the heroine in one of the novels I had read. I imagined myself about to embark on some fantastic, forbidden adventure never before experienced by any woman. But then I panicked. How could a respectable Muslim girl go out alone at night? To meet a young man? How could I do this to my father? Violate all the moral dictates of my religion? Its sacred laws? How could I risk dishonor? There would be no way to redeem myself or my family if I were caught.

"No," I said firmly to myself, "I will not go."

On the other hand, I thought, "I want to get to know a man before marriage! I want to be able to choose a husband for myself!"

I was afraid that if I hesitated I would miss my chance at happiness. To get to know the man I loved, to hear him speak directly to me, to know his intentions . . . I had dreamed of that!

"And besides," I said to myself, "how can I love Maher if I can't trust him! It's an affront to him to think that his intentions are dishonest!"

I would go.

Camille and Isabelle waited patiently to hear what I had to report. I told them that Maher wanted to meet me, and that I was experiencing the agony of indecision. I did not know what to do and asked them for their advice.

"In matters like these one has to take responsibility for one's own decisions," Isabelle responded.

"If you do go," Camille added, "be on your guard and don't give an inch, not even a kiss."

Hearing their warnings I was again afraid to go. As we approached Bahiga's house I pointed to the willow with its branches draped down to the ground in a thick green curtain. Anyone standing under it would be hidden from sight. Isabelle said it looked like a real lovers' hideaway.

"I don't think I will go," I said.

Isabelle looked relieved and said, "That would be best."

I was very uneasy. I felt dizzy and frightened, but no one noticed anything until Bahiga asked me to play my favorite piece on the piano before dinner. It was Chopin's "Barcarolle." I knew it by heart and had played it many times, but that night I could not concentrate. I hit the wrong keys, I forgot the notes and even the melody. My ears buzzed, and my head felt like an empty cavity. Even when Bahiga came to my rescue with the sheet music, I confused the notes. This had never happened to me before. I felt utterly out of control, I left the piano and collapsed in a chair, weeping. My friends rushed around me, but Camille told them that I needed to be left alone for a while. I was miserable. This beautiful, moonlit evening was a torture. Bahiga had set a table in the garden. Normally, I would have loved eating in the open air, but I listened to my friends chatting gaily and could barely participate in their conversation because I was so preoccupied with Maher.

I brooded and wondered if he might be standing under the tree listening to us, trying to make out which voice was mine. I was tormented by the thought of letting him down. I feared disappointing him. He would perhaps withdraw his love and I might never see him again . . . I would be deprived of his cherished face in the early morning . . .

Just then I heard Mademoiselle say to Bahiga, "To do a Gobelin stitch, you work with two threads and prick your needle on the underside first . . . " Bahiga was starting a tapestry to cover a chair for her husband's birthday and asked Mademoiselle to come into the house to see the wools she had bought.

When they both went in, I felt Maher's silent, irresistible pull. I looked at my friends and jumped up.

"I'm going!" I blurted out and dashed off in the direction of the tree.

Isabelle came running after me.

"Wait, I'm coming with you," she shouted. "I've told Camille to say we've gone to your house to get a shawl if Mademoiselle returns before we do."

I had acted so impulsively, it had not even occured to me that Mademoiselle and Bahiga would want to know where we had been!

As soon as we were out of sight, Isabelle took me by the hand and we ran down the hill. I saw a shadow move under the tree, and someone started toward us. My fingers tightened around Isabelle's.

"I'll wait by the gate for you. Don't be long."

She wrenched her hand free and disappeared.

"Ramza," Maher murmured.

I took a step toward the voice, and was instantly swallowed up by the deep shadows. A pair of hands reached for mine. They were trembling. We stood motionless and speechless. When my eyes got used to the dark, I began to make out Maher's features. My heart beat so hard it hurt me, and my hands in his expressed my solemn commitment to Maher. Our lives, I thought, were now forever linked.

I waited for Maher to say something, but I didn't quite know what. When he remained silent, I made a movement to go.

"For the love of God," he blurted out finally, "please don't go yet. I was so afraid you wouldn't come! I want so much to tell you that I love you, that I want to marry you! Please promise to meet me again so I can persuade you of my devotion!"

Maher only let go of my hands when I had assured him that I would return the next night. Isabelle was waiting for me. We ran to my house to get a shawl and returned just as Mademoiselle and Bahiga were coming out. I was flushed and out of breath. My eyes glowed. Mademoiselle looked at me with concern.

"I think we had better go home," she said, "You look like you have a fever."

I did not resist. I was grateful to retreat to my room and my thoughts. The ease with which I had been able to meet Maher without anyone getting suspicious emboldened me. The following night I returned but, without Isabelle, I was very much on my guard. Maher was waiting for me. We had a brief, whispered conversation. He asked me dozens of questions on my tastes, my interests . . . He also asked me if I would willingly accept him as a husband. When I said, "Yes," he impetuously pulled me into his arms and kissed me on the forehead. I extricated myself instantly and ran away, but I felt as if a fire had consumed me. Even in the safety of my room, I still felt the pressure of his hands on my shoulders, and the warmth of his breath on my face. I decided right then that I would not see Maher again until he had formally asked for my hand in marriage. But I didn't have the courage to give up our morning greetings across the garden, and I smiled at him from my balcony. When he signaled to me, pointing in the direction of the little gate, though, I shook my head. I was consumed with thoughts of him day and night. I was afraid of meeting him and afraid that if I did not, I would lose him.

I discovered that from the balcony of my father's room, I could see the entrance of Bahiga's house. When it was empty, I went out on the balcony to watch for Maher's return. I felt a thrill when I heard the sound of hooves on the pavement and I saw him trot by, molded into his brilliantly white summer uniform. He was a picture of manliness! I dreamed of his coming home to me one day and pictured myself waiting for him at the door.

One afternoon, Isabelle came to fetch me saying, "Come, come quickly, we have something to show you!" She was smiling in that mysterious way I had seen before, but I couldn't get her to tell me what it was all about. When we got to her house, we ran up to the roof, four steps at a time.

"Shush, don't say a word!" She covered my eyes, and led me forward by the hand.

"Now, open your eyes!"

I had to stifle a cry of surprise. In the garden next door were two young men, in white trousers and open shirts, playing tennis. One of them was Maher, a Maher I didn't know. I saw a vigorous young man, dressed informally, animated and totally absorbed in his game. I realized with a pang that Maher had a life that did not include me and that he was not obsessed with our love as I was. It was clear that hours went by when no thought of me even crossed his mind. I fretted. Had I discouraged him that first night by running away? Could it be that he had lost interest when I refused to meet him?

Even the thought of losing him made me dizzy. I felt as if I had taken a step on firm ground and found myself falling into a bottomless pit. The following morning I decided to act. I signaled Maher to meet me at the garden gate that same night and waited impatiently for the sun to set. It had been cloudy, still, and dreary that day, with not a breath of fresh air. At dusk, I rushed out of the house to meet Maher and came face to face with my father, who took my arm and strolled with me two or three times past the place in Bahiga's garden where I felt Maher must be waiting. I was in agony and so irritated with my father that I barely answered his questions. He talked on and on, though, seeming not to notice anything out of the ordinary, fortunately for me. Finally, I excused myself saying I had a headache. I went to my room and left it again almost immediately, taking the service stairs into the garden. I crossed the kitchen without meeting anyone, and ran to the little gate. I was taking a terrible risk. What if my family noticed I was missing? The danger of this was nothing to me compared with the thought of losing Maher.

It was a very dark night. At the gate I did not see Maher. I called his name softly, but no answer came. Had he abandoned me? I lost my head. I ran into Bahiga's garden and was almost to the house when Maher appeared. I threw myself into his arms, he covered my forehead, my cheeks, my neck with kisses, and I offered him my lips. A sudden noise startled us and we sank deeper into the shadows, listening, our hearts beating wildly.

Finally, Maher whispered, "Are you going to the beach with your friends tomorrow?"

I said, "Maybe . . . "

Anxiously he said, "Go with them. I'll wait for you in the nearby Bedouin tents."

I knew the Bedouins whose tents he was talking about. They were shepherds. I had seen them often looking for a spot in the dunes where their sheep and goats could graze. I agreed without hesitation. I was ready to do anything to keep Maher. I was heady with excitement and when I saw Mademoiselle that evening, I grabbed her, twirled her around, and covered her with kisses saying, "I love you, I love you, I love you!" Mademoiselle was alarmed at my sudden euphoria. I had been dejected a few nights before, and she could not understand my mood swings. She looked at me quizzically. "You're overexcited, Ramza! What's happening to you?"

"I'm happy!" was all I said.

25 · BEDOUIN TENTS

On Sunday morning Mademoiselle Hortense and Madame Henriette went to early morning mass at the Catholic church in Bacos. Mademoiselle agreed to drop me off at my friends so that the three of us could go to the beach together, making me promise not to go near the water. In answer, I held up a book I was taking along to read. I had no intention whatsoever of reading, of course, nor could I have concentrated even if I had wanted to.

As soon as Camille and Isabelle were in the water, I wrapped myself up in a black *melaaya,* and dashed in back of the cabins that faced the sea. I saw two tents in the distance and, further to the east, the shepherds with their herds. I scampered up the sand dunes and felt a lump in my throat when the camp looked forsaken. I hesitated and was about to turn back when Maher emerged, his figure silhouetted against one of the tents. He called me. I walked toward him, my heart racing, and suddenly felt disgusted at the thought of going into one of those tents. I had heard all sorts of tales about the Bedouins, and I was afraid the tent would be dirty and flea-ridden. I could not have been more wrong. It was clean and had a bright-colored wool rug on the floor. Maher pulled me into his arms and his lips touched mine. At that moment I felt I was committing the greatest folly of my life, but I could not stop myself. When I was finally able to get a good look at the man I loved, I found him as handsome as I had remembered. He was dressed in civilian clothes that morning. I admired the cut of his grey jacket, his tiepin, his ruby ring, his slender, brown hands, the silver handle on his ebony cane, and the soft kid gloves which I felt a sudden longing to caress as if they were his hands. He wore a carnation in his lapel. He offered it to me, watching as I inhaled its spicy perfume.

"How beautiful you are, Ramza!"

I was wearing a white cambric dress with a wide, blue taffeta sash and white kid booties. My *melaaya* had fallen around me on the ground as had my white head covering and veil. With my face so exposed to Maher's gaze, I felt as if I were delivering my entire being to him!

"Maher, when are we going to get married?" I asked, worried by the enormity of what I had just done.

"As soon as possible, my beloved," he answered.

"You must not delay in asking my father for my hand," I said urgently.

He hesitated and then said, "You know that as soon as your father has received my request, we shall not be able to see each other again until after the wedding. Had you thought of that, Ramza?"

Even though I knew our customs well, the thought that I would not be able to see Maher after we were engaged had not occurred to me, nor did I reason at that moment that we were meeting clandestinely anyway. I just thought of how my father would restrict my movements. I would be watched with greater vigilance and would neither be able to go to Bahiga's house nor even see Bahiga, perhaps. The thought of being deprived of Maher's company, even briefly, was so intolerable to me that I suggested he ap-

proach my father only when we were almost ready to leave
for Cairo. We agreed to meet at the garden gate or under
the Bedouin tents, which the shepherds were only too glad
to rent.

When I got back to the beach, I confessed my plans to
my friends. Isabelle listened without commenting, but
Camille told me I was being foolhardy.

"You don't know men, Ramza," she warned, "They always want more than they get, and when they get it nine
times out of ten they don't marry the girl. You're so in love
you will find it hard to resist."

Camille then gave me countless examples of girls who
had been seduced and abandoned. I had no idea how accu-
rate her statistics were, but her advice made me more careful, even though I refused to give up seeing Maher. I, too,
remembered stories I had heard about dishonored girls who
had brought catastrophe down on their families and were
condemned to live as social lepers for the rest of their lives.
Nothing could redeem them. I knew that however much
my father loved me, he would not be indulgent in this respect. He would curse me and, without his protection, I
would be defenseless. That is why, even though I was hopelessly in love with Maher, I carefully resisted his advances. I
must confess that Khedive Abbas' hunting trip on his estate
at Lake Mariotis also helped me to get a hold on myself.
Maher, of course, being a member of the khedivial guard,
had to follow and was absent for fifteen days. I had asked
him to write to me care of Isabelle or Camille. He had
promised, but only kept his promise once, and then his note
was brief and trivial. I was hurt and disappointed. I used to
wait impatiently for my friends to return from the post office and was pained when they appeared empty handed. I
began to doubt Maher's love for me, to paint a somber picture of what my life as the wife of a soldier would be like,
and I envied my friends.

In spite of my discontentment, I managed to find excuses for Maher. I had to persuade myself somehow that I was not a fool for loving him. I flaunted his virtues before Isabelle and Camille in an effort to reassure myself that he was worthy. I could not ask Bahiga about him for fear of arousing her suspicion, and alone, I went back to the places we had met looking for traces of him. I remembered his face, his voice, his sweet breath, the taste of his kisses, and I ached. Without him, the days seemed endless. I listened for the sound of horses' hooves outside our door, I jumped when I heard a carriage go by, and swallowed my hurt when none stopped in front of Bahiga's house. I kept thinking I saw Maher on the street, and I was so agitated that I worried even myself.

Finally, one night, I saw a light on in his room. I went out on my balcony and there he was, silhouetted against the door. He saw me, sent me a kiss, and motioned me to come down. I could not resist. The household was still awake, and although slipping out then was a risk, I went.

I had meant to reproach Maher for not writing, but before I could open my mouth, he had taken me in his arms, and I forgot everything. I was alarmed at the intensity of my desire for him and realized with a shudder that I not only had to guard against Maher but against myself.

That night, I told him it was time to send word to my father, swearing I would marry him, come what may.

26 · WOMEN'S BATH

One Saturday night Bahiga spent the night at our house because her brother and her husband were away. In the morning Narguiss suggested we go with her to San Stefano. I particularly disliked the women's bath on Sunday because it was even more crowded than usual. It was

Narguiss' favorite day, however. She insisted so much that we finally gave in, but I was sure that Narguiss had something up her sleeve. We arrived at San Stefano at the peak morning hour, and ran into all of the women Narguiss had befriended. They stopped to exchange greetings, dawdled, and paused to chat with the merchants who crowded the premises, hawking cheap lingerie, costume jewelry, or reading cards, reading palms, telling fortunes, selling food or drink . . . These women relied on a regular clientele among the bathers with whom they developed friendly relations based on gossip and small services. As we made our way to the baths, Narguiss introduced me right and left. I felt the eyes of women who looked me up and down so knowingly that I wondered if I were not just part of the merchandise.

Narguiss never bathed because she was afraid of the sea. She insisted, however, that Bahiga and I get into our bathing suits. When we came out of the cabin, I noticed she was in deep conversation with a large, imposing woman. She stopped talking when she saw me and, once more, I felt myself being undressed by her companions' probing eyes. Bahiga nudged me and gave me a knowing smile.

"That's Amina el Torkeyya. She's the best matchmaker in Alexandria. Did you notice her looking at you? I think she may be here because of you!"

I had heard of this woman. She was once a slave in the Toussoun family. Someone had pointed her out to me, as she rode her strange little buggy drawn by a mule. I had been told that she was very successful in her negotiations, and that people were always after her business.

Of course, my first thought was that Amina had been sent by Maher's family. But that was not logical. They already knew me. Rationally, I knew that. I was in love, though, and willing to see only what brought me closer to Maher. I persuaded myself that Amina el Torkeyya had come to San Stefano for the reasons that I wanted her to be here for, and I played the matchmaker's game to the hilt. I let my hair fall attractively around my shoulders, smiled sweetly at Sitt Amina, paraded up and down the beach with Bahiga, and dragged her into the water. I frolicked so happily in this place I had previously so much disliked that I even embarrassed myself with my own playacting.

When Bahiga and I finally went to rest on the beach, I saw Sitt Amina's eyes follow us.

"She's negotiating a bride for my brother too, you know."

I was startled. But then I thought to myself, "Bahiga's teasing me. Everything must be going as planned."

"You know," she said, "At one time Maher wanted to marry. He asked for the hand of the daughter of a high government official—the khedive's head of protocol, in fact. My father refused. He would not even approach the family and told us that, although we were richer than they were, they would always look down on us. He said that such marriages were always a source of trouble."

When I heard Bahiga say this, I suddenly felt anxious. This same difference in class applied to Maher and me.

"My father told Maher that such a wife would always look down on us," Bahiga continued, "Her family would never let him forget that Maher had had the honor of being accepted by a pasha's daughter!"

I bit my lip.

"And whom does the family want your brother to marry?"

Bahiga said, "I haven't met her yet, but it seems she's an only child, the daughter of a very rich wood merchant in Alexandria. If the negotiations are successful, Maher could leave the khedive's service and go into business with his father-in-law."

I froze.

"Is Maher pleased with this idea?"

Bahiga answered, "Why shouldn't he be? She's an heiress!"

My fury rose instantly. Had we been alone, I would have struck Bahiga. Instead, I got up saying that I was cold and dashed back to our cabin as fast as my legs would carry me. I passed in front of the matchmaker without a glance. Narguiss called out to me, but I ignored her. I dressed quickly, trembling with rage, and sat in the cabin to wait for Narguiss and Bahiga. I was desperate to get home.

So, Maher was betraying me! He was getting ready to marry someone else! I thought that explained why, only the day before, he had said that he wanted us to stop meeting. He had been so innocent, so cool as he spoke . . .

"We can't risk being caught and compromised," he had said.

The rogue! I would let him know what I thought of him!

27 · CONFRONTATIONS

The rest of that Sunday was pure torture. I had to spend it with Bahiga against whom I turned all my anger. The angrier I became, the more patient she was. I was beside myself with irritation and frustration. Camille and Isabelle were away with their parents, and there was no one else I could confide in. I cursed their absence that day. I needed their calming influence and their advice. Had they been with me, they would probably have protected me from my impulsive action. But, left to my own devices, I decided to confront Maher without delay.

I watched for his homecoming. As soon as I saw a light in his room, I left Mademoiselle and Bahiga in the drawing room, and rushed across the garden to Bahiga's house. It was deserted except for the hum of voices coming from the kitchen. I walked up the stairs, saw a sliver of light under

Maher's door, and knocked. Maher opened it and recognized me instantly. He froze. I can remember his face at that moment as if I had seen it yesterday. He went pale and looked shocked. The only conceivable reason I could commit such an indiscretion would be to announce a catastrophe!

"Ramza! What has happened?" he cried.

I did not answer. I will never forget how determined, and also how terrified I was. I walked straight into his room and pushed the door shut behind me. When I saw him go pale, I was sure it was because I had caught him at his game of deceit. I looked him straight in the eye and said, "When are you getting married to the daughter of the wood merchant?"

As soon as I had spoken, his face broke into a smile and a look of utter relief came into his eyes.

"You terrified me, Ramza! I was sure the house was on fire or someone had died!"

"Answer me!" I cried angrily, "You talked about getting married and you were deceiving me all the while. Did you mean to abandon me after all the promises we made? Or did you think I would become a second wife, Maher?"

He laughed softly and tried to take my hands.

"Don't touch me!" I cried.

"Ramza, who told you this stupid tale? It was Bahiga, wasn't it? How could you have believed her?"

"Bahiga would not lie to me."

I wanted to hurt him and added, "Besides, I understand that your family is very fussy about you marrying into their own class!"

Maher looked hurt.

He cried, "Ramza, I beg of you, please believe me, I knew nothing about these negotiations until yesterday evening! When I found out I refused categorically. I'm a man! I can't be forced into marriage!"

Seeing his face change, I began to soften.

"Listen, in spite of the risk you've just taken, I'm glad you're here. I can tell you that I have asked Wassef Pasha to intervene on our behalf. He honors me with his protection, and has agreed to go see your father before my father does to ensure that we will be successful."

Wassef Pasha was then governor of Alexandria and a good friend of my father's. When I heard Maher outline his plan, my anxiety fell away. He took my hands in his and pressed them tenderly. His sweet warmth filled me with desire, and under the charm of his kisses, my willpower was gone. I melted into his arms and would have been his that night had he wanted me. But he pushed me away gently.

"Ramza, you must go. Are you aware of the danger you are putting yourself in? If you are discovered, your reputation would be lost forever!"

"So what?" I said carelessly, "That would force them to marry us!"

"That's not the way I want us to get married. You must be more careful."

Maher inspected the hallways and the stairs. The way was clear. I left, but I did so with a deep feeling of regret. I had been with him no more than ten minutes, yet I felt as if I had been absent from our house a lifetime. At home, Bahiga and Mademoiselle were still where I had left them. They were still talking quietly about their favorite topics, cooking and tapestry. I felt disconnected from them, removed from their concerns, and quickly found an excuse to escape to the familiar safety of my room. That night I could hardly sleep. I had a terrible feeling that I was not going to see Maher again.

In the morning Amina el Torkeyya came to visit, and Narguiss called me, but I refused to go, and we ended up quarreling as usual.

"I don't ever want to see such women in our house again!" I shouted. "Have I made myself clear, Narguiss? No more matchmakers!"

Narguiss looked at me in astonishment. My moods had been swinging wildly in the last few weeks, and she did not know what to make of what I said or did.

"I don't want to be looked over, bartered for, bought, sold, or locked up in a harem. The era of slavery is over, Narguiss!" I shouted.

"I was a slave, and I'm not the worse for it," Narguiss snapped back. "In fact I'm a happy woman," she said with complete sincerity, I think.

"Well, I don't want to be one! And I don't want that kind of happiness! I will marry a man I want and have chosen for myself!" I replied.

"And how are you going to choose him, smart aleck?" she said. "Can you tell me that? Where will you look for your handsome husband? In the streets? In the shops? Will you propose to him yourself? Ramza, when you want to buy a piece of jewelry, you call a jeweler. When you want a house, you go to a realtor. When you want a husband, it's a matchmaker you need!"

I stared at Narguiss. Her reasoning was consistent with the customs of our society, but I was up in arms against those customs and sick of the marriage marketplace.

Narguiss thought perhaps that she had subdued me. She said, "This Turkish woman is very skilled and knows all the families of Alexandria."

"So that was it!" I thought, "Narguiss has taken a liking to Alexandria and wants to find me a husband here so she can visit as often as she wants!"

Narguiss was not going to give up easily. Despite my anger, and even after our fight, she continued to scheme. I decided to tell her nothing about Maher, although later I realized that was probably a mistake. Narguiss cared a lot about me. I could have used her help as an ally. But I had been afraid, given her talkative nature, that she might inadvertently drop a word to my father. I was determined to guard against that.

In the afternoon Camille and Isabelle came to visit me. I told them what had happened in detail. And although they were amused by my confrontation with Narguiss over the matchmaker, Camille disapproved of my nocturnal foray into Bahiga's house. I saw Isabelle's look of admiration, though, and I was flattered. A little later, Bahiga joined us with her ever-present tapestry in hand. She was in a flap.

"I don't know what's happened to my brother," she said, "He sent a soldier over to pick up his things, and with a message that he was staying at his barracks for a while."

Camille and Isabelle gave me a probing look. I felt faint. Was Maher running away from me? Had he lied to me the night before about Wassef Pasha's visit to my father? I no longer knew what to think. I was so distracted that day that I did not notice that the level of activity at home had increased. The kitchen was a beehive, there were continuous deliveries being made, and the servants were involved in frenzied preparation for something. Finally, I found out that Wassef Pasha was coming to dinner.

I can remember to this day the feeling of relief I experienced at that exact moment, and how immediately happiness returned as I thought, "Maher has not betrayed me after all!" He had moved out of a sense of discretion while the negotiations were taking place. How that thought comforted me!

That night I lay awake wondering what my father and Wassef Pasha had said to each other. At dawn, I dozed off and ended up missing my father at breakfast. I felt annoyed with myself. Although I knew he would never say a word to me directly, I was counting on being able to find out the outcome of Wassef Pasha's visit by deciphering the expression on my father's face. I went to his room, but he had left. It was Mademoiselle I ran into instead. She handed me a note without saying a word. It was from my father.

"I am leaving for Cairo. Make sure Ramza does not see her friend, Bahiga . . . " I read.

The note was brief, with no explanation.

"What has happened between you and Bahiga, Ramza? What could poor Bahiga have done?"

"Bahiga has nothing to do with this," I said, feeling happy and, I am sure, looking so radiant that Mademoiselle was confused. She looked at me quizically.

"I'm going to marry her brother!" I said and explained the custom of keeping the bride away from her future bridegroom's family until matters had been formally settled.

"But, Ramza, why should you be deprived of Bahiga when you are going to become sisters?" she persisted.

"Custom, Mademoiselle!" I answered flippantly. "You are surprised, I know. But that's how it is. They think Bahiga might act as a go-between. Obviously, no one trusts a bride, but I don't mind waiting this time while they go through the formalities. I know my bridegroom already, and I love him."

All at once I saw Mademoiselle's eyes fill with tears. I thought she might be wondering if I would abandon her once I was married. I kissed her and told her we would always be together, and that I was counting on her to raise my children. We discussed love and marriage, and she reminisced about her own brief summer of happiness, her eyes filling over and over again with tears.

"Did he ever kiss you, Mademoiselle?" I asked finally.

She blushed to the roots of her grey hair and cried, "Oh, Ramza, what a question!"

"Tell me, Mademoiselle!" I insisted, "You know that in novels couples who are engaged always kiss."

Finally she whispered, "No, he never kissed me. He couldn't have. My mother was always with us."

I smiled knowingly and thought, "Poor Mademoiselle Hortense! In a few weeks I have come to know more about love than you have in a lifetime. I have been kissed!"

The day after our little interlude, Mademoiselle and I were returning from a visit to our French friends when she

was called in to see Narguiss. I was not included. All the
women of the household were gathered, talking loudly,
laughing, and passing samples of fabric around. A seam-
stress was trying to measure them as they gesticulated and
bantered. Narguiss, authoritarian matron that she was,
looked completely in her element as she orchestrated the activities and gave orders right and left. No one heard me
come in. They were all so busy gabbling! I recall standing
happily by the door dreaming of the day when Maher and I
would be married.

New dresses were only ordered for the entire harem for
religious feasts and on the occasion of a wedding, and I saw
no other wedding in sight than my own and finally asked
Narguiss why everyone but me was getting a new dress.

She laughed heartily and when she said, "Have patience,
my girl. Your turn will come," I was truly exasperated.

"Narguiss, I've had enough of all this secretiveness. I
know what's going on, so why don't you just come out
with it!"

"You've always known better than anyone one else,"
she replied with good humor.

"So, did my father accept without a fuss?"

"Accept what?" Narguiss asked.

"Maher's proposal of marriage," I answered boldly. I
was so naïve!

"Maher, Muhammad, Moustafa . . . I don't remember
his name," Narguiss said elusively, and laughed.

"Oh, all right, all right," I finally said, giving up. "Keep
your secret!"

Narguiss gave orders that I was to be taken to Hannaux,
one of the elegant department stores that had opened in Alexandria. Mademoiselle was instructed to go with me and
to buy me a wedding gown. We chose one that was delicately trimmed with seed pearls, with matching satin shoes,
and a fan in the shape of a bouquet of flowers, fashionable at
the time. Despite all the good cheer, I noticed that Made-

moiselle seemed sad and asked her what the matter was. She just shook her head and said it was nothing, and I thought no more about it. Even today, I am suprised at how self-ishly unconcerned about her I was. I've noticed since that people who are happy often are!

Wassef Pasha had come and gone. When a week went by without a visit from Maher's stepmother or any other female member of his family, I began to worry. It would have been unthinkable for members of the bridegroom's harem not to call on Narguiss if matters were truly under-way!

28 · THE DEAD MAN'S RIGHTS

One morning as I stood on my balcony, hoping that Maher would appear, I saw Bahiga's little servant girl trying to get my attention. She pointed to the garden gate. I understood instantly, and raced down with my heart beat-ing wildly. There was a letter on the ground. I snatched it up and ran with it to my room. I opened it joyfully, only to discover that it contained the worst possible news I could have imagined.

"Your father told Wassef Pasha that he could not accept my suit because he was held by a previous engagement. I am heartbroken. Wassef Pasha kindly offered to intercede on my behalf if I wanted another bride, even the daughter of the prime minister, but I told him that if I could not have you, I would never marry."

I was thunderstruck. What previous engagement was my father bound by? I found it hard to believe what I had just read. For a moment I thought it might be a pretext for discouraging Maher without refusing him outright. But then I remembered the dresses, the preparations, my wedding gown. Wedding plans had been made, but to whom? My eyes filled with tears, and I got angrier and angrier. Did Narguiss and my father think that I would just let myself be sold off like a slave? Or married off without being consulted? I would fight back! I would not give up Maher! I sat down and feverishly wrote Maher a four-page letter in which I assured him of my love and my commitment to him. I pleaded with him to remain steadfast, also, and concluded by saying that I too would never marry anyone else.

When I left my room to deliver the letter, I bumped into Mademoiselle Hortense in the hall. She looked at me strangely, as if the expression on my face had frightened her, as if she had seen a ghost.

"What's the matter, Ramza?" she asked.

I pushed her into my room.

"Who is my father planning to marry me to? Do you know, Mademoiselle?"

Her eyes instantly filled with tears.

"You do know! You know I love Maher, and you know that my father has refused his suit saying that he was bound by a previous engagement. Who can that be?" I asked bitterly.

Mademoiselle would not answer.

I put my hand on her arm and shook her saying, "Who is it? You know! Who am I engaged to?"

She knew she had to tell me. She did so reluctantly, though, in her smallest, saddest whisper.

"I heard that you had to marry Medhat's brother."

If the sky had fallen on me, I would not have been more surprised or outraged.

"Medhat!" I cried.

He belonged to a closed chapter in my life. I saw a dead man rise out of the forgotten past. He was returning to haunt me. I pressed Mademoiselle for more information, but she knew nothing else. I ran to find Narguiss in the kitchen and violently dragged her out of it. She was alarmed at my vehemence. I remember she too looked at me very strangely, but she did not resist.

"What has happened, Ramza?" she asked.

"I want to know who I'm being married to?" I asked Narguiss point-blank.

"Please trust us, Ramza," she answered, "He will be an excellent husband."

"Excellent or not, I want to know who it is."

"I can't tell you," Narguiss answered, "Your father would be angry."

"If you can't tell me then I'll have to ask my father."

"Don't even think of doing that, you miserable girl!" Narguiss cried.

"Then tell me!" I insisted.

Finally, when Narguiss saw it was no use trying to discourage me, she told me a most incredible tale in which I played the leading role. It seems that six months after Medhat's death, Narguiss started to look for a new husband for me.

"How can I explain this to you, Ramza?" she said, "When a girl gets to be a certain age, she must get married. This is how things are."

I did not argue. I wanted to hear the rest.

"When Medhat, God have mercy on him, had been dead half a year, I set out to find you a husband and discovered an obstacle that stood in the way. Medhat's family had not asked for the presents they gave you to be returned."

"And why didn't we send them back?" I asked.

"That's impossible! It's just not done! It would be considered an insult," Narguiss said.

"Well, how can Medhat's presents stop me from getting married?" I asked.

"As long as the family has not retrieved them, the engagement is not broken."

"The engagement with whom?" I cried, "With a corpse?"

"When you become engaged, it's not just to a man!" Narguiss said, "You make a commitment to a whole family."

I could not help laughing when I heard this, despite my anger and despite my anguish.

"You mean to say that if Medhat's presents are still here, his family can decide on my future, on what I can do with my life?" I cried.

"That's right! I tried to extricate us. You have to act delicately in such situations. I did the best I could. I sent Sitt Khadiga, the matchmaker, with the message that we would be much obliged if they would take back their gifts. But they never did."

"Did you have a groom in mind when you did this?" I asked Narguiss.

"Of course," Narguiss answered, "He was rich and came from a very good family! Sitt Khadiga affirmed this herself."

"I see! And how much was he offering to pay for me?" I said, challenging Narguiss. She pretended not to notice my indignation.

"We don't know, because the negotiations never got under way."

"And, just what does that mean?" I asked Narguiss.

"It means that Medhat's family is still eager for a union with us. After I sent word to them, they let us know that they were not prepared to give up their preemptive rights to you!"

I was stunned. Who wanted to take possession of me now? Medhat's father? Narguiss explained, and as she did, I could feel my hands clench into fists as they used to do when I was a little girl listening to my mother's tales of golden slavery.

"Medhat's father sent an intermediary, Mazhar Bey, to offer your father one or the other of his sons, Kamel el Din or Fadel, as your bridegroom."

So Medhat's family had given my father a choice between two brothers! How considerate of them! I decided it
would be wiser to keep my thoughts to myself and pursue
my questioning of Narguiss as calmly as I could.

"So, they gave my father a choice . . . "

"Well," Narguiss went on, "the choice is clear. The
youngest of the brothers, Fadel, is studying law in Paris and
still has three years to go. Kamel is the name of the oldest.
He will finish medical studies in Paris this winter. When he
returns to Egypt, Medhat will have been dead a year. We
can decently celebrate your wedding at that time because the
year of mourning will have lapsed."

"All of these preparations are for this coming winter?" I
asked, puzzled.

"No," Narguiss answered. She had become her talkative
self again.

"Kamel el Din is coming back to Cairo for a visit. We
decided to take advantage of this and celebrate the *Katb el
Kitab*. You know this will be in the month of Ragab,
Ramza. It's said to be particularly propitious for marriages!"
Narguiss concluded.

My aunt had regained all of her good humor. The
worry that I had caused her when I abruptly dragged her
away from the kitchen had vaporized. The way she rambled
on made it clear to me that she would never understand me,
would never learn! No matter how much I argued with her,
no matter how much I explained, I realized that she simply
could not comprehend my indignation at being treated like
merchandise!

I was being disposed of like a piece of furniture. My
marriage to a stranger was being planned and preparations
for a wedding were being made without consulting me. I
had not even been told! I was offered a husband I knew
nothing about, it was assumed that I would love and serve
him willingly and gladly, and I had no say in the matter
whatsoever! Kamel el Din had never seen me, but he was

going to marry me to fulfill a brother's promise. I had never seen him, but I was being given to him because our families wanted to be joined.

"If this brother dies," I thought, "will the youngest one take his place, and then the father?"

I was furious. I felt sick and swore that this marriage would never take place.

"We will have the *Katb el Kitab* without any festivities, of course, because Medhat's mother is still in deep mourning." Narguiss droned on. "In fact, she still doesn't know about these new plans. Once the contract is signed, your bridegroom can visit you. He can come every day if you like, Ramza. Your father has consented to this. You can have tea together. He's very handsome! Everyone says so! You'll be so happy!"

I listened to Narguiss, but it was as if she were speaking to me in a dream. Everything seemed unreal, until I shook myself and looked Narguiss straight in the eye.

"You can be sure, Narguiss, that I will never marry this doctor."

She looked stunned.

"But, your father . . . the word he gave . . . "

"I have reached my majority, Narguiss, and my father is no monster . . . He will not force me. I don't want this marriage at any price. I'll speak to him."

"Don't do that, Ramza! Let me handle this . . . In any case your father is not home now."

I was not sure whether or not Narguiss was lying and went to find out for myself. My father was gone. At the door, I remembered the letter I had written to Maher. I could feel its thickness pressing against my ribs where I had hidden it inside my blouse.

I decided to deliver the letter to Bahiga myself. I was forbidden from going to her house, but I resolved then and there to stop at nothing. She was, after all, Maher's sister and my oldest friend. I felt I could confide in her. I ran down to the garden gate and, moments later, I burst into Bahiga's room.

Bahiga froze when she saw me but then sprang up and threw her arms around my neck.

"Oh, Ramza," she cried, "I thought you were angry with me, when you stopped coming! I went to your house, but I was not allowed to see you! What has happened? What have I done?"

"Your brother said nothing to you, then?" I asked Bahiga.

She was stupefied.

"My brother? But I haven't seen him in eight days!"

"Are you sure he wasn't here this morning, or yesterday evening?" I asked. I wondered how the servant girl had gotten the note I had received. Maher must still be in Alexandria.

"I haven't set eyes on him since he left for the barracks," Bahiga assured me, "But he sends a soldier every day to pick up his mail."

"Well then," I said, pulling out the letter, "Here is a letter for Maher. Tell the soldier to deliver it to him personally and as quickly as possible."

Bahiga was speechless. She just looked at me in utter disbelief.

"Yes," I said, "Maher and I are in love. We're determined to get married."

I saw Bahiga's face change. She did not know whether to rejoice or cry. As we looked tearfully at each other, I heard Mademoiselle Hortense's familiar footstep in the hallway.

"Quick, hide this letter. Please make sure it gets to Maher," I said to Bahiga, "I'll explain everything later."

Mademoiselle had followed me to Bahiga's. Knowing I was not supposed to be there at all, she decided it would be better for me not to be there alone at least. She looked deeply worried and wanted to help. She did not understand what was happening and was pained. She wanted to help and did not know what to do except to put herself at my disposal. I took her hands in mine and kissed her.

"You were right. It is to one of Medhat's brothers that they want to marry me. The wretches think they own me! They made the first payment on an installment plan, and now they want the goods to be delivered. What does a Frenchwoman like you think about all of this?"

Mademoiselle was silent, but tears ran down her face. When Bahiga heard what I said and saw Mademoiselle crying, she was totally confused and with good reason, of course.

She said, "But, Ramza . . . then it's not Maher you're going to marry?"

"Maher asked my father for my hand," I explained, "but my father refused, saying that I was already spoken for. Medhat's family still has rights over me. But I'm not going to submit! Maher and I love each other. I have no intention of sacrificing our love to some senseless custom!"

As I said this, Bahiga's face changed again. This time she looked horror-stricken.

"Don't look at me like that, Bahiga," I cried impatiently, "Don't you realize that I persuaded my father to rent this house to be able to see Maher? We have been meeting ever since I got to Alexandria!"

"Oh, Ramza," she cried, "How could you have done such a thing! What if your father had discovered you!"

"I have no regrets," I said firmly. "I will marry Maher! I swear it!"

"But, what if your father continues to refuse . . . " Bahiga whispered.

"I'm going to do my best to persuade him, but if I fail, then I know exactly what I have to do!"

Mademoiselle stared at me, bewildered. Bahiga blanched.

"Oh, Lord! How could I have been so blind! Why didn't you say something to me, Ramza? I'm sure to lose you now! They will never allow me to see you! And Maher?

God knows what he will do! I will lose him too . . . " she lamented.

"Instead of moaning and crying," I said firmly, "try to think of how you can help us! Will you ask your husband to intervene on our behalf? I know my father respects him."

"The respect is mutual," Bahiga said. "My husband tells me that the pasha often visits him in his office downtown."

"Will you have the courage to speak to your husband, Bahiga?" I said cutting to the chase.

"Are you sure you won't be afraid of displeasing him?" I said.

"Oh, I'll speak with him," Bahiga said confidently, "Abd el Salem is always on the side of lovers!"

I was amazed to hear Bahiga say this. Seeing my surprise, she explained.

"As a young man my husband fell in love with one of his cousins. She was in love with him, too. They wanted to get married, but the families refused and she killed herself. On the eve of her wedding to someone else, she dropped dead. She had poisoned herself. Abd el Salem himself told me this story. I've often heard him say that people should never be married off against their will!"

"Well, then," I said. "Ask him to plead my cause or I'll follow his cousin's example!"

"Oh, Ramza! You can't be serious!" Bahiga cried, her eyes brimming over with tears.

I shrugged my shoulders and said, "Of course I'd rather get married than kill myself, but I will have Maher or no one!"

This declaration brought fresh tears to Bahiga's eyes as well as Mademoiselle's. And, in the end, it was I who had to console them both. In doing that, though, I regained my confidence. I was optimistic at that moment that everything would turn out for the best and started coaching Bahiga on what to say to her husband. We agreed to stay in touch through Mademoiselle and Isabelle because I knew that I would be kept under strict supervision.

Unfortunately, Abd el Salem's interview with my father was a failure. My father—I learned this from Mademoiselle who had heard it from Isabelle who had spoken to Bahiga—had categorically refused to reconsider. He gave strict orders forbidding me to see Bahiga or any other member of Maher's family as well as my French friends.

Abd el Salem sent word that he had done his utmost. My father had resented the intrusion into his affairs. He would under no circumstance allow me to marry Maher. Abd el Salem's "brotherly" advice to me was: "Submit."

"I will not give up!" I told Mademoiselle. "I will plead my own cause." I decided to write a letter to my father, then speak to him. Although I have no copy of that letter and never found one among my father's papers, I remember my arguments well. I spent all night writing draft after draft, trying my utmost to find words that could express my feelings and, at the same time, not alienate or hurt my father. I scratched out sentences, rewrote them, tore up one letter after another. Finally, I had a bright idea. I would begin my letter with something he himself had said to me: "My daughter, remember that involuntary obedience is slavery. It can only lead to self-abasement!" I continued by invoking the tender affection he had always manifested toward me, by reminding him of the education he had lavished on me, and the satisfaction he had expressed in seeing me develop. I concluded by saying that it was he who had first encouraged my assertive personality. I also added that there was no way I could marry Kamel el Din, even though I had full confidence in my father's judgment of what was good for me and wanted very much to please him.

"Medhat would always be a ghostly presence between us . . . " I remember writing.

Of course, I said nothing about my meetings with Maher but confessed that we had seen each other, that I had inquired into his character and believed him to be honest and upright, and that his family was like a second family to me because of my affection for his sister, Bahiga. I wrote that I did not feel I was acting impulsively, that I was motivated by love. I reminded my father of his own love for my mother, and how it had been reciprocated. I begged him not to deprive me of a similar joy with a man I loved in order to hand me over to one about whom I could only think of with revulsion.

I showed the letter to Mademoiselle the next day. She said, "I can't imagine your father not being touched by this letter."

I agreed and was sure I would completely win him over to my point of view. I was feeling confident when I went to his study and left my letter on his desk. That evening even Narguiss let me explain my wishes to her without flinching. She said she would do her best to help me, and we hugged each other and made up our differences.

My father came home late that night. I did not undress, waiting for him to send for me, but he did not. Nothing happened and, finally, I undressed and went to bed but could not sleep. I went over and over again in my mind what I would say to my father the next day. I had an answer to every one of his questions. I knew just how to respond to every objection he might raise. As I saw it, I would win hands down, and my father would call Maher, embrace him like a son, and give us his blessings. He would marry us without delay, right there and then . . .

How easily I conjured up our happiness!

29 · ELOPEMENT

The next morning my father was already in his little sitting room next to the library when I cracked open the door with a trembling hand. I was much less confident than I had been the night before. My father was standing, as if he were waiting for me. I knew instantly that he had read my letter and that his reaction was negative. I knew my father well. I could tell by the expression on his face that nothing would go as I had planned. I had let my imagination run away with me! I gritted my teeth and got ready for a confrontation.

It was brief.

Before I had time to say a word, my father spoke.

"Ramza," he said sternly, "I don't want to hear another word about this brother of Bahiga's! It's a shame that he has been able to see you, to speak with you, and to sweet-talk you the way he has."

"Father," I cried, "he did nothing of the sort! I had a chance to observe him, and I have chosen him. I would like your permission to marry him!"

My father's answer was sharp.

"I have an only daughter. I will not surrender her to the son of a shopkeeper, to a boy without education, an insignificant officer without a future! Miserable girl, do you want to spend the rest of your life following him from one Sudanese garrison town to another? Is that your ambition?"

"My ambition, father," I answered, "is to marry a man I have freely chosen, a man I appreciate and love. I refuse to become a member of Safwat Pasha's harem! How can I willingly join a family where I am handed down from one brother to the next like some inherited chattel!"

Instantly, my father's face softened, and his eyes filled with tender concern. He smiled with that special affection he reserved only for me, and I'm sure now that he thought I objected to the way the negotiations with the Safwat family had been carried out. In fact it probably did not occur to him that I actually wanted Maher. Rather, he must have been convinced that I was determined to avoid marrying Kamel el Din because he was Medhat's brother.

I felt my anger melt, too. I loved my father and did not want to hurt him.

"I've spoiled you, Ramza!" he said. "I let you learn to think for yourself and so I feel responsible for what you've become. I really do owe you some explanation. I want you to understand what I've done on your behalf, and why I've done it even though it is not customary for a father to discuss these topics with his daughter. Remember, Ramza, that we belong to the Orient. Getting married in our world is not just forming a couple with a handsome boy. You become a member of a family. Your place in Egyptian society, the consideration with which you are treated, the impact you have, depends largely on the status of the family you marry into.

"If I have accepted Safwat Pasha's request, Ramza, it's because his family is one of Egypt's top families, honorable in every way imaginable. Plus, I was certain that you would not have to make any sacrifices as a result of a union with them. You are not going to marry an old man, or an imbecile, a cripple, or an old fashioned traditionalist! I know your tastes, your way of thinking . . . I tried to choose someone who could make you happy! Believe me, Ramza! Kamel el Din, like the late Medhat, has studied in Europe. He is modern in his thinking, and he seems to be headed for a brilliant future in which you could play a part. Also, he's young. There is nothing about him that could displease you! I can't think of a better partner for you!"

My father paused, then added, "You see, I'm discussing with you just like a French or English father would with his daughter. I want to give you the full picture. In all fairness I should also tell you that even if I wanted to refuse Safwat Pasha's offer, I couldn't at this point. The gifts which were sent are a symbol of the pact made between our families. They bind me. They bind us, you and me, to Safwat Pasha. The family has refused to have those gifts returned to them, and I have no good reason not to honor our committment to his family."

"Father," I answered, "I understand your reasoning, but

I love Maher. I cannot love anyone else. If you have given your word, so have I. I swore to Maher that I would marry no one else."

I no sooner said this than I saw my father's face turn crimson. He was furious. He glowered at me with eyes like live coals. I thought he would strike or strangle me, but he did not. He grabbed my arm and shook me furiously instead.

"Enough! Enough! Go to your room and stay there! Tomorrow I'm taking you back to Cairo! You will never, do you hear me, never marry that miserable rogue!" he shouted, and stormed out, slamming the door behind him.

I ran to my room and collapsed on my bed, sobbing, but soon stopped. I realized that I was all alone and that instead of crying, I should be deciding what to do. My father had gone out, Mademoiselle was at church for early morning mass, and Narguiss never left her room at that hour. I decided I would run away.

I dressed, covered myself from head to toe in a black *melaaya*, and put a black *boro* over my face. This veil was so opaque that it completely masked my features. There was no way anyone could recognize me. Nothing, as you know, can make a person look so anonymous as the costume worn by Muslim women!

In my handbag I stuffed my most precious jewelry and all my money. I had quite a bit because my father never failed to give me some every day. Near the kitchen, I grabbed a basket, put it on my head as I had seen the servants do when they went shopping, and left quietly by the service entrance without anyone being the wiser.

My goal was to find Maher and to elope. But how would I find him? I was careful not to go to Bahiga's house and headed toward the streetcar station in our neighborhood in Bacos. I knew there was a carriage stand there where I could hire a closed coupe, typically used by women at that time. I climbed into one and directed the coachman to the quarter of Mustafa Pasha, where I knew Maher was garrisoned.

Just as we left, I saw Mademoiselle coming out of church and starting toward home on the sidewalk closest to me. I stopped the carriage just long enough to open the door and pull her in. She was stunned. She did not know what I was doing, and I decided not to put her on the spot by telling her. I remember, though, that as soon as I had her next to me I felt less anxious and more confident.

As we approached the barracks, I saw a young officer on the street. I took my courage in my hands and stopped to ask him if he knew Maher. As it turned out they were friends and he offered to look for him. He warned me that it could take awhile, and I said I would wait.

Fifteen minutes later, Maher appeared. He was surprised to see me. But, when I told him I had run away from my father's house and that I was determined to get married, he was flabbergasted. I saw him hesitate and I thought he was getting ready to refuse but then, seeing my resolve, he agreed.

Mademoiselle did not understand what was going on because Maher and I had spoken quickly in Arabic, but she did not ask any questions. Dear Mademoiselle Hortense! Maher left us waiting to go and arrange for leave, and when he came out, he was dressed in civilian clothes. He climbed into a hackney and told our coachman to follow. And before the end of the day, Maher and I were married.

When we arrived at the office of the *mazoon*, who was a scrawny, grizzled sheikh, I was afraid of complications. The *mazoon* knew right away, of course, that we were eloping because we had come to him rather than having him called to the house, and that we had no family with us. Maher went in to see him while Mademoiselle and I were ushered into an adjoining room. He came out to tell us that the *mazoon* had been reluctant at first but had changed his mind when Maher put a tempting sum of money on the corner of his desk.

"I see that nothing can stand in the way of that which is destined, my son! You are complying with the Prophet's commandment to marry, multiply, and increase the numbers of the faithful on this earth. God Bless You! God Bless You!" he had said.

Maher then reported that for an additional sum, the *mazoon* would find two witnesses and an agent, a *wakil,* to represent me and certify that I was of age. The witnesses testified that they knew me well and that I was, indeed, of age and free. The *wakil* stood beside Maher as my representative, instead of my father, with his hand in Maher's under the ritual handkerchief. The *mazoon* read the opening verses of the Qur'an, the Fatha, then the habitual sacred texts for marriage ceremonies, while Mademoiselle and I waited in the next room. The witnesses only came to ask if I agreed to take this man as my husband. My role in all of this consisted of nothing more than saying "Yes." The *wakil* then went back to the *mazoon*'s office with my affirmative answer. I could hear him saying, "According to the authority invested in me by Ramza Farid, I now entrust her to you as your legally wedded wife."

The next step was going to the courthouse. We had to register the marriage and, luckily, found a judge in his chambers. He was old and stern. He too guessed that we had eloped and did not approve. He warned us that marriages contracted in this way were subject to annulment and made my heart skip a beat.

"My father would not want to provoke a scandal," I reassured myself. "Now that I'm married, he will have to accept Maher."

We agreed to leave for Cairo immediately. Only then did I tell Mademoiselle who, of course, had already guessed. I'm sure she had not spoken up because, on the one hand, she did not want to thwart my plans and, on the other hand, she was fearful of being considered an accomplice. She kissed me and wished me much happiness, and came with me to the train station. I told her confidently that I would send for her as soon as I was settled, and kissed her good-bye. She smiled, but said nothing. I watched her standing motionless on the platform as the train began to move. We had not been apart a single night since Mabrouk Agha had escorted her from Alexandria to our house on the Khalig. I had no regrets, though. I believed I had acted deliberately, and I was ready to take the consequences of my actions.

Only one thing mattered now, and that was making a life with Maher. I was willing to give up everything for him, my family and the comfortable life I had led. I was ready to follow Maher anywhere. I would not have turned back then, even though I knew I might never see my father or Narguiss again, and was not even sure I could keep the promise I had so impetuously made to Mademoiselle on the platform.

In the train, I could not travel with Maher. At that time the cars were segregated, and women could only ride in the compartments reserved for the harem. We met in the hallway, however, and discussed what to do once we reached Cairo. We decided to go straight to Maher's father's house.

Although we were not expecting congratulations, Maher's father reacted with a violence that went beyond our worst fears. He spared neither of us, and accused Maher of dishonoring him. He ordered me to dispatch a telegram to my father asking him to come and get me.

"Maher will divorce you quietly, and our family will try to contain the scandal," his father said.

I looked to Maher for support, but he did not open his mouth. I waited to hear him say he would not divorce me, but he stood before his father like a little boy, his eyes glued to the ground. I was shocked. He seemed all at once to have crumbled, becoming a shadow of the man I loved. I held back tears of frustration, and refused either to send word to my father or to go back home. Somehow, Maher's weakness reinforced my determination. I would not be subdued.

I would fight for the life I had chosen to live with the man I loved. But, of course, I also felt betrayed by Maher and feared for our future happiness.

30 · SHEIKH ABD EL MOUTEI

Finally when Maher's father saw that I was not going to give up, he said we could stay, but not together.

"We're married," I cried.

He shot me a searing look and spat out, "Such a marriage is worthless in my eyes!"

I turned to Maher and asked anxiously, "Do you agree to this?"

Maher was very pale, and was only able to whisper lamely, "It might be best for the time being."

My father-in-law asked me if there was anyone that I could stay with. At that point there was nothing I could do but agree to go. I had to think of what to do next. I mentioned a few names. Maher's father chose to take me to Sheikh Abd el Moutei because he was an old friend of my family's and also because he knew him. When it was time to get in the carriages, I realized that Maher was not coming, and I refused to go.

"If you want me to follow you," I said to his father, "my husband will have to be with me."

Finally, the three of us proceeded to Sheikh Abd el Moutei's house in Darb el Gamamiz, not far at all from our old house on the Khalig. In some ways, it was like coming home. I had been very fond of the old sheikh when I was a child, and he of me. He was a colossus of a man, always in a good mood, full of humor and kindliness. I had remembered him as having fairly liberal views, and I was prepared to do all I could to win him over to my cause.

Maher's father made this difficult for me from the start, however. Without so much as an introduction, he spat out his venom as soon as we arrived.

"I'm here to place someone in your care, a wretched girl who has married against her father's will!"

Sheikh Abd el Moutei looked surprised by Maher's father's intemperate outburst, followed by mine.

"I'm of age! I have the right to marry whomever I please!"

Without answering, Sheikh Abd el Moutei shook his head disapprovingly. But Maher's father was beside himself, and retorted.

"I too have a daughter. If she had been in your place, I would have strangled her!"

I quickly realized it was useless to discuss anything with this angry man and asked to speak to Maher privately. This further enraged my father-in-law who forbade Maher to exchange a single word with me. Sheikh Abd el Moutei, who had remained calm throughout the exchange, took charge. He took Maher's father aside, and discreetly ushered Maher and me into his office. Out of some sense of modesty, I left the door slightly ajar.

"Maher," I began, "We are married! I'm determined to protect the happiness we want together! I don't want to go back to my father now! If he pushes for divorce, I'll fight it to the bitter end! I urge you, don't betray me! Don't weaken! Don't abandon me!"

Maher assured me that he was as determined as I was to fight for our happiness.

"Well then," I said, "Why do we have to be separated? Let's get out of here. Let's find a place to live and be together before God and man!"

But Maher refused. He insisted on trying once more to win over both our fathers and receive their blessings. He tried to persuade me that we would never be happy any other way.

"Happy are those who go forth having been blessed by

both parents," he said, quoting a proverb to stress the point. Maher could argue persuasively and did so on that day. There was nothing more to do but to let him go. As I watched him leave, though, my eyes were suddenly blinded with tears, and I felt utterly bereft. I feared the loneliness of my struggle, faced with a hostile world, cursed by the father I loved, maybe even abandoned by the husband I had left everything to win.

Sheikh Abd el Moutei looked at me, stroked his beard, and shook his head.

"You've taken a bad turn, Ramza," he said quietly. His words reawakened my combative spirit.

"There are people a thousand times guiltier than me!" I cried, "All I've done is legitimately marry a man I know and love, a man I wish to spend the rest of my life with! Is that a crime?"

Sheikh Abd el Moutei continued to look at me and shake his head.

Emboldened, I thrust forward my argument, "It seems more criminal to me, Sheikh Abd el Moutei, to have that old man, Medhat's father, who has never seen me, do his utmost to acquire me for his household, like a chattel that has to be delivered! And his son! He would have me without knowing me, just because I was his dead brother's fiancée! And what do you think of my father who insists on this marriage? Who discounts my feelings? Who will not consider my objections to a marriage that is repugnant to me?"

"Our customs contain more wisdom than you think, Ramza," he answered. "Young people are dazzled by passion. They are easily misled. That's why parents stand a better chance of choosing a suitable mate for their children, than the children themselves."

"Parents are full of prejudices! They're blinded by their desire to join together property or sacks of money! The happiness of young people doesn't mean a thing to them!" I cried.

"Happiness often depends on knowing how to judiciously combine all of the interests that you so despise, Ramza. Lovers rarely make good marriage partners . . . To be honest with you, I know you will never be happy with this young man. You're expecting a lot of him because you love him, but he won't be able to give you much."

"You don't know him!" I cried, feeling stung.

"That's true, that's true. I saw him for the first time just a little while ago; but I know men, and I have some experience of human nature, Ramza. He would have to be far superior to others of his kind—kinder and more intelligent in every way—in order not to blame you one day for ruining his life!"

"Ruining his life? . . . But I'm going to make him happy!"

"You will love him . . . at least for a while. Making him happy is another matter!"

"I can't imagine happiness without love! I can't even conceive of life without this man!"

"What do you want me to do, Ramza?" Sheikh Abd el Moutei said finally. "Do you want me to tell you that I approve of what you've done? I cannot. Do you want me to help you? All I can do is speak to your father. But, in the meantime," he said almost jovially, "Go look for Khadiga and Soheir. You'll find them in the harem. You know the way! You can stay here as long as you wish."

31 · COURT CASE

My father arrived in Cairo the day after my elopement. Mademoiselle and Narguiss told me later that they had been terrified to tell him of what I had done. They had put off breaking the news to him until late that night, and said that his fury could not be contained. He reproached them scathingly for their lack of vigilance.

"I will have the last word in this affair," he cried, "Or I will kill her myself!"

The first thing he did when he got back to Cairo was to try to invalidate my marriage by filing an annulment suit against Maher and me. Although Sheikh Abd el Moutei might have persuaded him not to do this, he was too late in speaking with my father. The affair had already reached the courts. Sheikh Abd el Moutei, however, told me that my father no longer spoke of killing me, and that he had made this threat in the heat of passion.

"You must know that if your father had acted on it, Ramza, he would not have been blamed, and he would probably not have been found guilty by the courts because he was safeguarding his honor and tradition," Sheikh Abd el Moutei added, softening his revelation by telling me that my father wanted me to come home.

"Your father said you could come home, Ramza, but that you must stay out of his way."

I could just hear my father saying, "I never want to set eyes on her again!" And, I was just stubborn enough to consider going home and confronting him, but decided it was wiser to lie low just then. Although I had little freedom of movement in Sheikh Abd el Moutei's harem, I felt an exhilarating sense of independence at being away from home. I was not ready to give that up.

Luckily, Mademoiselle Hortense came to stay with me at Sheikh Abd el Moutei's soon after I went there. She had asked my father's permission to let her come, arguing that it was not right for me to be left alone, without a single member of my family to keep me company. I saw her come with an incredible sense of relief, and her company was precious to me during the trying weeks that followed.

The struggle between me and my father was terrible. We were made of the same stuff, both stubborn and authoritarian. I loved him, and I remain certain, to this day, that his affection for me was just the same as before when he was not blinded by his fury and egged on by public opinion. He had a lawyer, and I too hired a lawyer, who was recommended to me by the devoted Sheikh Abd el Moutei. Although this young man was dressed in clerical garb, that is he wore a *kaftan,* overcoat, and turban, he had liberal views. He was ready to plead my case with conviction. His name was Sheikh Mustafa el Maghrabi.

I saw very little of Maher during that time and began to fear that his father's influence would prevail. I worried that he would submit and divorce me; and I knew that if he did, I would die of shame. And so I decided to enlist Sheikh Mustafa's support, who promptly took it upon himself to broach the subject with Maher. They conversed at length, and Sheikh Mustafa advised Maher, encouraged him, and stiffened his back bone, at least for a while. He reminded him that we had a goal, a higher ideal, and that we not only wanted to validate our marriage but to set a national precedent!

My marriage soon became a hot topic of conversation throughout Cairo. As the date of the hearing approached, I felt the excitement of the fight mounting in me. And, to be quite honest, I nearly forgot about Maher. I managed to get hold of a number of law books, which I studied avidly. I discussed the issues in detail with Sheikh Mustafa, and even communicated my zeal to him. He warned me that the judge presiding was anything but sympathetic to me, though, and that we would not win hands down.

"He has daughters," Sheikh Mustafa said, "you can count on his being afraid of the precedent you are setting."

I knew that parents and judges were among my fiercest adversaries. But I was equally aware that I had struck a chord to which some of my sisters in the harem were ready to respond. I began to receive anonymous letters from them. They congratulated me and encouraged me. They wrote about their lives, about feeling trapped inside a "golden cage," about themselves as "prisoners of tradition," or "victims of custom," and urged me not to give up the fight.

Meanwhile, I spent hours pouring over the intricacies of the *sharia*, the canon. With Sheikh Mustafa's help, I read and studied the passages covering personal status laws and those relevant to women. Sheikh Mustafa could find nothing in how Maher and I had proceeded that could give reason for annulment. He pointed out that we had a perfectly valid marriage contract, that I was not a minor, that we were of sound mind, and that Maher had paid an appropriate dowry. For someone of my class, at that time, it was no less than 500 Egyptian pounds up front, with an equal amount set aside for me in case of divorce. We had followed the laws, he told me, even though we had violated the customs.

When I saw Maher, which was far too infrequently for comfort, we made plans for the future. Both Sheikh Mustafa and I felt that we could not lose. We had prepared ourselves carefully. We had looked at every facet of the issues surrounding the case, and were persuaded they were sound. So Maher and I planned. We tallied up our assets and found that I had two hundred pounds over and above the five hundred pounds he had given me as a dowry, and my mother's jewelry, which was extremely valuable. On his end, Maher owned one hundred acres of some of the best cultivable land in the Delta and a house in Shoubra. He received a yearly income from renting the house to people in town and the land to tenant farmers. He also had a seasonal share of the sale of the crops and his military stipend. We decided we had quite enough to live on, and based on that, I persuaded Maher to ask for a transfer to the Sudan. We could remove ourselves from Egypt for a few years until passions and rumors had died down. I was so eager for that day!

Despite all of these preparations, I felt extremely nervous on the day our case was tried. I could not attend, of course, since women were not allowed in court. I waited anxiously at home, and made Sheikh Mustafa promise that he would come right over with the verdict. I posted myself by a window, and when I saw two figures approach who looked like Maher and my lawyer, I ran down to meet them. The news was not good. I could tell at once, before they spoke, from the expressions on their faces even at some distance, that we had lost.

Sheikh Mustafa was beside himself.

"The judge never even listened to my plea! His decision was already made! That judgment was iniquitous! If they think we are going to give up so easily, they're wrong! I'll appeal this decision tomorrow morning!"

Maher was very pale. He had been deeply humiliated by my father's lawyer, who had dragged him and his ancestors through the mud. When he spoke, his voice was tight with anger.

"He called us earthworms! He smeared my father and called me a mean soldier who got into military school only because it was letting in riffraff for lack of anyone better . . . "

It would seem that my father's attorney had said that Maher's ancestors were nothing but peasants who had accumulated wealth through hoarding and avarice, whereas our family traced its lineage back to the Prophet himself. This, it would seem, made us incompatible under Muslim law. My father even produced a *firman* from Sultan Abd el Hamid confirming his status as a *sherif*, a descendant of the Prophet's grandson, Imam el Hussein. This *firman* reinforced the argument in favor of annulment. Even though Sheikh Mustafa assured me of the obvious, saying that the issue of class was nothing but a ploy to discourage young men and women from following our example, I was heartbroken. And even though he pressed Maher not to take the attorney's slurs to heart because they were nothing more than legal acrobatics, Maher was stung to the core. I suffered also on his behalf and would have done anything to wipe the insults from his memory. I would have washed them with my blood if I could have. But they had been branded on his heart, and he was inconsolable.

My greatest fear at that moment was that Maher would somehow hold me responsible for his humiliation. Something told me that what he had heard in court that day would create a chasm between us that could not be bridged.

When the press announced the verdict of annulment, my case became the subject of heated debate between supporters of traditional values and liberals who favored modernizing. The polemics even reached Turkey, where they revived an old conflict between the liberal party of the Young Turks and Sultan Abdul Hamid with his traditionalist policies.

Daily, impassioned articles made front-page news. I was attacked venomously by conservatives and praised with an equal lack of restraint by my defenders. Sometimes, I couldn't help being flattered by the attention; but mostly I feared that the publicity would compromise my happiness with Maher, as well as my chance for reconciliation with my father.

When I shared my apprehension with Sheikh Mustafa, I found out that he was optimistic. He had appealed the decision and was sure that no judge would uphold the verdict in the face of the strong public opinion in our favor. One day he came over to Sheikh Abd el Moutei's house, his eyes glowing with pleasure. As soon as he saw me, he cried, "The khedive is on our side! He has given you his support and vows to do everything in his power to ensure that love triumphs!" I was skeptical about the khedive's power and was surprised by his lack of consideration for my father, whom I knew he respected. But then, I reasoned, the khedive was only thirty; he was young and would naturally be on the side of youth.

As it turned out, however, Khedive Abbas' motives were political. The British Consul General, Lord Cromer, had intervened on behalf of my father in the case, and this was enough reason for Khedive Abbas to side with us. He despised Cromer, as did the nationalist press. They took up my banner also, and equated my personal struggle with Egypt's struggle to free herself of the yoke of colonialism. In fact, at that time, the papers were full of sensational headlines. There are two I remember well: "From the bellies of slaves, only slaves can be born," and "Liberate our mothers and our daughters, and liberate our wives that they may give birth to free men." There was so much talk of freedom! Somehow, my case was kneaded in with the larger issues, my tentative feminist ideals amplified and embellished. I went from being an ordinary young woman confronting her father over marrying the man she loved to a symbol of independence for a nation and something of a heroine.

I must confess that a part of me liked being considered a heroine, but the more public support I had, the more inflexible my father became. I heard that he had angrily announced that he would marry me off to the superintendent of his estate. I knew Selim Effendi! He was a wiry old weasel, at least sixty years old! Although I did not take my father's threat altogether seriously, it stiffened my determination to go on fighting for my freedom.

It seemed to me that the harder I struggled on behalf of our happiness, the quicker Maher lost his resolve. I grew increasingly exasperated with his weakness, his reticence, and his fearful attitude. He hardly dared to visit me anymore. And when he came, he kept a safe distance between us, even if we were alone in Sheikh Abd el Moutei's parlor.

One day, when he came to visit me, I could no longer contain myself. I asked him point blank if he still loved me. He assured me that he loved me more than ever, that I should not doubt him, that I needed to be more patient.

"You know," I continued, "I sometimes wonder if we're married! Did I really sign that contract in Alexandria, or was I dreaming?"

"What can I do?" he murmured, "My father is furious every time I come to see you . . . "

I exploded.

"Do you mean to tell me that you're still hanging on your father's coattails! I wrenched myself free from my father! Do you think it was easier for me than for you! Here we are, struggling for the emancipation of women . . . Do the women have to do the job for men as well?"

Maher went deathly pale. I had wanted to shock him. I realized I had gone too far.

"Please try to understand me, Maher," I said more gently, "I love you! Nothing will keep me from truly becoming your wife! If you are afraid of living with me in Cairo, ask for a transfer. I'll go with you to the Sudan, or to the ends of the earth!"

His face relaxed. He asked me again to be patient.

"I'm counting on the success of our appeal, Ramza. Once we win our case, my father will have to accept our marriage . . . "

"Accept?" I cried, trying to contain my anger, "Don't you realize that half the judges are in my father's pocket, that the British support him, that they're masters here? What do you think our chances are?"

I was feeling particularly despondent that afternoon. I thought our chances of winning were poor, and I wanted to do something drastic. I tried to reason with Maher, to persuade him to act with me.

I said, "We can't rely entirely on the courts, you know. What will you do if our appeal fails? If our marriage is annulled? The only recourse we have is to live together now as husband and wife, to have a child, to show that we're proud of ourselves!"

"I urge you to look for an apartment! We must live together as man and wife! It's the only way we can validate our marriage."

To my surprise, Maher agreed. Days passed, a week went by, I waited; but there was no sign of Maher.

Meanwhile, I felt increasingly hemmed in at Sheikh Abd el Moutei's. The harem was hospitable, Soheir and Khadiga were kind, but they were illiterate and interested in nothing but their housekeeping. In spite of Mademoiselle's presence with me, I found the company of the sheikh's wife and daughter wearisome. They did not understand me or the issues I was grappling with. When they gave me advice, as they did from time to time, they found nothing better to tell me than to turn back.

"Give up, Ramza. Leave this Maher and go back to the safety of your father's house!"

Sheikh Abd el Moutei became more and more uncomfortable the more publicity my case got in the newspapers. In fact, he was outraged, saying to me that the matter had gone altogether too far and that my attitude toward my father was not acceptable. Every time he picked up a paper and read a headline, he reproached me, until one day I answered back.

"Have you forgotten that you are under my roof, Ramza?" he said indignantly.

"Not for long!" I snapped back, unable to contain myself.

As you can imagine, I was extremely upset and agitated. The sheikh's home, which had been a safe and hospitable haven, suddenly felt like a prison. His harem was like all the others, a place where women were shut up, cloistered. I could not stand to be there a moment longer, and I castigated myself for the weeks that I had remained.

"What a fool you've been! Here you are, championing freedom for women and living shut up in a harem like all the others! What a contradiction! How absurd!"

Without any hesitation, I gathered up my things and, with Mademoiselle in tow, I left.

32 · BREAKING FREE

When we left Sheikh Abd el Moutei's house, I was furious. I launched on a tirade against repressive customs. Mademoiselle climbed into the carriage I hired, and I piled in behind her. She listened patiently as usual, but did not answer. I did not want to see the sadness in her eyes. She had gone with me without complaining, but I knew these last few weeks had been hard for her. I am certain she would have followed me to hell, but of course I was only taking her to another part of the city.

My grandmother's old *khalfa,* Tahasin Hanem, lived in Abasiyya. Gaulizar had generously endowed her when she became too old to work, and Tahasin had purchased a house for herself in this new neighborhood and had helped her married daughter buy one there also. When Mademoiselle and I arrived, the shutters were closed on all the windows. We called, and a watchman came out. He told us that the old *khalfa* was too sick to live alone and had moved in with her daughter. He pointed out the house, and we found them. Tahasin Hanem was very pleased to see me, and agreed to rent me her house. She also lent me her servant girl, whom I dispatched straight away to Narguiss to let her know my whereabouts.

Mademoiselle and I moved in immediately, opened the windows, and began to arrange the house to our liking with the help of Tahasin's servant. In the afternoon, Narguiss sent me the daughter of one of my old nannies. Zoheida had married and stayed in the family and now came to help. Along with her husband, she moved into a room at the side of the house. They had arrived with a box from Narguiss which contained two hundred Egyptian pounds in gold coins for me. Dear, kind Narguiss! I had spent all my money on lawyer's and court fees and was beginning to sell

my mother's jewelry to survive. I can still remember the
sudden urge that came over me at that moment to see my
aunt, to hug and kiss her! I imagined the meeting, the quarrel, the reproaches, and the reconciliation!

Four days after I moved into Tahasin Hanem's house,
Maher stormed in looking utterly miffed.

"I have searched high and low for you! I was frantic!
How could you have left without consulting me? You could
have written me a word, told me where to find you! Even
Sheikh Abd el Moutei had no idea where you went!" Maher
cried furiously.

I listened. I stayed cool and did not even bother to look
at him. I was sewing when he came in and continued. This
exasperated him, and I was quite pleased to see that he still
cared enough about me to worry.

"Capriciousness, your name is Ramza!" he cried. "One
never knows what you'll do next! You act on your own as
if I didn't even exist!"

"I see so little of you that I have no choice but to act on
my own."

Maher blushed and changed the subject.

"Surely you don't plan to live in this out-of-the-way
place all by yourself?" he ventured.

"I have a couple of servants living with me for want of a
husband!" I said, watching for his reaction.

He started. I knew he was stung when he turned his
eyes from me and pretended to be interested in how my
little house was furnished. It was, in fact, very cozy. I had
taken some trouble to move things around and cheer it up
with linens and rugs that Narguiss had sent and flowers that
Mademoiselle had picked in the overgrown garden.

He complimented me.

"I was taught to keep house and cook, you know," I
said, sarcastically.

"Would you invite me to stay for dinner then?" he bantered.

"No," I answered dryly, "I have to safeguard my reputation. Besides, I don't think you should stay any longer. It would be compromising."

I got up and made a move to retire. He put out his hand to stop me.

"You're being cruel, Ramza!" he cried, "What have I done to deserve this?"

"Nothing. Nothing at all," I answered irritated. "You have been moderate to a fault! Go on being careful and return to your father's house before he discovers you've come to see me and takes his bedroom slipper to you!"

This was the ultimate insult. Maher blanched. I saw his hands tighten into fists. How well I knew this reaction, which was so much like my own when I was angry!

"Don't provoke me, Ramza, or I'll be the one to strike you!"

His voice was hoarse. He came toward me menacingly.

"What gives you the right to speak to me this way?" I answered back, "Certainly not your place as my husband!"

We were standing face to face, our eyes drilling holes into each other. He was so close I could feel his breath, tight and rapid. Without warning he grabbed me and lifted me off the ground. I struggled, but not too much. This, after all, was the moment I had longed for and waited for! Dear Maher!

Two weeks of bliss followed, at once a fleeting moment and an eternity, and I lived them for Maher and Maher alone. I calculated the hours and minutes he was absent. I used a battery of wiles to prolong his visits and contrived dozens of ways to stretch our meals together. When I saw him glance at his watch, I thought of a stream of things I had to tell him. I sent the servants out on errands, knowing Maher could not leave before they returned, and when words failed, I turned to music. I had brought my mother's old oud with me. I strummed it and sang him his favorite songs.

I snatched snippets of time where I could find them and even tried to dupe the sun. I hung thick drapes on the bedroom windows to keep the light from waking him too early and thought nothing of his being late for work. When he was in my arms, I wanted to keep him there forever. I was love-crazed, and anything that stood in the way of my pleasure was intolerable to me. I felt, even then, that this joy would be short-lived. I wanted to savor every instant of it.

I took no precautions to disguise my intimacy with Maher. When I was told that my father had been informed that Maher was staying overnight, I felt no shame. I was glad. I had resolved to live as an emancipated woman. This was my declaration of independence.

Sheikh Mustafa continued to work on the case he was planning to present for the appeal. The court set a date, and two days before the hearings the khedive expressed his support for us in public. He invited Maher to ride with him in his open automobile for everyone, including my father, to see that he was on our side. They drove through the streets of Cairo to the palace at Inshaas. And because there were very few automobiles in Cairo at the time, people rushed out to gawk. The khedive being driven in his car through the capital was a public event!

"Can my father still consider Maher unworthy of becoming a member of our family after this?" I wondered.

The evening before the court was to convene, Sheikh Mustafa and I worked together to polish the argument he would present. By the time we were finished, it sounded more like a political tract than an attorney's appeal. We said that the verdict, based on "social incompatibility," was nothing more than a pretext. It was based on the antiquated notion that a father could dispose of his daughter like a slave.

We wrote paragraph after paragraph urging the emancipation of women. We prepared ardent speeches saying Egyptian women demanded freedom of choice, that our na-

tion would not know the meaning of democracy, of freedom, if women remained enslaved. They must be given
their rights as human beings and those rights included the
right to a husband of their own choosing.

I was elated. Both Sheikh Mustafa and I were optimistic. But the next day I was not quite so confident.

Maher, who had spent the night, left at dawn. I knew
the debates in court were going to be heated. I wondered if
my notoriety would not, in the end, work against me. I
began to panic, to imagine the worst possible scenarios.

If the court upheld the first decision, my father could
take me home by force, with a police escort . . . Medhat's
brother could insist on a wedding to spite me, then divorce
me, saying I was not a virgin . . .

The thought made me blush!

"Never," I said to myself, "I will never submit to this
humiliation! I will stay one step ahead of them. I will publicly declare my intimacy with Maher!" Oh, how I wished
then that I were pregnant! I would have shouted it from the
rooftops!

"If I am wrenched away from Maher," I promised myself, "I will refuse to marry anyone else. If I am delivered
against my will, I will kill myself rather than submit!"

I tried to calm down, repeating, "Sheikh Mustafa is optimistic, Sheikh Mustafa is optimistic . . . "

But then I thought, "What if we fail? Maher and I could
always run away! They would never succeed in separating
us! We could go abroad! We could go to Europe if other
Muslim countries refused us asylum! . . . "

I knew I would not hesitate to do anything or go anywhere to keep Maher. But, what about Maher? Could I
count on him when push came to shove? The realist in me
said no. When I was quite lucid, I saw Maher for the fearful,
timid young man he really was. I realized that he would
never have the courage to give up his family and his security, leave behind his friends and familiar surroundings, or

turn his back on his homeland for my sake. He would not be able to make that sacrifice to keep me. These dark thoughts tormented me. If we lost the appeal, I would be lost, too; but I did not once regret giving myself to Maher, whom I truly considered to be my husband. I decided that, come what may, I would not be the one who would give him up.

33 · AFTERMATH

The next day, my worst nightmare was confirmed. My marriage was annulled and my reputation dashed to the ground. The verdict, which was an affront to the khedive and to Egypt's liberal thinkers, left me with the brutal reality that I was no longer legally Maher's wife. Sheikh Mustafa, who came to see me as soon as the verdict was handed down, was appalled. He blamed the judges for dismissing the evidence in our favor and for not really considering the appeal. He launched into a diatribe against regressive values, but I was no longer able to listen. I had lost interest.

I waited anxiously for Maher, but Maher did not come. Finally, feeling utterly dejected, I asked Sheikh Mustafa to look for him, and I went to my room to pack. I was unsure about what to do next, but I held on to a glimmer of hope that Maher would come, and that we would leave this house together.

I had just finished telling the servants that I did not want to be disturbed when Shahine Pasha arrived. He was governor of Cairo and a close friend of my father's. I could not refuse to see him.

I put on my veil and went out to meet him. He had an officer with him. Instantly, I felt trapped. I reacted just like a hunted animal looking for a way to escape.

Shahine Pasha eased my mind a little when he said, "I'm here to see you as a friend, Ramza. This is an aide-de-camp to the khedive. He came to deliver a message from him."

After exchanging civilities, the officer said, "I am here on behalf of our sovereign to convey his deepest regrets to you about the outcome of your appeal."

I responded bitterly, "Why didn't he oppose this odious judgment?" I could not help my outburst, even though I knew that the khedive had done all he could by openly endorsing Maher. I knew also that he did not have the power to force the judge's hand. Still, I was angry. I felt betrayed and diminished.

That day, I resented the whole world. I was exasperated with the khedive and irate with my father, Maher, my lawyer, as much as with the judges themselves. And finally, I reproached myself as well for not planning more carefully, for not fighting harder.

I sat, lost in fantasies of retaliation. Shahine Pasha's high voice pulled me back into the moment.

"Your father came to see me, Ramza. He wants you to come home," he said not beating around the bush.

I clenched my fists. "Of my own accord or by force?" I asked.

"I am obliged by law to have you arrested if you don't go home of your own free will, Ramza," he answered matter-of-factly.

"Now?"

"As soon as I receive a court order."

"So you'll come and arrest me? In the name of the law? Like a common criminal?" I said, shocked.

"I'm sure it won't come to that. But you must understand that the reasonable thing to do is to return to your father's house," he concluded.

I had to use all my willpower to keep from shouting that I would follow Maher, married or not. The presence of the khedive's aide-de-camp kept me in check. An outburst in front of this young officer, who was also a stranger, would have been quite improper.

It was a good thing I said nothing. It occurred to me that, if I wanted to escape, speaking out would certainly compromise my chances.

I decided to remain poised and respond carefully to Shahine Pasha's declaration that I should go home.

I said, "Is it wise to make me come face to face with my father quite so soon? Don't you think his irritation and anger would cause him to lock me up or marry me off, or do something rash? Shouldn't we let matters settle for a while? You know he once threatened to marry me to his steward, who is more than sixty years old!"

"You have nothing of the sort to fear, Ramza," Shahine Pasha answered. "Your father is not likely to do anything that will further displease the khedive. Besides, you know that there is a law that protects you from being forced to marry against your will. Your father has to have your consent. He's a responsible man. He's responsible for you. He doesn't want to cause another scandal. He's well aware that you're not the sort of girl one marries against her will or even locks up!"

Shahine Pasha paused. I gritted my teeth and tried to control my temper. I was outraged at the thought that all my father cared about was the scandal.

Almost as an afterthought, he added, "I've known your father a long time. We were in school together. It's true he's touchy, but the smallest gesture of goodwill goes a long way with him. You have to know how to approach him. It would take so little to please him, Ramza! He asks for nothing better than to have his only daughter back! He's cherished you far too much to remain your enemy for long!"

"Then why doesn't he let me stay here? Live the way I want to?" I piped up.

From the look on Shahine Pasha's face, you would have thought I had proposed prostituting myself.

"Come now, Ramza," he answered curtly, "you know perfectly well that's impossible! Don't even think of mentioning it to your father! Your rightful place is in his house!"

There was nothing more to be said.

I was a woman. Even the idea of living alone was scandalous. If I was not under a husband's yoke, I had to be under my father's. It did not count that I was of age, that I was educated, that I had a will of my own, that I wanted to be free.

I could feel an argument forming on the tip of my tongue. But before I could say a word, I was stopped by the sound of voices in the next room. They were women's voices. The loud, sonorous one belonged to Narguiss, I was certain.

Shahine Pasha immediately excused himself and left. When I turned around, I was face to face with two women, unveiling. My Aunt Narguiss, as I had guessed, was one. Tewfikeh Hanem, Shahine Pasha's wife, was the other.

Instantly, I understood why they had come. Shahine Pasha could not force me home before receiving a court order. He had sent his wife and my aunt as bodyguards to make sure I would not attempt to run away. I bit my lip. I was deeply vexed. But I was forced to hold my tongue because of Tewfikeh Hanem's presence. Had I been alone with Narguiss, however, I would have exploded. Narguiss and Tewfikeh Hanem embraced me and covered me with kisses in an exaggerated show of affection. I hated them both just then and particularly Narguiss, who was acting like a hypocrite. It was so unlike her!

"I couldn't leave you alone on a day like this, Ramza," she said. "Tewfikeh Hanem and I have come to keep you company."

They had, in effect, come to restrain me. They would spend the night. They were moving into my house without so much as "by your leave," and, true to character, Narguiss made herself right at home and took over. She had brought with her all sorts of foodstuffs as well as two servants, who went straight to the kitchen and busied themselves with preparations for cooking.

In the midst of all this confusion and emotion, I continued to hope that Maher would come. I could not imagine what was keeping him. Instead, it was Maher's father I was confronted with and, to this day, I feel rage and humiliation when I recall the scene!

Zoheida had answered the door. She ran back to me and whispered, "Maher Bey el Khashaab wants to see you." Maher had come! He had not let me down, after all! I rushed out, my heart beating wildly, and I found myself face to face with the man who, no doubt, hated me more than anyone in the world. There was Mourad el Khashaab, Maher's father.

I was startled. Had Zoheida misunderstood the name? Had Maher's father used this low trick to smoke me out? I would never know. But, when I saw him, I froze and for a moment could not utter a word.

He gave me a hard look and brought down the axe.

"Maher says to go back to your father!"

I will never forget that moment as long as I live. I flinched as if I had been stabbed, and my voice came back to me.

"I don't believe you!" I cried.

He answered disdainfully, "Maher doesn't want you! Get that through your head!"

"You're lying!" I cried, "If you weren't, Maher would be here telling me himself! He was just here this morning! I'm sure of him!"

He laughed, cynically.

"You're sure of him?! Because you slept with him?! That's how he found out just what kind of a woman you are! If the court had not annulled your marriage, Maher would have divorced you! One doesn't marry a slut!" He spat out the insult.

I stood stock still. I desperately wanted to keep control, to strike back at him, but my nerves gave way. I broke into sobs.

Maher's father turned to leave. At the door he shouted over his shoulder: "You will never see Maher again! He's gone! He's miles away from Cairo!"

Narguiss, always curious, heard the commotion and came running in. The last thing I wanted now was to be caught falling apart! I quickly dried my tears. But Narguiss, in a rare moment of discretion, turned and walked out.

I wanted desperately to believe that what I had heard was a pack of lies, but I knew better. I was all too aware of Maher's limitations. Late that evening, Sheikh Mustafa returned. He had not located Maher, but he had heard that Maher had been transferred. He would command a post in Qosseir, on the Red Sea.

"I can't believe it. It's impossible! The khedive would certainly have opposed such a maneuver! It's so obviously designed to keep us apart!"

Sheikh Mustafa sighed. He patiently explained that the khedive himself was under attack.

"All the khedive wants now is to forget the whole affair," Sheikh Mustafa said reluctantly.

I felt betrayed on all fronts, but particularly by Maher.

"He left without even saying good-bye . . . " I murmured, almost to myself.

Sheikh Mustafa just shrugged his shoulders.

"I saw him in court this morning. He looked pale and slipped out as soon as he heard the verdict. He looked ashamed and left like someone running to hide."

"I can't believe he's left, unless he was taken away by force," I said.

Sheikh Mustafa did not respond, but got up and took leave of me. I walked to the door with him. Outside, a little ways from the house, I saw a figure standing immobile. My heart jumped, but it was a soldier in police uniform. Other figures lurked in the shadows who had not been there earlier. It was clear that I was under surveillance. When I turned to come back into the house, I saw a door quickly being pulled shut. Someone had been spying on me. I ran to catch the offender. It was Narguiss.

"Who is the man who just left?" she asked, attacking before I could reproach her.

I looked at her without answering. I knew that Narguiss was curious by nature and had, undoubtedly, been listening behind the door. I knew I had to be careful now, even with Narguiss, and I put a lid on my temper.

"That was my lawyer," I said drily, without further explanation.

Try as I did, I could not believe that Maher had left Cairo without coming to see me one last time. I retired to my room. It was a soft, moonlit night. Oh, if only Maher were with me!

Instead, I sat alone. I watched the window and waited. I saw the guards milling around outside. I cursed them because I thought that Maher might be within reach, looking for an opportunity to come in. I knew the guards would have been given orders not to let him by. And as the evening wore on, it occurred to me that Maher himself might be held captive.

"That's the only reason he hasn't come!" I thought, and my heart suddenly felt much lighter.

I stayed up all night waiting hopefully. But at about three o'clock in the morning, my anxiety returned. I felt desperate, in fact. Maher had not come and would not come. I was no longer able to make excuses for him and felt alone, like a hunted animal without hope of escape. The option of returning to my father in defeat made my whole being rise up in arms. I remembered the story of a girl like me who had been so humiliated that she poisoned herself. And the return home that I imagined was far worse, I am sure, than it could possibly have been in reality. Yet, I saw myself being locked up or given lowly chores to perform under the gaze of servants I had once supervised. I saw myself a slave where I had been a queen and resolved that under no circumstances would I go home.

34 · ESCAPE

Because I had spent the evening mourning my fate and could cry no longer, I resolved to pull myself together and do something before it was too late. I knew my father would not wait to exercise his right to take me home. Shahine Pasha would secure a court order in the morning, and I would have to leave this house of my own free will or by force. I decided to escape.

The house was quiet. The dawn call to prayer would not be for another hour or two. I heard snoring in the room next to mine, where Narguiss and Tewfikeh Hanem slept. Mademoiselle had gone to bed early in her bedroom across the hall. She would not be up until six o'clock to go to mass. I wondered if I should leave her a note but decided not to. If she knew my plans, she might find herself compromised.

There was no movement outside the house or on the street. The soldiers guarding me were nodding off after their long night watch. I looked around me and saw my suitcase open on the floor where I had left it only a few hours ago—days, it seemed! The dresses I had pulled out of my wardrobe were draped on the back of a chair. The room smelled of departure. How I wished at that moment that I were leaving with Maher!

The idea of running away excited me into action. A pitcher of water and a washbasin stood on the small, marble-topped table by the window. My towel and Maher's towel were on the rack beside the table. I poured myself some water, washed, and changed my clothes. I gathered a few essentials, tied them in a bundle, and cracked open my bedroom door. The hallway was deserted. I veiled my face, wrapped myself from head to toe in the black *melaaya laff* I had used in Alexandria when I eloped, and stepped out. Disguised as a commoner, no one would take any notice of me.

I tiptoed into the kitchen with my shoes in hand. It was empty. The servants, too, were asleep. I took a wash basket, put my bundle and shoes in it, placed it on my head as I had seen the washerwomen do, and tried to decide on the safest way out of the house. The front gate was illuminated by a gas lamp, and I avoided it. Instead, I took the little service door, directly opposite the pantry, which opened out onto a dark alley and pulled the door half shut behind me. The wind caught up my *melaaya,* and the cold flagstones under my bare feet made me shiver. I listened. I heard nothing at first but my own heart thumping, and then the sound of regular breathing. It was a guard. As my eyes got used to the dark, I saw him slumped over where he sat to the right of the door. I stood still and observed him until I was sure he was not going to move, pulled the door closed quietly behind me, and slipped into the night.

When I finally emerged into a lighted street, I heard the call to prayer echoing from one mosque to the next. I was far enough from home so that no one could tell where I had come from. And as the sun came up, the first streetcar of the day clattered by and stopped. I boarded along with servant girls and washerwomen going to work. I had no idea where I could take refuge, or who would take me in now. I was not sure how to find out where Maher was, and there was no one I could ask.

"If Maher has been shipped to Qosseir, I will figure out a way of reaching him," I thought. I was not ready to give him up if he still wanted me. I did not have a precise idea of where Qosseir was located. I tried to remember Sheikh

Nassif's geography lessons when Zakeyya and I pored over the atlas of Egypt he grudgingly bought for us. Qosseir was a port on the Red Sea, somewhere in the South . . . Maher had told me that it was a Godforsaken place, where young officers dreaded being sent. I supposed that there must be boats to Qosseir from the port of Suez . . . But then I did not really know where Suez was precisely either. I decided that taking a boat would be risky anyway. I could not picture myself, a lone woman, on board a sailboat for a trip that would last no less than two or three days. There were no railway lines to Qosseir, but I remembered seeing, on the map, a narrow strip of desert between the Nile and the Red Sea. If I could get to a town in that region, I would surely find a way of reaching Qosseir.

My grandmother had described that strip of desert to me, telling me how she had crossed it on a camel, in a caravan transporting pilgrims to Mecca. If I could get to the southern town of Kena, along the Nile, I was sure to find a way to the Red Sea. My grandmother had done it, and I would do it, too. I wondered, though, what route Maher had taken.

Before I knew it, the streetcar had stopped at Cairo Station. I got off, hoisted the basket on my shoulder, gripped a corner of the *melaaya laff* in my teeth, the way I had seen women do it in front of the mosques I visited with my grandmother, to free their hands, and went to the ticket counter. I bought a ticket in a third-class carriage and headed for the platform where the train bound for Upper Egypt would pull in.

I was on my way into the unknown!

When I reached the platform, I was told that the train for Upper Egypt was not due for an hour. I worried about the delay. Once Narguiss and Mademoiselle discovered that I was missing, they would sound the alarm and send the police after me. I spotted an animated group of women chattering loudly on the platform, and recognized their ac-

cent as being the southern drawl of Upper Egypt. I decided
to join them in order to seem less conspicuous, standing on
the platform all alone. I had no difficulty making friends.
They were jovial and told me that they had come to Cairo
for a wedding. They were waiting for the train to go home
to Manfaloot. I told them I was going to join my husband
in Kena, and that I was from the South myself. Of course, I
adopted their accent to make my story plausible.

When the train pulled in, they all let out a volley of cries
for joy, and I did likewise. We boarded, helping each other
with baskets and bundles. When the train moved, whistling
and puffing smoke, the cries for joy went up again. We
were a lively bunch in that third-class compartment. Other
women joined us during the journey. We talked, laughed,
shared food, and told stories the entire way. I recounted
tales I had heard, that were passed from harem to harem and
that never failed to entertain the listeners.

As the train moved through the Egyptian countryside, I
felt increasingly lighthearted. I laughed harder than anyone
at the jokes and stories, totally forgot my worries and my
status as a fugitive.

When we reached Manfaloot, my companions got off,
but in Assiut a fat, jolly woman sat next to me, and we
began to talk right away. She had spent two weeks with her
oldest daughter who had just given birth to her third child.
Sitt Zeynab was going home to Kena where she still had
younger children at home. Her husband was a jeweler, and
they were rich. She asked me about myself. I made up a
story, of course, but it was not really so far from the truth. I
said that my husband was in the military, in Kena. He was
about to be transferred to Qosseir, and I was going to see
him before his departure. By the end of the trip, Sitt
Zeynab and I had become fast friends. The train pulled into
Kena late at night. I walked out of the station with my
friend and looked around. Of course, no one was waiting
for me. I expressed my despair to Sitt Zeynab.

"Could the letter I sent not have reached my husband?" I said.

It was impossible to go looking for him at the barracks at such a late hour. Should I spend the night sitting up in the station? My friend protested that it was out of the question.

"You will come home with me. There is plenty of room. My home is your home," she said.

My friend's invitation saved me. There was no way I could have stayed at the station, no way I could have walked the streets all night, and certainly no way I could have gone to a hotel! As a woman alone, I would immediately have been suspect.

When we got to Sitt Zeynab's house, she introduced me to one of her daughters, Nabila. I shared her room that night and Nabila instantly took me into her confidence.

We stayed up late, talking. Nabila was only sixteen but was already experiencing the painful dilemma of so many of the young women of Egypt. She was smitten with the son of a neighbor, a draper whose shop was next to her father's. She was afraid that, according to custom, her father would marry her to her first cousin, who was twenty years older than she was.

Poor Nabila!

Despite what I thought and what I myself had done, I did not dare recommend that she go against her father's wishes. I knew this was a decision that a girl should make on her own and only if she was strong enough to bear the consequences.

I lay awake that night recalling the events of the day. I tried to imagine what had happened in Cairo while I was on the train. I wondered where Maher was. In Qosseir, in Suez, on board a ship on the Red Sea, crossing the desert? Could he possibly be in Kena, just a few steps away from me? The thought that he might be close by made me impatient for morning. I could hardly wait to start looking for him. The thought also crossed my mind that he might still be in Cairo, or Alexandria. What if his father had lied to me? What would I do then? Should I even risk going to Qosseir? How would I get there if I decided to go? It was farther from Kena than I had supposed, five days away according to Sitt Zeynab. The camel caravans that departed from Kena and stopped in Qosseir on their way to Mecca in my grandmother's day were no longer using that route. Such convoys traveled infrequently now, and when they did, they departed from Kift, not from Kena.

My pursuers could easily catch up with me before I even had a chance to leave the Nile Valley. I was determined to find Maher, come what may and, at the first sign of morning, I asked Nabila to accompany me to the barracks. I was hoping for nothing more than information leading to Maher's whereabouts. We walked to an encampment composed of only some tents in the desert. And as we approached, I was nearly struck dumb when I saw an officer come toward us. Even at a distance, I recognized Maher. I stopped and clutched Nabila's arm.

"That's him! That's my husband!" I whispered.

Maher nearly walked past us. He could not know the identity of the women hidden behind the veil, nor could he suspect that beneath the thick folds of an ordinary black *melaaya* a heart was beating wildly at the sight of him!

"Maher," I cried as he walked in front of me.

At the sound of my voice, he froze. His mouth fell open and he looked stupefied. I was afraid that he might be angry or annoyed with me. But instead, I saw his eyes brighten with amazed pleasure, and he smiled.

I had been ready to reproach him bitterly, but his smile disarmed me. I dropped the speech I had rehearsed, and we walked silently side by side with Nabila following discreetly some distance away. I was tongue-tied. It was Maher who finally broke the ice.

"You know, Ramza," he said, "I wanted to say good-bye to you before leaving. Everyone said I shouldn't. They warned that I might compromise you . . . "

"I didn't ask anyone's advice," I said, finding my tongue. "I was determined to find you, and I did, all by myself!"

"How did you find out I was in Kena?" he asked. "Was it my father who told you?"

I laughed.

"Your father . . . " I was about to tell him how his father had humiliated me but changed my mind.

"No one told me anything, and I said nothing to anyone either! If I hadn't found you here, I would have gone to Qosseir to look for you!"

"That would have been difficult . . . " Maher said.

"Believe me, I would have done it! Now, let's be honest with each other, Maher. In spite of everything, I still consider myself your wife, and I'm ready to follow you anywhere. The question is, do you want me? I need a clear answer," I said, then added, "And don't tell me to go home! I did not take all these risks to turn around and slip under my father's yoke again. I have decided either go to Qosseir with you, or take the train to Aswan today if you don't want me. I would go to Khartoum. I'm educated. I can work. I can be independent."

Maher did not answer right away. I began to wonder and suddenly worried that he might humor me and then betray me. I stopped and confronted him.

"Maher," I said, "Forgive me for suspecting you . . . But I won't censor myself any longer . . . If you have any intention of sending a telegram to your father or mine, think again! I'm warning you, I will not be restrained! I'll kill myself first!"

"Ramza, how can you think such a thing!" he protested.

"When do you leave for Qosseir?" I asked.

"Tomorrow morning," he answered.

"Are you going to take me with you? Yes, or no?" I said at last.

He squeezed my arm. "How can I leave you behind? I was certain you were lost to me! Now that you're here, how can I abandon you?"

His words were balsam to my ears. I loved him. He sounded so sincere, and I asked for nothing better than to believe him.

35 · VOYAGE

We departed Kena at dawn the following day. I was still anxious that I would be found, arrested, and prevented from leaving with Maher. I even feared a trap of some sort. But there was no trap, and nothing happened. I began to wonder if they would be waiting for me at Qosseir . . . Then, all at once, I resolved to stop thinking about my pursuers or about the dangers of being caught. Qosseir was five days away, and I would be a fool, I decided, if I did not live them fully with Maher.

The voyage was pure enchantment. Our party consisted of Maher and myself, two other officers, a dozen soldiers, and two women who were the wives of noncommissioned officers already in Qosseir. One of the women left Kena with us. We picked up the other one in her hometown of Kift. A *tachtarawan* with two places had been rigged up for the harem. I hated it. It was a tiny enclosed room hoisted on the back of one of the camels and resembled a cage. I was eager to get out of it and, as soon as possible, I offered my place to my traveling companion from Kift. She was pleased, and I was relieved to ride directly on the animal's back. A white female camel was prepared for me instead with a sheepskin on the saddle. Maher instructed me on how to let my body sway in rhythm with the camel's for a comfortable ride. I was as happy as a child at play.

As soon as we left the cultivated Nile Valley, the world I entered was unknown to me. Most of us live crowded in the Nile Valley, unaware of the desert and its riches. No

one ever talks about it, and I am ashamed to admit that until
the day I left Kena with Maher, I knew nothing about it
either. I was astonished at the unimaginable beauty of the
landscapes, the spectacular sunrises and sunsets, and the
changing light on the stark, rocky hills and canyons. The
silence was breathtaking, and the star-filled nights were like
nothing I had ever experienced.

My worries had evaporated. I felt drunk with freedom
and love. Maher had told me that in the desert no laws applied; once we left the Nile Valley, we were no longer under the jurisdiction of the courts.

"No one can arrest me out here," I thought, and in one
of those flashes of great lucidity, it occurred to me that I
was living some of the most beautiful days of my life. How
well I remember wishing that our journey would never end!

Ramadan eve fell on our second day out, and although
we were not obliged to fast because we were traveling, our
soldiers did, and we joined them. At sunset, we camped at
the water wells of Guita. The soldiers, who were mostly
Nubians, improvised a little celebration with singing and
dancing to mark the advent of the fast the following day. I
cooked *mehallabiyya* pudding, using noodles and sugar we
had bought in Kena and fresh camel's milk. Everyone ap-
preciated the sweet and complimented me on my cooking,
including Maher. And I was delighted. All I wanted then
was to be a good wife, Maher's wife!

On the first day of Ramadan, hours before the sun came
up, we ate our last meal until sunset. It consisted of dried
dates followed by strong, sweet tea, which the soldiers prepared; and before the sun rose, we were on our way. We
traveled in a single file some of the time, as the path nar-
rowed between the mountains. This was my first experience
of a mountainscape. I was enthralled by the colors of the
rock, which went from black to violet to blue green, changing every hour of the day. What I saw did not perhaps compare with the majestic alpine peaks my father spoke of so

often or the arid and fantastic Mount Arafat that my grandmother described when she recalled her visit to Mecca. But
to me it seemed a land of magic and infinite beauty. And,
how could I avoid being enchanted by it! I was seeing it for
the first time with the man I loved, and I was radiantly
happy.

Maher rode beside me, cantered on the edge of our
small caravan, and looked manly every moment. I admired
the grace with which he held his body for long hours in the
saddle, and I could not get enough of looking at him. I liter-
ally drank him in with my eyes. I thought he was the hand-
somest of men, the only man worthy of being my husband!

On the afternoon of the fifth day, we reached Lambaga,
the fountain of Qosseir. Date palms and mimosas, pungent
with yellow blossoms, were growing on both sides of a
small stream and around the natural spring where travelers
stopped to fill their goatskins with water. Although our little party dismounted, rested, and watered the camels, we
did not drink. We would break our fast in Qosseir, after
sunset.

The mountains had become more precipitous as we approached our destination, and after we departed Lambaga,
we traveled on a narrow pass until late afternoon. When we
emerged, the Red Sea was before us. I saw the fort from a
distance and a handful of houses scattered on the tawny-
colored sand. This was Qosseir. It was a tiny patch between
the desert and the sea, and at that moment, I wished it to be
even more desolate!

I had had Maher to myself for five, full, heavenly days
and dreaded coming into a town where I knew that my
freedom would once again be impeded. The sight of
Qosseir gave me a sharp pang, and a sudden feeling of panic
flooded through me. For a moment I truly feared for our
love. What would happen to us in this place? Later, I was to
understand that this feeling was a premonition. How right I
had been to be apprehensive!

36 · QOSSEIR

As commander of the post, Maher had his lodgings inside the fort. Our home was really meant as bachelor quarters. It was a small pavilion consisting of two rooms furnished with some camp beds and a few regulation tables and chairs. When we arrived everything was covered with dust, and that first night we slept on the grass mats we had used to camp.

"We are at least behind closed doors," I thought, "and in our own house."

Maher seemed dejected at the prospect of my living in this way, but I looked on the experience as a challenge. He had hired the wife of a sargeant and assigned an orderly, an old Nubian soldier named Abdallah, to help me. But even before they arrived, I began to clean and organize.

"I will show Maher how enterprising I can be, and when he comes back tonight, this pavilion will be a home!" I said to myself.

In the afternoon, I went to explore the *souk* in town. I needed to buy some underclothing for myself and shop for material to make linens for the house. I was also determined to serve Maher a traditional Ramadan meal when we broke our fast that night and bought some dried fruit to cook a compote. I wanted so much to please him, but instead my efforts were met with indignation. Maher was angry that I had gone out alone.

"Did anyone recognize you?" he asked. "I would prefer it if you didn't go out without me from now on!"

I was tempted to answer back, to tell him that I was not going to be locked up by him or anyone else, but my love for him kept me from it. Instead, I explained that I had not once lifted my veil, and had used my voice only to order what I needed in the shops. There was no way anyone could

have known who I was! Still, Maher looked glum, and we
ate in silence.

After dinner I suggested we go up to the roof for a
breath of fresh air. The crescent moon was out, the stars
were extraordinarily brilliant, and the air very pure. The
dark mountains seemed to press the narrow band of desert
beneath them against the sea. The water glittered in the distance, and a cool breeze brought me voices of women sitting around braziers on other rooftops and of children
walking by with brightly colored Ramadan lanterns. Every
now and then, I heard someone singing. I inhaled deeply
and stood looking around me in wonder. I wanted to share
the wild silent beauty of this landscape and the festive feeling of Ramadan with Maher. But, when I turned to speak
to him, he was asleep on one of the two lounge chairs. Instantly, my pleasure fell. I, too, sat down and began to
yawn.

Although we received mail once a week, I had no reason
to expect any letters because I had told no one where I was
going. But the mail included newspapers that I awaited eagerly. I was beginning to feel the sharp edge of isolation and
was hungry for news from Cairo.

"What are people saying?" I wondered. "What are the
reactions to my disappearance?"

As the days went by, I missed Mademoiselle and Narguiss more and more, but I missed my father particularly.
There was little I could discuss with Maher. I had not taken
any books with me, and I was also beginning to worry seriously about my father's silence, which was uncharacteristic.
I knew him. He was the sort of man to have mobilized the
army or to have followed me to Qosseir himself . . .

When Maher smiled and took me into his arms, I forgot
everything. Then I was the happiest of women, but Maher
grew increasingly irritable and less attentive. I began to
wonder if his father had not been right, that I had forced
myself on him, and that he really did not want me any-

more. He was gone most of the day, and escaped into sleep at night. Although I was deeply hurt, I continued to find excuses for him.

"He's tired," I thought, "he's worried. He's irritable because of fasting all day . . . "

The wives of the noncommissioned officers began to talk. Why had Maher not introduced me to the wives of the dignitaries of the town? The wives of the governor or the judges? How could it be that I was left alone without female companionship day after day? They sometimes ventured a word to me, and I assured them that I elected to lead a quiet life. Although this was true to some extent, I was secretly alarmed by Maher's attitude. Did he keep me hidden because he was ashamed of me? Because he did not really consider me his wife? I knew him to be very susceptible to public opinion. I was a woman about whom too much had been said already. In my darker moments, I was certain that he was planning to get rid of me. The less my presence was felt in Qosseir, I reasoned, the more easily he could send me away without having to answer too many questions. It would have been easy to say he was divorcing me, but he could not do that because our marriage had been annulled. I was increasingly tortured by anxiety, and when I got tired of rattling around our little house alone or climbing to the terrace to gaze for hours at the mountains and the sea, I covered myself up and went out. I did not feel there was any danger of my being discovered. As soon as I was out of the fort and mixing with other veiled women on the street, I was anonymous. I was particularly attracted by the port. I liked the sound of the waves crashing on the jetty, and the activity of the fishermen drying their nets with their small, colorful boats bobbing up and down in the water behind them. I could watch them for hours.

One day a cutter glided into the port to unload a shipment. I had never seen one before and was captivated by the elegant lines of this vessel. I wondered where it had come from? Was it from Arabia, or Bahrain, or maybe even India? I stood hypnotized until the cargo was unloaded and the crew lifted anchor, hoisted the sails, and cut out for the open sea. Standing there, I had forgotten who I was and where I was and why I was there. I had forgotten that I had a husband, that I had run away from my father and my family, that I had abandoned everything for the sake of love . . . I had forgotten about the restrictions placed on me because I was female, about being covered from head to toe, and yet, inside the armor plating of the *melaaya,* and behind the protective veil, I was once more a little girl dreaming of departures.

The next morning, I saw people crowding around a camel caravan on the edge of the town. My heart raced because I thought it was the mail train that had perhaps arrived during the night. But Abdallah explained that these camels belonged to members of the Ababda tribe.

"They are very independent and fierce," he told me, "and they graze their sheep and goats all through this desert, and rarely come to Qosseir except to trade their baskets and rugs for supplies."

When I heard this, I threw on my clothes and my veil, and ran out to see them. I was amazed at these black men who were only dressed in loin cloths. They held spears and round shields in their hands, they had a bush of kinky hair, and very fine features. I shall never forget their eyes, which burned with extraordinary pride. The Ababda, Abdallah told me, lived outside the boundaries of any law. They were eternal rebels, and I found myself envying them, and oddly enough after they departed, I felt desolate.

The last thing I wanted to do at that moment was to go home. I walked toward the beach instead and stood staring out to sea. The water was calm, the air was soft and warm, and I remembered the sirens my grandmother had told me about. They fascinated people and their call was irresistible. All at once I thought I heard them urging me to escape, and

I felt anguished. Standing on this narrow strip of land between the mountains and the sea, I was trapped, and love was my prison. This thought frightened me, and I felt a desperate need to see Maher, to be with him, to hear his voice, and to feel his arms around me. I started back for the fort, almost running.

Maher would never tell me just where his office was. It was clear to me that he did not want me going there. Yet, that day, I could not stop myself. I went to the barracks, I asked a soldier where Maher was, and he took me to a door with a sign on it that read No Admittance. Gingerly, I pushed open the door and saw Maher was draped on a divan. He and his colleagues were joking and laughing. As soon as they saw me, they froze, and Maher jumped up, looking furious. He had recognized me despite my heavy veil.

I started a sentence. I wanted to speak to him for a minute. Brutally, he interrupted me and ordered me to go home. I was stung. He had shamed and embarrassed me. I walked out of his office, slamming the door behind me. I was not going to go home!

When I left the fort, I had tears running down my cheeks and my veil was plastered against my face. I was so hurt, I could hardly breathe. I thought I was going to suffocate and felt utterly desperate and alone. I dragged myself to the southern end of the town where I knew there was a sheltered cove. I sank down on the sand, took off my veil, and cried my heart out. The waves lapped at the shore, and I had the feeling that I wanted them to take me somewhere and nowhere at the same time. If Maher did not love me, what was I doing in this Godforsaken place? I asked myself this question, yet I longed for no other place. I had no desire to return to Cairo or to go to Alexandria . . . The whole world was a hostile place. I looked up and saw the Ababda men in the distance. They were going South, plodding in single file along the foot of a cliff.

"If only I were one of their wives and could follow them into the desert," I cried to myself. I had never felt so helpless!

The sun had set, when the canon announcing the *iftar* shocked me back to reality.

Suddenly, I thought, "Maher will be hungry!"

He would be waiting at home. I knew that with his huge appetite he did not tolerate fasting very well. He would be getting frantic.

Then I said to myself, "Let him suffer a little!"

Despite everything that had happened and despite my mean thought, my heart was full of love and I began to find excuses for him again.

"He wanted to save face in front of his colleagues. After all I came into his office without warning . . . "

I decided that I had been too quick to conclude that he did not love me, and began to feel better. The streets were deserted, as everyone was breaking fast. The soldiers guarding the fort were eating at the gates, and when I got home, I discovered that Maher had not waited for me. He was just finishing his meal when I came in.

"What are you doing here?" he asked, furious. "Why don't you go back where you came from!"

"Fine, Maher, now I understand!" I lashed out, "You won't have to say that twice!"

I was just as angry as he was, and my fighting spirit had returned. I was almost to the door when he caught up with me. He grabbed me by the shoulders and pushed me back into the house. He had hurt me, but the pain filled me with joy.

"He does love me, after all!" I thought, then I heard a key turn in the front door. He had locked it.

"I forbid you to go out!" Maher shouted. "Is that clear?"

"Then don't leave me alone all day," I answered.

"I have work to do," he said.

I started laughing.

"Yes, I saw how busy you were!"

He flushed. I knew I was infuriating him.

"Don't bother lying to me, Maher. You're bored with me. I know it. So let me distract myself as best I can, or let me go!"

He cried, "I'm master here! I will not let you go out and create more scandal! You've done quite enough as it is!"

"You're blaming me, Maher? Have you forgotten that I'm the one who acted like a man, when you could find nothing better to do than stand on the sidelines, wailing like a woman!"

He threw himself at me intending to strike me. I fought back. I bit him. I scratched him. Yet, all the time I loved him. In the end our fight turned into a lover's spat, and the two days that followed were happy ones with frequent visits from Maher. I responded to his attention by staying home.

37 · BAHIGA'S LETTER

A week later, Maher received a letter from his sister that contained the worst possible news for me. I had been watching impatiently for the mail, and met Maher eagerly at the door. The minute I saw his face, though, I knew something was wrong.

He was pale and he avoided my eyes.

"What's happened, Maher? Do they want to separate us again? Are they telling you to send me back to Cairo? I won't do it! You will support me, won't you?"

"That's not it . . . It's a letter from Bahiga . . . "

"Speak up. What's happened?"

"It's your father . . . "

"What has he done now?"

"He's had an accident."

Maher said this, crumpling the letter, but I tore it out of his hand. I recognized Bahiga's handwriting and realized as soon as I had read the first few lines that it was really meant to fall into my hands. It was phrased carefully so as to let me know Narguiss' position regarding me and to avoid frightening me away.

" . . . the shock of her disappearance was terrible. He died that same day of a cerebral hemorrhage . . . I am enclosing the article that appeared in the newspaper . . . I took the train to Cairo as soon as I read it . . . I went to Narguiss . . . We talked about Ramza . . . The question of inheritance came up . . . What to do about . . . If you know where Ramza is, break the news gently to her . . . Insist that she return to Cairo without delay . . . Tell her she has nothing to fear . . . Narguiss wants her back and will be waiting for her with open arms . . . "

I was shocked and could not believe the words I had just read. My father could not be dead! It was impossible! One did not just up and die in this way! I reread the letter, and I'm ashamed to say that, for a moment, I wondered if this could be a trap to get me back to Cairo. But, no, Bahiga's letter rang true, and the intolerable certainty of my father's death went through my heart like a dagger. I had killed him! I collapsed, weeping desperately, and Maher took the letter from my hand and reread it.

"You have to leave, Ramza!"

I looked up at him in horror.

"I don't want to leave you!" I said, crying, and instantly his face turned to stone. I knew that he, too, thought that I had killed my father.

"You think I've killed him, don't you?" I asked.

He turned away without answering.

"I fought for our happiness, Maher! Even against my father, and God knows how much I loved him! . . . "

I reached for Maher's hand, but he withdrew it.

"Get ready to leave tomorrow," he said flatly.

"You are coming with me, aren't you?" I said without thinking.

I confess that those words escaped my lips like a bitter cry of joy. The memory of being with him in the desert day and night . . . I was so afraid of losing him!

"I will go with you to Kena," he answered, "I can't stay away from my post longer . . . "

"Resign, Maher! I'm rich enough for two!" I blurted out.

What had I said! I would have given anything to take back those words, but it was too late. His face became contorted and he shouted, "I'll never touch that money! I'll never leave the army!"

"Then I'll stay with you!"

"You have to go home!"

"Then come with me. Ask for a leave of absence."

I was struggling desperately. I was certain that if I left him, even for a few weeks, I would lose him forever.

I reached out to him, but he was inflexible and his eyes refused to meet mine.

"I'll take you as far as Kena," he repeated.

"Then you'll abandon me?"

He hesitated, then answered, "I'll put in a request for leave. I'll come to Cairo when I get it."

"Then let's wait and leave together," I said.

"You have to go home now," he insisted. "In any case, we can't be seen together. Our marriage was annulled, don't you remember?"

"A court order is not a divorce, Maher," I said. "We can find a *mazoon* or a judge to remarry us in Qosseir. No one will stand in our way now!"

How stubbornly I fought through my pain for the happiness I thought was possible with Maher, but Maher only shrugged.

"Even if I wanted to," he said, "legally I've been declared unworthy of you. Or had you forgotten?"

I realized instantly that Maher was carrying a grudge, that he had been mortally wounded and had not healed. I remembered what Sheikh Abd el Moutei had said to me . . . The way Maher's voice broke just then, the way he tossed those words at me, like an accusation, made it clear that he felt I was to blame.

I was both indignant and hurt, and also I suffered for him.

"That's absurd, Maher," I cried, "you know I had nothing to do with any of those abominable manipulations! I promise you, I will move heaven and earth to wipe out any trace of the humiliation you suffered!"

"No one can ever do that . . . " he murmured.

"What do you mean? . . . "

For an instant, I caught his eye. I think when he saw my face so disfigured with anguish, he decided to stop for fear his words would kill me.

"We'll leave tomorrow morning . . . " was all he said.

"And then?" I asked.

He did not answer, and I repeated my question.

"Then? We'll see . . . " he said.

I was a coward still. I did not have the courage to face the truth and did not ask him to explain. I never found out where Maher slept that night. And even though custom dictated that, because I was in mourning, my husband had to stay away from me for forty days, I knew Maher had other reasons for retreating. When I finally went to bed, I tossed and turned and suffered the torments of the damned. All night I saw my dead father's face before me, as if he were in the same room. When, at last, I heard the morning call to prayer, I got up, relieved, despite my grief and the knowledge of what the day held in store for me.

Our voyage back to Kena was lugubrious. Maher and I rode side by side on our camels in silence. We were still fasting; and when we stopped for prayers or after sunset to break fast, then sleep, Maher joined his soldiers and left me alone. I prayed alone. I ate alone. I slept in my tent alone with Maher camped outside the flap, and we pushed hard to get to Kena. Needless to say, I had lost all interest in the scenery and only wanted the trip to be over as soon as possible.

On the afternoon of the fourth day, we reached Beer Ambar. We stopped to water our camels and to perform the third prayer of our five daily prayers. I could see green fields in the distance, and I knew we were not far from the Nile Valley.

When it was time to leave, I got up my courage and spoke to Maher. I pleaded with him to listen to me. I had had plenty of time to meditate and reflect during those four days of silence. I was determined to hear the truth about his feelings and to decide the fate of our marriage before reaching our destination. My voice trembled as I spoke, and when I questioned him, I knew his answer would shatter my dreams.

"Maher, I am going to ask you a question, and I want an honest answer . . . " I began.

"This is not the time, Ramza . . . " he said, but I insisted.

"Do you, or do you not want me to be your wife?" I asked point-blank.

Maher did not answer right away. The silence that followed was excruciating. He seemed unable to speak, yet the answer to my question was clear. At that moment I realized that it had been clear all along. Blinded by my love, I had been unable to see the truth. Maher did not want me from the time his father turned on me. Perhaps he had never wanted me. Our elopement had been my idea. It was I who had run after him in Kena and forced him, in a sense, to take me to Qosseir. It was I who hired a lawyer in defense of our marriage. Neither Maher nor his father had wanted to win the case. I had fought alone and lost alone.

Still, I was certain that Maher had loved me. His love

could not silence his wounded pride, however, nor was he strong enough to brave public opinion or overcome his own prejudices. And what I further realized as we crossed the desert in silence was that Maher would always live in fear of my bold determination. He would always wonder what I might do because of what I had done. In his eyes, even if we remarried, I would remain the scandalous wife, the one that deep down he would always be ashamed of because I had broken all the rules. I was not the docile, obedient, wife-servant willing to live cloistered and silent behind harem walls.

Finally, when Maher found his voice, he said, "You see, Ramza, as long as your father was alive, we still had a chance of gaining his approval. My father's would have followed. But that's impossible now. We've killed your father! He died condemning us! My own father has cursed us and will continue to do so until his dying day. We can never hope for their blessings . . . "

Maher spoke almost in a whisper, his eyes averted. He could not look at me. His message was clear, however, and I knew what was left for me to do.

"Well, Maher," I said. "that decides it. I won't bother you anymore, but I want you to know that I am acting of my own free will. Neither my father's wrath nor any court order would have made me give you up. But I, Ramza Farid, declare to you now that I no longer can be, nor wish to be your wife. Call two soldiers as witnesses and divorce me."

Maher flinched and protested.

"I will never subject you to such an affront! There's no reason to do this, Ramza! Even if we never see each other again, we have no legal bonds to dissolve. The courts never recognized our marriage in the first place . . . "

I interrupted him.

"That judgement has no validity in my eyes, Maher. I never accepted it when it was delivered, and I don't now. It is not in the power of the courts to rend asunder those whom God has joined through love. And I'm going to tell you something else. Knowing what I know, had we lived where women had the right to do more than obey, it is I who would divorce you now. And you can be certain that my voice would not tremble, delivering the words. So go ahead, do it . . . "

When I stopped speaking, he stood transfixed. I looked at him intently. I wanted to drink in his features so that his face would be forever etched in my memory. Even though I was leaving Maher, he would remain a part of me for the rest of my days.

I then covered my eyes with my hand and said, "Go ahead! Speak! Deliver the death blow!"

"Oh, Ramza," he said trying to make light of my words, "always the prima donna! It's literature and drama with you to the end, isn't it? Let's go, or we'll miss the train!"

His attempt at irony rang false.

"Maher," I said, "This is the last thing I will ever ask you to do. You're a soldier; have the courage to strike, since I'm not allowed to!"

"I don't have the right to! I don't want to!" he cried.

"Could it be that you're a coward? Come on, let's get it over with!"

Finally, in a dull, almost inaudible voice he pronounced the repudiation. "I divorce you. You are no longer my wife. You are now as a sister and as a mother to me."

Before he could repeat the ritual phrase three times, though, Abdallah, who was serving as one of the two witnesses, spoke up.

"Enough! Enough! Do you want to kill her? One day you'll go back to her!"

Although Maher had whispered the terrible words only once, I knew that whatever happened in the future I would never return to him, and I would never take him back if he came to me. I had covered my face with my heaviest black veil, and I knew that Maher would never again lay eyes on me.

A few hours later we were in Kena, and by the time I got off my camel, Maher was gone. I looked straight ahead, forcing my eyes not to search for him. It was Abdallah who came to the station with me, bought my ticket, and put me on the overnight train to Cairo. I was dry-eyed, and felt that I had emerged victorious, even though my heart was in shambles. I had tried to preserve my marriage, and when that proved impossible, I had orchestrated my own deliverance.

My tears only came at dawn, and they were a great release. When I was done crying, I looked over on the couchette and there, beside me, was my black veil. I picked it up and crumpled it with loathing. I was tempted to toss it out the window but resisted the impulse. The time to be free of it had not yet come, and as we approached Cairo Station, I automatically covered my face. I swore, though, that I would not rest until that heinous symbol of the jealous despotism of fathers and husbands was removed from the faces of my sisters in the Orient. I promised to fight with all my energy, with all my resources, to ensure that no woman would ever be forced to wear the veil or endure the slavery that was considered her natural lot in life.

EPILOGUE

The night is one of those limpid southern nights, soft and starlit. It settles over Aswan. The town, the velvet ribbon of the Nile, the black boulders, the gardens, the terrace where we sit, everything slides gently into darkness. And Ramza is silent. Huddled in the wicker chair beside mine, her eyes are half closed. She is again an old woman lost in a dream.

What visions haunt her now, I wonder? Is she imagining generations of young women, like endless fields of ripe wheat, rippling before her eyes? Is she seeing their faces free, turned toward the sun, their laughter filling the air? Or does she feel removed from the struggle?

After revisiting her past with me, is she thinking of herself as the exile come home to die?

Could this little wrinkle forming at the corner of her mouth, almost a smile, mark a tender recollection? Is she remembering Indje, Narguiss, that harem world that she knew so well, that she loved and hated, almost in another life?

And the tear trembling beneath the fading eyelid? Is it called up by her memory of the handsome young officer whom she never saw again after they parted on the edge of the Egyptian desert so many years ago? Maher, whom she continued to love? Who was the symbol of freedom and happiness for the twenty-year-old Ramza? Oh, that impossible happiness!

Contemporary Issues in the Middle East

This well-established series continues to focus primarily on twentieth-century developments that have current impact and significance throughout the entire region, from North Africa to the borders of Central Asia.

Recent titles in the series include: